ELVIS PRESLEY, CIA ASSASSIN

by
Andy Rausch

Burning Bulb
PUBLISHING

Elvis Presley, CIA Assassin
By **Andy Rausch**

Burning Bulb Publishing
P.O. Box 4721
Bridgeport, WV 26330-4721
United States of America
www.BurningBulbPublishing.com

Cover designed by Gary Lee Vincent with the following licensed elements from Fotolia:
  - Top secret document template © pilarts
  - Elvis look-alike impersonator © Maridav
  - Gun logo and woman © St.Op.
  - Chitarrista 2 © alexonline

First printing.

Paperback Edition ISBN: 978-0-69221-271-4

Printed in the United States of America

Library of Congress Control Number: 2014939872

Also by Andy Rausch

The Suicide Game

Riding Shotgun

When I was a boy, I always saw myself as a hero in comic books and in movies. I grew up believing this dream.
—Elvis Presley

INTRODUCTION

I first met Charlie Trimble when I was working as a beat reporter for *The Washington Post*. Charlie, a retired Central Intelligence Agency operative, assisted me with numerous stories as an anonymous source. Remarkably, no one ever called any of the allegations made by this unidentified person into question, so Charlie's identity remained a secret.

Then, in October of 1999, Charlie asked me to assist him with a memoir about his career as a C.I.A. operative. That book, *My Secret Life in the C.I.A.*, which Charlie wrote under the *nom de plume* A. Nonymous, became a colossal bestseller. It sold an embarrassing number of copies, was translated into more than twenty languages, and remained on the *New York Times* bestsellers list for an astounding twenty-three weeks. It was even optioned by Brad Pitt's production company to be made into a movie. (It never went before the cameras, but the checks cleared just the same.)

All the money he made had little effect on Charlie. He remained in his apartment, kept wearing the same clothes that hadn't been in fashion since the mid-seventies, and he continued driving the same old crappy blue Chevy Nova.

The money changed my life dramatically; I got a new house, a few new cars, and even a new actress wife to play Marilyn Monroe to my Arthur Miller. But the money didn't make me happy. What I really wanted was to write fiction, but no one wanted to buy my half-assed novels, even if I was a *New York Times* bestselling author.

"You need to write another non-fiction book," my agent told me.

But what? It wasn't every day that a story as compelling as Charlie's fell into a writer's lap. So what would be my encore?

"I might have a follow-up project for you," Charlie would say from time to time. But then when I would ask him what it was, he refused to answer. "It's not the right time," he once said. "Some secrets go to the grave with us, and some secrets...well, they live on after we are in our graves."

That was when he handed me the key. It was just your average run-of-the-mill key connected to a plastic "Keep On Truckin'" keychain.

"What is this?" I asked.

"Not now," Charlie said. "But one day, I promise you, all will be revealed."

And that was the end of it. Sure, I thought about that key and the mystery that surrounded it from time to time, but after a year or so, those thoughts came to me less and less frequently.

Charlie and I remained good friends, but it turned out he was keeping another secret from me.

Charlie had bone cancer.

He never once mentioned it, but nonetheless he had it. He would disappear from time to time and, looking back, maybe I should have seen the signs and suspected that his health was failing. But I didn't. I just figured it was some sort of secret spy business.

On July 15, 2004, Charlie's daughter, Sarah, called to inform me that Charlie had passed away. When I told Sarah I had no idea her father had been ill, she was less than surprised. "Daddy didn't tell anyone he was sick. I guess he thought if he pretended that he wasn't in poor health, then maybe he'd be okay." Sarah and I both wept throughout this conversation. A few days later I flew to Miami to attend Charlie's funeral, and that was that—or so I thought.

I missed my friend, but my thoughts never returned to the key he had given me. That might sound strange, but it's true. Then, about a week later, a lawyer named Donald Goines, who was employed by Charlie's estate, came by to see me. So I invited him inside and we talked over coffee.

"Your friend, Charles Trimble, left you something in his will," Goines said.

I was speechless. I had always believed Charlie thought of me as the son he'd never had, but I'd never even considered the possibility that he would leave me something.

Goines opened his briefcase and removed an envelope, handing it to me.

"He wanted you to have this."

I opened it and found a receipt for the First National Bank just down the street from my house. On it Charlie had scrawled: "safety deposit box 237."

And then I remembered the key Charlie had given me. After Goines left, I ran upstairs to my office and removed the key thumbtacked to my bulletin board. I then turned and left the house, climbed into my new Porsche, and headed to the First National Bank. When I got there, I asked to see safety deposit box number 237, and was led to a tiny room filled with locked deposit boxes. The woman who had escorted me to this room left, and I went on a hunt for the box.

Once I found it, I braced myself, wondering what awaited me.

I opened the box and found that it was full of government documents held in manila folders. There was a typed note taped to the top folder. It read: "Johnny boy, here is your next book. This story needs to be told."

And that was how I came into possession of the government documents that started my nine-year investigation of C.I.A. Operative #67357, better known to the world as Elvis Presley.

Still unsure of what I was now in possession of, I bundled up the files and carried them out of the bank. I then sat in the parking lot in my Porsche for the next three hours reading document after document, barely able to believe what I was reading. If these documents were real, the famed rock singer Elvis Presley faked his death in 1977 and became some sort of spy/assassin for the Central Intelligence Agency.

Surely this couldn't be real, I thought. This had to be some sort of elaborate trick being played on me from beyond the grave. But it wasn't. I knew in my heart that, as ridiculous as this all sounded, it was true. It wasn't Charlie's style to play such a cruel joke on someone, and the sheer work it would have required to forge those documents made the whole thing seem unlikely—especially for a joke Charlie would never live to see the outcome of.

No, these documents were the real deal. There wasn't enough in those files to fill an entire book, but they would certainly serve as a great jumping-off point. I had a good idea even then that such a book would entail ungodly amounts of research and probably hundreds of interviews, most of which would likely never go on the record.

But it was a start, and I knew there was a great book there if I was up to the task of writing it. And it would turn out that I was—but just barely.

The book you now hold in your hands turned my life upside down. In the nine years it took to complete it, I lost my Marilyn Monroe, my fortune, and my once-sound mind. I would ultimately become exceedingly paranoid, searching for government agents in the shadows, wire taps on my phone, and bombs in my car. This book would cause me to have a mental breakdown and spend several months in an institution.

But please don't dismiss this as the work of a madman. The story told within these pages will be difficult for you to believe, but it is true. Knowing that many readers would use my questionable mental health as an excuse to disbelieve the revelations I offer here, I decided to present only the facts. In other words, I'm butting out. You will not find my personal opinions and assertions within these pages. Instead this book was assembled as an oral history of sorts, finding its narrative in the words of those who knew Presley, as well as a variety of documents, both personal and governmental.

I was warned by numerous people not to unearth the Presley/C.I.A. connection, but I chose to press forward. My search for the truth would ultimately become an overpowering obsession for me, and I would find it difficult to focus on much of anything else. Not surprisingly, I was stonewalled by literally hundreds of interview subjects, and even told by more than one person to "fuck off" or go fuck myself. One gentleman, a lifelong friend of Presley's and a member of the so-called Memphis Mafia, even punched me in the face. And yet I persisted. I was vaguely threatened by extremely frightening people, and threatened in a way that was less than vague by others.

Most of the people I interviewed just out and out lied to my face, and others feigned bewilderment and astonishment regarding the issue. But the keys to telling this story, I would find, would be the handful of knowledgeable people who risked their lives and careers by speaking on the record; not the least of which was Presley's confidant and C.I.A. comrade Bo Whitaker. Whitaker's assistance on this project was invaluable, and we spoke nearly every day over a three-year period, right up until the mysterious boating accident that claimed his life in May of 2009.

To be truthful, all of my most valued sources are now deceased. Make of that what you will. None of them appear to have been murdered—at least not that I can prove. They all died accidental deaths under questionable circumstances. A boating accident; an automobile accident; a fall in the shower; a freak snow-blowing accident; a bow-hunting accident; and so on. Two of my most valued sources apparently took their own lives. Another was an apparent victim of auto-erotic asphyxiation.

Perhaps now you will understand my paranoia. Even as I write this I can hear strange sounds outside my window. Is it a government operative sent to murder me? Probably not, but it could be. Maybe it's even Elvis Presley himself, wielding the famous sequin-handled Colt .45 automatic that so many people told me about.

So you decide: did Elvis Presley fake his death and become a C.I.A. operative? Read the recollections of those in the know and pore over the documents and transcripts I've compiled, and decide for yourself.

—Jonathan Woodson,
February 19, 2013

EDITOR'S NOTE

Author Jonathan Woodson died before finishing this work. The remainder of the book was then painstakingly assembled in accordance to detailed notes found inside the author's home. A full year was spent organizing the missing documents and quotations, and we are confident we have done justice to Woodson's original vision.

We attempted to investigate the claims made within this volume, but were unable to prove or disprove the quotations and their context as Woodson and nearly all of his on-record sources are dead.

Because Woodson alleges in his introduction that the accidents which befell these individuals were perhaps something more than accidental, it becomes necessary to explain the author's own death so as not to add credence to these theories. On February 19, 2013, Jonathan Woodson died in a freak electric dishwasher accident. Although such deaths are extremely rare, the coroner's office has concluded that this is indeed what happened in this instance.

EDITOR'S NOTE PART TWO

Due to the deaths of the editors who assembled this book based on Jonathan Woodson's notes, we remaining editors here at Hill House Publishing wish to disassociate ourselves from the project. We had absolutely nothing to do with the publishing of this book. In addition to this, we are all huge Elvis Presley fans and loyal Americans who kind of think Woodson was a dick.

Should any interested parties wish to speak to someone about the publishing of this book, we suggest Hill House Publishing chief Tony Piccolo. He can be reached at the following address:

Tony Piccolo
1422 Cumber Hill Road
New York, NY 10002

DEDICATION

This book is dedicated to the late Tony Piccolo.

WHO'S WHO

GINGER ALDEN—Singer and model who was Presley's fiancee at the time of his "death" in 1977.

BISHOP—Central Intelligence Agency operative known as a "cleaner." He discreetly cleaned up messy killings and murder scenes.

DANNY BONADUCE—A member of the Partridge Family.

CARL BRADSHAW—A car salesman and member of Presley's bowling team.

ALBERT R. "CUBBY" BROCCOLI—The producer of the James Bond film series.

DAVID CASSIDY—A member of the Partridge Family (and the name of Bo Whitaker's pet monkey).

CHUCK COLSON—Special Counsel to President Richard Nixon who later served time in connection with the Watergate burglaries of 1972.

LT. DICKEY CROMWELL—A former member or the Memphis Police Department.

SGT. LARRY DAVENPORT—Non-commissioned officer from Milford, Minnesota, who led Presley through the Vietnam jungle.

EARL DUNLEAVY—A UFO enthusiast.

SHARON JEAN DUNLEAVY—The wife of Earl Dunleavy.

JOE ESPOSITO—A close friend of Presley's and a member of his entourage.

DR. CHARLES FENDRICK—The plastic surgeon who performed Presley's facial reconstruction surgeries.

LAMAR FIKE—A close friend of Presley's and a member of his entourage.

SAM GOULD—A C.I.A. officer sent to Area 51 to help Presley adjust to his position. "Sam Gould" is not his real name.

LT. COL. DEMNEY HOLCUM—United States Air Force commander at Area 51 from 1966-1977.

LT. DEWAYNE JENKINS—A former member of the Memphis Police Department.

BUD KROGH: An official of the Nixon White House administration who was later imprisoned for his role in the Watergate scandal.

MARTY LACKER—A close friend of Presley's and a member of his entourage.

EDWARD LAFTONTAINE—A C.I.A. officer sent to Area 51 to help Presley adjust to his position. "Edward Lafontaine" is not his real name.

GORDON LIDDY—President Nixon's intelligence chief who (along with Howard Hunt) orchestrated the Watergate burglaries in 1972.

ERIKA LINDSKEY—A C.I.A. assassin from the years 1974 to 1985. "Erika Lindskey" is not her real name.

CPL. TOMMY "DOC" MARCUM—A field medic from Parsons, Kansas, who accompanied Presley's squad into Vietnam.

LESLIE MARTIN—A member of the organization known as C.R.E.E.P.

CAROLYN MERRILL—The president of the unofficial "We Love Elvis Presley Fan Club" from 1971 to 1986.

TOSHIRO MIFUNE—A legendary Japanese actor best known for his collaborations with director Akira Kurosawa. These included *The Seven Samurai*, *Yojimbo*, and *Rashomon*.

DEL NEWMAN—The leader of the organization known as C.R.E.E.P.

GEORGE C. "DR. NICK" NICHOPOULOS—Elvis Presley's personal physician from 1969 until his "death" in 1977.

BOOTS PELTIER—Presley's handler at the C.I.A. from 1971-1980. "Boots Peltier" is not his real name.

SGT. PAT PETERSON—A former member of the Memphis Police Department.

DARNELL "PINKY" PINKLEMAN—The owner and proprietor of a Knoxville, Tennessee bar named Pinky's Bar and Grill.

PRISCILLA PRESLEY—Presley's wife from May 1, 1967 to October 9, 1973. She later became an actress and is perhaps best known for appearing in the *Naked Gun* films.

REZA RAHIMI—A C.I.A. operative stationed in Iran from 1975-1981. "Reza Rahimi" is not his real name.

SGT. RUDY RANDOLPH—Helicopter pilot in Vietnam hailing from Richmond, Virginia, who flew Presley in to Bravo base camp.

PVT. TYRELL "JUNIOR" REDDING—A member of the extraction team sent to Hanoi with Presley. Redding hails from Atlanta, Georgia.

JERRY SCHILLING—A member of Presley's entourage who also handled his money and later managed the Beach Boys.

RUDY SHATZINGER—A New Mexico radio deejay and member of Presley's bowling team.

BILLY SMITH—A close friend of Presley's and a member of his entourage.

RAY WALKER—A member of Presley's back-up band, the Jordanaires.

RED WEST—A close friend of Presley's and a member of his entourage. He also wrote songs for Presley (such as "Separate Ways") and appeared as an actor in sixteen of his films.

SONNY WEST—A close friend of Presley's and a member of the his entourage. He was also a musician who first recorded the songs "Rave On" and "Oh, Boy!"

BO WHITAKER—A member of Presley's entourage and one of his very closest friends. Whitaker was initially put on the payroll as a bodyguard, and then later joined the C.I.A. alongside Presley.

CHALKY WILSON—The C.I.A.'s top assassin in the 1970s.

TOBY WONG—One of Presley's contacts through the C.I.A. and a trusted friend. According to Bo Whitaker, Wong was the guy who could "get you anything." Wong is believed to be a former spy for the Chinese government.

CHAPTER ONE
CRIME FIGHTER (1968)

BO WHITAKER: Elvis and I grew up together, and as far back as I can remember, Elvis wanted to be some sort of super spy. When the James Bond books first came out in the 1950s, I remember them having a real big impact on Elvis; particularly *Casino Royale*. He used to say, "That James Bond cat, that's who I wanna be, man." Then when that first movie [*Dr. No*] came out in the early sixties, Elvis really started saying these things.

And he didn't just want to play James Bond in a movie, he wanted to *be* James Bond, man. But he did try for a while to get in those movies before setting his sights on actually becoming a real-life government agent.

ALBERT R. "CUBBY" BROCCOLI: A mutual friend of ours—I believe it was the director Norman Taurog, but it may have been Hal Wallis—introduced us when Elvis was performing in England. He said, "You produce those James Bond movies?" I said yes, and Elvis said, "The way I see it, the movies got it all wrong. That Sean Connery, he's no good as James Bond. He's not good enough." I asked him who he had in mind, and he said, "Well, me, of course." Then he asked me if I had seen any of his movies, and I confessed that I had not. He said, "You should watch *Fun in Acapulco* or *Harum Scarum*, because those are my best performances." I told him I would watch those films, just to appease him.

17

Later, when Sean left the series and we were looking for a new Bond, I remembered Elvis and considered him briefly. At least until I saw his films, and then we cast George Lazenby instead.

BO WHITAKER: When Sean Connery left those movies and they cast that damned George Lazenby fella, it almost killed Elvis. It almost killed him, man. He was just beside himself. I remember him screaming, "Fuck Cubby Broccoli!"

This is a letter Elvis sent to Albert Broccoli, dated August 13, 1968:

Dear Cubby ass-hole shit Head,

I can't believe you cast this guy in your new James Bond movie. I don't Know what you are Thinking. I am one of the Best actors working today and I told you I wanted To Be the next James Bond. You screwed up. Nobody messes With Elvis Presley man. I Could have made You're movies real popular here in The United States where I am a Huge celebrity. So what it's you're loss, Buddy.

Sincerely Yours,
Elvis Presley

RED WEST: Elvis was real mean when he got ticked. When he found out that other guy had been cast as James Bond, he punched a mirror and cut his fist. But that didn't stop him. He took a golf club and beat the hell out of his expensive high-fi stereo and then he moved on to the new TV set he had just bought for Priscilla. When I asked him what was wrong, he just said, "Those cocksuckers got some asshole to play James Bond, man." He was just really, really mad about the whole thing. It didn't set well with him at all.

PRISCILLA PRESLEY: Yeah, Elvis definitely destroyed the TV set he had gotten me for my birthday. He came into the room in a rage and just broke that TV all to hell. I remember I was real angry because *As the World Turns* was on and I was watching that. It was a real good episode, too.

BO WHITAKER: I don't think Elvis ever got over that shit. I remember him telling me, "If I can't play James Bond in a movie, then maybe I could be a real-life spy." I thought he was out of his damned fool mind, but I said, "Yeah, Elvis, maybe you can. That sounds like a great idea." He would just say shit sometimes that made you kind of scratch your head and go, what the hell? I figured this was just one of those times. Truthfully, I just thought he was doped up on the painkillers, man. I had no idea he was serious.

JERRY SCHILLING: I'll be damned if he didn't take that spy stuff as serious as a damned heart-attack. He started buying guns. Lots and lots of guns. I asked him if he was planning on attacking Bolivia, and he just said, "You never can be too careful, man."

PRISCILLA PRESLEY: I didn't like all those guns in the house. I would say, "Elvis, you got more guns in here than the entire Mexican army put together." He'd just grin and say, "Well, I got more money than the Mexican army, too. I can afford 'em."

BO WHITAKER: Priscilla didn't like those guns in the house one bit, not with her trying to raise a baby there. She used to get real mad and cuss him and they'd get in an argument over those guns. And I think you know what eventually happened... Priscilla left, and the guns stayed.

RED WEST: I remember one day Elvis bought something like thirty-two rifles and six or seven pistols. I looked at all those guns and I asked him what he needed them for. He said, "I need 'em for my work." I said, "What kind of work?" And he just said, "You and me are on a need-to-know basis. I'll fill you in when I think you need to know." I loved Elvis, but sometimes he could be really weird...really out there. He really believed he was a spy, even before he met with President Nixon. One day we were all sitting around and joking and one of the guys—I forget which one—said, "Elvis really thinks he's some kind of a spy or something." And right at that moment Elvis walked into the room and said, "Listen, you S.O.B., if you ever say anything like that I'll blow your goddamn head off." And he meant it. Everyone just stopped laughing and kind of looked around, wondering what the hell was happening.

In Alanna Nash's book Elvis Aaron Presley: Revelations from the Memphis Mafia, *entourage member Marty Lacker recalled:*

> The night of Sonny's wedding, I picked up Elvis and Sonny, and we holed up in the preacher's office, waiting for everybody to come into the sanctuary. Elvis was standing there, and he was dressed in all black, except for a white tie and those amber glasses. He had on a suit made of crushed velvet, with bell bottom pants. His hair curled up in the back, it was so long. And he had gold on everywhere—his sheriff's badge belt with diamonds, this second belt with gold eagles and chains, and some kind of chain around his neck. And he had his guns on, and he carried this fifteen-inch long, Kel-Lite police flashlight, black metal.
>
> The preacher came in and said, "Sonny, it's time to go." And then he said, "Mr. Presley, if you'll come with us, also." So Elvis started walking out of the office to go into the sanctuary.
>
> When he did, I took hold of the flashlight. I was going to take it out of his hand so he wouldn't walk out there with it in front of everybody. Well, he pulled the damned flashlight back. He wouldn't let me take it. I said, "Elvis, this is a wedding. You don't need this flashlight." He said, "If I'm not taking my damn flashlight, I'm not going." I started to laugh, and Sonny was looking at him like "God, man, are you nuts?"
>
> I said, "Elvis, you can't take this flashlight up on the altar with you. It's not right, and it won't look good. It's going to mess up the wedding." I was laughing, hoping to joke him out of it.

He thought a minute, and he said, "Goddamn, I hate to give this up." And I just took it out of his hand. So he went up there without it, but he still had his guns on. He had two gold guns in his shoulder holster, a pearl-handled pistol in the waist of his pants, and another one in the back of his pants. And the derringer in his boot. I'll bet he was the only best man in the history of Memphis to go to the altar with five guns on him, just to stand up for the groom.

BO WHITAKER: Elvis set up a firing range out behind Graceland, and he would have all us guys out there to shoot with him. He was a pretty damned good shot, even then. He used to say, "I can shoot the pecker off a coon at a hundred yards." That was his little saying and we used to hear it all the time.

LAMAR FIKE: We was all out behind the house shootin' at soda cans. I was never a very good shot, and Elvis used to kind of make fun of me. He'd say, "What are you gonna do when the damned Russians come knockin' on your door?" One time I said, "Well, Elvis, if I answer the door and there's Russians right there, I guess I'll just shoot 'em on account of them being a lot closer than those goddamned cans out there." He just looked at me kinda irritated, but he didn't say too much else about it. He used to take that shit really seriously. He actually thought maybe the damned Commies were gonna show up on his doorstep one day, and by god he was gonna be prepared.

BO WHITAKER: One thing was for sure—if we ever get attacked by soda cans, Elvis was gonna be ready for 'em.

JERRY SCHILLING: One day we were shooting at some pictures of the Beatles that Elvis hung up out behind the house, and Elvis leans over, serious as can be, and says, "You know, Jerry, one day I'm gonna be a secret agent." And that made me laugh. Elvis was always sayin' funny shit like that, so I just figured this was one of his jokes. But he didn't laugh at all. He was serious.

LAMAR FIKE: I remember those photos of the Beatles. Elvis used to shoot 'em in the face with his .22. I don't know why, but he seemed to really hate the Beatles. Maybe he was jealous, I don't know. He used to say, "That S.O.B. John Lennon is the one that said the Beatles was bigger than Mr. Jesus." That used to really irk him. He used to offer us four or five hundred dollars for the first person to shoot the Lennon photo through the eye. He really, really hated Lennon. He didn't care for any of them, but Lennon was the one he liked the least.

JERRY SCHILLING: One day Elvis walked out to where those pictures of the Beatles were hanging and he pissed all over them. He said, "Look, guys, it's raining in England, man!"

BO WHITAKER: People forget that Elvis was a black belt in Karate. Even back then, back in '61, maybe '62, he was training to be a spy. Of course we didn't know it then. We just thought he wanted to kick some ass. He used to say, "If those Commie bastards show up here, I'll give 'em a kick to the balls and a chop to the face."

What people don't know is that Elvis was always real concerned with Communists. He felt there was a plan to take over America, and he felt like a lot of entertainers were in on it. Especially the Beatles. He'd say, "Look at those little foreign sons of bitches, man, with their sloppy hair and messed up clothes. I'll bet you a Cadillac and a bucket of chicken"—he liked saying that, that he would bet someone a Cadillac and a bucket of chicken—"that those little bastards are Commies."

RED WEST: He thought there were Commies everywhere, so he only trusted his friends and family. He was just sure that most of the people in Hollywood were Commies, so he started carrying guns on him at all times.

BO WHITAKER: Elvis was sure that Tiny Tim was a Communist. He wasn't too sure about Dinah Shore, either. And he *really* thought Rip Taylor was up to no good. He used to say, "Something ain't right about that boy. I'll bet he's a Communist." But then he said that about Liberace and Rock Hudson, too. And Jim Nabors.

PRISCILLA PRESLEY: He believed there were Communists all around us. I remember one time we were eating at this nice restaurant in Palm Beach and the waiter brought Elvis the wrong thing. The waiter was real sorry and said he would run back to the kitchen and get Elvis meatballs. Elvis just leaned over to me and said, "I'm pretty sure that guy's a Communist. That's why he brought me the wrong food. It's all part of their conspiracy." I tried to tell him that the waiter not bringing him meatballs would in no way further the Communist cause, but he was just dead certain it was part of some big conspiracy. He said, "The Commies hate meatballs." I asked him why and he said, "Who knows what goes on inside the mind of a Commie?"

A lot of people would say it was all the drugs Elvis was on, but I was there. I know; Elvis was absolutely obsessed with Communists, and he thought they were everywhere. He used to say, "It's just like *Invasion of the Body Snatchers*. They're hidin' all around us, man."

BO WHITAKER: He put anti-Communist messages in a lot of his songs. He didn't write most of them, but he'd ask Jerry Leiber and Mike Stoller, or even Dolores Fuller, to add those messages in there. Listen to "Hound Dog." What he's really talking about there is Communism. That's why he says you ain't no friend of mine, because he was talking about a Commie. That whole damn song was about Communism.

JERRY SCHILLING: One night we were all at the Memphian watching a movie, just me and Elvis and the guys. I think the movie was *Mary Poppins*. Elvis started freaking out. He was broken out in a cold sweat. He grabbed his pistol and said, "Everyone in here's a fucking Commie. I'm gonna shoot every last one of these S.O.B.s." We had to fight with him to get the gun away. He was seriously gonna shoot everyone in the theater.

BO WHITAKER: I'm pretty sure it was Elvis seeing Dick Van Dyke up there on the screen that set him off. He really hated Dick Van Dyke, because one time Dick Van Dyke cut in front of him in the cafeteria at Warners. Elvis said he took the last piece of meatloaf. "I'll be damned if I didn't want some of that meatloaf," he said. That's when he decided Dick Van Dyke had to be a Communist.

So, I think that's why Elvis went crazy in that movie theater. It was either that or all the drugs Elvis was on at the time.

RED WEST: He definitely wanted to be some sort of lawman. He collected badges from different police departments and branches of the government. He used to ride along with the Memphis police officers in their squad cars. You know, they took citizens out on ride-alongs so they could see what they did, but Elvis took those ride-alongs real seriously. He used to pack three or four guns with him whenever he'd go. He was on some real Dirty Harry shit.

LT. DICKEY CROMWELL: Sure, we used to do ride-alongs all the time. Usually it was members of the city council, people like that. But then Elvis started going on ride-alongs. To be real honest, we were all excited as hell about that. I mean, who wasn't an Elvis fan, and getting an autograph from him was a great way to get in good with your girlfriend. Everyone liked it, as I recall, except for my partner, Pat Peterson. He didn't care for Elvis one bit. He used to say that his wife had a thing for Elvis, and she would pretend he was Elvis whenever they made love. He said he didn't mind so much because at least he was getting sex, but then seeing Elvis there in the squad car used to piss him off real good.

SGT. PAT PETERSON: My wife never had a thing for Elvis. Dickey just made that up. He's full of shit.

LT. DICKEY CROMWELL: So one night we're out on patrol, Pat and me, and we got Elvis with us in the backseat. I'm pretty sure he was high on something, but we didn't say anything because, you know, he was Elvis. Well, we pulled over a car for speeding. Right off the bat Elvis was unhappy. He was saying, "Look at that sports car. I'll bet they's Communists in there."

SGT. PAT PETERSON: So we chase this car for something like two miles before they finally pull over, and Elvis is steamed. When we finally pull them over, Dickey and me get out of the car with our guns drawn. I told Elvis to stay in the car, but he didn't listen. He got out and ran up to the car before we could even get to it. The guy in the car opens his door and starts to get out, and Elvis grabs him and throws him to the ground. He pulls out a .45 and sticks it in the guy's mouth. He says, "Make a move, sucker, and you're dead."

LT. DICKEY CROMWELL: I believe his words were, "I'll fill you so full of lead you'll be able to use your pecker for a pencil." Pat probably doesn't remember it all that well because he's an alcoholic. The man gets up at six o'clock and he drinks his breakfast, if you know what I mean. That's why he got kicked off the force.

SGT. PAT PATTERSON: Dickey's a goddamn liar. I never got kicked off the force, I quit. And as for me being a drunk, I hardly even drink. Sure, I have a Natty Light every now and again, but who doesn't?

I think Dickey's just sore because I didn't come to his wedding. But Christ, that was forty years ago! Who gives a shit, you know? Dickey always was a no-good prick.

LT. DICKEY CROMWELL: So Pat and me look at each other like, what the hell? Why does Elvis have a gun? So we go to pull Elvis off, and he gets real mad and starts yelling at us and calling us names. He called me the no-good son of a motherfucker.

SGT. PAT PETERSON: And he said we were Commie bastards. Those were his words, "you damned Commie bastards." Meanwhile this guy we pulled over is just lying there on the ground staring at us, wondering what the hell was going on.

And it turns out the guy was deaf, which is why he didn't hear our sirens. So Elvis almost shot the guy for not pulling over, and it was all on account of his being deaf! And he was like, "Sorry, man. I shouldn't have done that." Taking Elvis on ride-alongs got to be a real strange event. All the cops talked about him doing crazy shit like that, but no one ever did anything about it on account of him being Elvis.

LT. DEWAYNE JENKINS: One time Elvis went out on patrol with me and my partner, Otis, God bless his soul. Looking back on it, I'm pretty sure Elvis was high on something. And we're out riding around, and he says, "Can I drive the squad car? I always wanted to drive a damned squad car." I said, "We would, but we could get in real big trouble." But Elvis says, "I'll give you both a hundred bucks each if you let me drive the squad car for a mile or two and turn on them sirens." Well, a hundred bucks was a lot of money in 1969, so we said, "Yeah, what the hell?" So we took him out on the highway and let him drive the squad car.

Well, he starts following this little Volkswagon bug and he says, "I think we got us a criminal right there." And he pulls out a pistol and starts firing out the window at the car. First we said, "You can't shoot at civilians, Elvis." Then Dewayne says, "You know you ain't supposed to bring that damned gun with you anymore, anyway." Elvis keeps shooting, and he looks at Dewayne and says, "Now how the hell am I supposed to do any police work without a damn gun?"

We tried to get him to stop shooting, and the car was swerving all over the road. He almost hit the cars driving in the other lane three or four times. Finally the Volkswagon went off the road and hit a tree. When we caught up to it, the driver—it was an old woman—was dead. Elvis just says, "You guys don't have to thank me."

Lucky for all of us, Elvis never managed to hit the car with a single bullet, so we were able to just pretend we found her there dead. Then Dewayne got to thinking and he pulled out a bottle of hootch and poured it all over the woman to make it look like she'd been drinking. And Elvis said, "Dewayne, you're pretty smart, man, you know that?"

In his book, The End of Elvis, author R.D. Riley writes:

> After going on a number of ride-alongs, Elvis started to believe he was actually a police officer himself. One day he turned to his manager, Col. Tom Parker, and said, "I'll be damned if I'm not the best police officer in the whole damn city of Memphis." Parker just looked at him and shook his head. By this time he was used to Presley saying these strange things, but this one still caught him off-guard.

BO WHITAKER: I think those ride-alongs made him really start to feel like he could be some sort of law-enforcement officer. He'd been talking about this shit for a long time, but now I think he really believed he could do it in a way he hadn't before. I think those ride-alongs are what really gave him the balls to eventually go talk to the president.

PRISCILLA PRESLEY: I used to tell him he couldn't be a cop or a secret agent or anything like that. He'd say, "Why?" And I'd tell him because he was famous. I mean, people mobbed us everywhere we went. Everyone knew who he was. It would have been impossible for him to go into a regular line of work, let alone be a secret agent.

Whenever I'd say that to him, he'd have one of his fits and start destroying things. One time he tipped over the refrigerator. Another time he shot the TV screen. One time he punched Red. He'd say, "Priscilla, you're just trying to hold me down. You just wanna destroy my dreams." Then he'd call me a damn Communist.

CHAPTER TWO
MR. BURROWS GOES TO WASHINGTON (1970)

BO WHITAKER: On December 19, 1970, Elvis and his daddy got into a real big tussle. I've heard it was because Elvis was spending a bunch of money on the guys, and Vernon didn't like that. He'd just bought ten brand-new Mercedes for about $80,000 apiece. Priscilla says the argument was over the Colonel. She says Elvis was ready to fire him because he was tired of him meddling in his affairs, but Vernon wouldn't let him. Then I've also heard that the whole damned argument was just over some orange juice. The story goes that Vernon saw Elvis drinking out of the carton and he about blew a gasket. He said, "A grown man don't drink outta the carton, Elvis." Elvis got pissed and started yelling back, and it turned into this big blow-out with Vernon saying, "I don't like the orange juice with the pulp anyway. Why you always getting that damned orange juice with the pulp?" But who knows what it really was that got them going. They were both hard-headed suckers, and if you got either one of them going, watch out, man.

RED WEST: So Elvis gets ticked and just disappears. No one can find him anywhere. Vernon come in there and said, "I can't find Elvis. He's not in his room. Has anybody seen him?" And no one had. Then, finally, the phone rang and the maid gives it to Sonny. Sonny answers and talks to Elvis. Then he comes back and says, "You ain't gonna believe this shit. Elvis went to Washington, D.C. with Jerry Schilling to see President Nixon." At first we thought it was a joke, but then we realized Sonny was serious.

BO WHITAKER: Elvis got mad and decided to go to the Memphis airport by himself. He had never done anything like that before. He hated traveling alone. Well, he got to the airport and he freaked out, probably because of all those people. So he calls Jerry Schilling, who was in Los Angeles. He says, "Jerry, meet me at LAX and bring some cash." He actually flew from Memphis to L.A. and then back to Washington, D.C.

JERRY SCHILLING: I didn't know what the hell was going on, and Elvis wasn't much help figuring it out. He was real cryptic on the phone. He said to meet him at the airport and to bring $500 because he had left the house without any money. So I get the money and meet his plane at LAX. He was acting really strange and was extremely secretive. He said he couldn't tell me what was happening, and he said it was for my own good. He said, "If they take you captive, you won't be able to tell them anything, man. It's called plausible denial."

BO WHITAKER: Elvis was out of his fucking mind. He was high and paranoid. He thought he was some kind of super-spy. So on the plane to Washington, Elvis starts writing a letter to President Nixon.

JERRY SCHILLING: We were on the plane and Elvis was writing his letter to Nixon on American Airlines in-flight stationary. He was very concerned that every word of the letter be just right. He'd say, "Hey Jerry, do you think the word 'respect' should be capitalized?" I'd say no, and then he'd say, "I think it looks more respectful if respect is capitalized. What do you think?" So I'd just agree with him. It was easier that way.

So he's writing this super-secret letter to the president, and he finds out that California Senator George Murphy is on the plane, too. So Elvis brought Murphy into the conversation. He says, "I'm writing a top secret letter to President Nixon." Murphy asks him what it's about. Elvis just says, "It's top secret, man." Then Elvis tells him he's gonna put his name in the letter as a sort of recommendation. He doesn't ask Murphy, he just tells him. Then he tells Murphy that he met Vice President Agnew a few weeks before that. "Do you think I should mention that, too?" Murphy just shrugs and says, "What the hell..."

This is the letter Elvis wrote to President Nixon, dated December 19, 1970:

Dear Mr. President,

First, I would like to introduce myself. I am Elvis Presley and admire you and Have Great Respect for your office. I talked to Vice President Agnew in Palm Springs three weeks ago and expressed my concern for our country. The Drug Culture, the Hippie Elements, the SDS, Black Panthers, etc. do not consider me as their enemy or as they call it The Establishment. I call it America and I Love it. Sir I can and will be of any Service I can to help the country out. I have no concern or motives other than helping the country out. I am on this plane with Sen. George Murphy and we have been discussing the problems that our country is faced with.

Sir, I am staying at the Washington Hotel, Room 505-506-507. I have two men who work with me by the name of Jerry Schilling and Sonny West. I am registered under the name Jon Burrows. I will be here for as long as it takes to get the credentials of a Federal Agent. I have done an in-depth study of Drug Abuse and Communist Brainwashing Techniques and I am right in the middle of the whole thing where I can and will do the most good.

I am Glad to help just so long as it is kept very Private. You can have your staff or whomever call me anytime today, tonight, or Tomorrow. I was nominated this coming year one of America's Ten Most outstanding young men. That will be January 18 in my Home Town of Memphis, Tenn. I am sending you the short autobiography about myself so you can better understand this approach. I would love to meet you just to say hello if you're not too busy.

Respectfully,
Elvis Presley

P.S. I believe that you, Sir, were one of the Top Ten Oustanding Men of America also.

I have a personal gift for you which I would like to present to you and you can accept it or I will keep it for you until you can take it.

JERRY SCHILLING: He tells me I can read the letter, but then says I can't show it to anybody. I say, "Who the hell am I gonna show it to? We're on a damn airplane, for Christ's sake." And he says, "I'm pretty sure the airline stewardess is a Commie." So I start reading the letter, and I get to the part about him giving the president a gift. I say, "What kind of gift are you gonna give Nixon?" And he reaches into his carry-on bag and pulls out this great big chrome-plated Colt .45. I say to him, "Elvis, you can't flash that thing around on the plane," and he says, "I'm Elvis Presley. I can do whatever I want, man."

BO WHITAKER: Elvis was in a crazy state of mind. He was obviously stoned. So he meets a soldier on the plane who's coming home from 'Nam. So Elvis says, "God bless you, son."

JERRY SCHILLING: He tells this kid what a hero he is and what a service he's done for his country. "Goddamn I love you boys for what you're doin' over there in Vietnam. You're a hero, son." Then he says, "I want you to be comfortable while you're at home," and he gives him his ring and his watch as gifts. Then he tells me to give him the $500 I brought. I say, "Hold up, Elvis. That's all the money we got." And he gets real serious and says, "Jerry, I said give this guy here the $500. He's a fuckin' hero, man." So I gave him the money, and later on Elvis says, dead serious, "Why the hell did you give that boy all of our money? Are you out of your goddamn mind?"

RED WEST: Elvis calls Sonny from the airport and tells him to fly out to Washington. "We're gonna meet with the president," he says. "Don't tell anyone. In fact, you should probably make sure you aren't followed. Get a taxi and just take it to three blocks away from the hotel. That way they won't know where you're going and you can see if anyone's tailing you." Sonny was real confused by all that secretive shit, but he said, "What the hell," and he did what Elvis told him to do.

In the book, The End of Elvis, Sonny West tells author R.D. Riley:

> I got to the airport in Washington D.C. and I was nervous as a colored fella at a KKK rally. I'm wondering the whole time who the hell is following us and what exactly is going on. So I'm looking over my shoulder, thinking we might be in some kind of danger.
>
> I was at the airport, waiting for my baggage, and I saw this old woman looking at me kind of funny. I try not to make eye contact with her, but she just kept looking. Then it dawned on me that she was probably one of *them*—you know, whoever it was that was after us. I thought maybe Elvis had been right all along—maybe it was Communist spies or something like that. Then I thought maybe she was with the mob, because Elvis had always been real nervous about them, too.
>
> She just kept staring at me, watching my every move. So finally, I just got up and tackled her. I punched her a couple times and smashed her jaw up real good. Then I grabbed my suitcase and I high-tailed it outta there.
>
> I took three different cabs to the hotel so I wouldn't be followed. Then I get there, Jerry tells me Elvis is just being paranoid and he's wanting to be a spy again. Turns out I punched the hell out of that old

woman for nothing at all. I was real heartbroken about that, but you know, Elvis was the boss. When he was crazy, we were all a little crazy, man.

JERRY SCHILLING: When Sonny came to the door at the hotel, Elvis almost lost his shit. He jumped about three feet high. He grabbed two pistols off the bed—one for each hand—and he ran over to the door. He said, "Them cocksuckers are here. Hide behind the bed, Jerry. I'll take care of this." So he yanks the door open and jumps out into the hallway—oh, and I forgot to mention, he had just gotten out of the shower so he was naked except for his oversized sunglasses—and he jumped on top of Sonny. He says, "I'm gonna kill you, you S.O.B. bastard!" Then he realized it was just Sonny so he let him up, but after he did, he said, "I could still kill you if I wanted to." Sonny asks why Elvis would want to do such a thing, but Elvis just says, "I'm just lettin' you know, man."

Sonny later explained his take on this incident in Kerri Bayer's book, Memphis Mafia Memories:

> When Elvis jumped on top of me, I pissed myself a little. Luckily I had just taken a leak at the airport, but still a little bit came out. That was the worst part. Well, that and having Elvis' dick and balls on my chest. That wasn't too good either.
>
> So we get up and Elvis looked me right in the eyes, still naked there in that hallway, and he said, "I just want you to know I could have killed you." I said yeah, I know—something like that. And he said, just as serious as can be, "I can *still* kill you." I said, "Why the fuck would you want to do something like that?" And he said, "You never can be too careful, what with them Commie brainwashing techniques and all."
>
> I don't think Elvis ever really trusted me again after that. I think he always believed I had become some sort of Commie on the plane trip to Washington.

Things just wasn't never the same again. You know, sometimes I could feel him just staring at me, or I'd turn my head and catch him looking at me. I'd say, "What's wrong, Elvis?" And he'd say, "I think you and I both know the answer to that one, man." But he never really said anything. He didn't fire me and he didn't kill me, so who knows what he was really thinking.

JERRY SCHILLING: Elvis decides he's gonna take the letter to the White House. So all three of us climb into a rented limo and go the White House. We have to go to the gate—they won't just let you walk up to the see the president—and the guard doesn't recognize Elvis. That really pissed him off.

BO WHITAKER: Later Elvis said, "I almost shot that cocksucker." I said who, because he was always wanting to shoot some cocksucker or another. And he said, "That guard at the White House, man." He was just really pissed about that whole thing.

JERRY SCHILLING: Elvis says, "I wanna see the president, son." And the guard says he can't allow him on the premises without permission. "Well, you better get some permission then." So the guard calls someone inside the White House and asks for permission. "What's your name?" the guard says, and Elvis is really steamed. He says, "What's my name?" And he grabs the telephone out of the guard's hand and talks to his superiors.

RED WEST: Apparently Elvis said, "Listen you cocksuckers, this is Elvis Presley. Let me come up there and see President Nixon." Because Elvis wasn't used to being told no. That was a word he just never heard. When he wanted something, he got it. We made sure he got it, whatever it was. But we didn't have any pull here in a situation like this.

Transcript of the security guard phone call between Elvis Presley and White House official Bud Krogh:

PRESLEY: Who is this?

KROGH: This is Bud Krogh. Can I help you?

PRESLEY: I'm Elvis fuckin' Presley, man.

KROGH: The singer?

PRESLEY: And actor.

KROGH: What can I do for you, Mr. Presley?

PRESLEY: I need to see President Nixon today.

KROGH: We might be able to set something up, but it won't be for today. The president's schedule is very busy and these things take time.

PRESLEY: You better make time, sucker.

KROGH: [Inaudible] ...day, Mr. Presley.

PRESLEY: Listen you cocksucker, I need to see Richard Nixon today.

KROGH: Matters like this take time.

PRESLEY: I'll give you till this afternoon then. I'll leave a letter at the gate explaining my intent to the president. The letter is for his eyes only. It's top secret, man.

KROGH: Uh, okay.

PRESLEY: I don't want you reading this letter. I know how you guys up there work. You read the president's mail before he sees it. But this is different...I'm Elvis Presley. For all I know you could be a damned spy or something.

KROGH: I assure you I'm not a spy.

PRESLEY: Okay then, thanks, man.

KROGH: No problem.

PRESLEY: I'll see you this afternoon.

JERRY SCHILLING: Sonny and I just looked at each other like, what the hell is this man doing? But we didn't say anything. People always accuse us of being yes-men. Well, that's not exactly true. It wasn't so much that we said yes as it was that we just never said no. We both thought what Elvis was doing was crazy, but we kept our mouths shut.

BO WHITAKER: Sonny said the ride back to the hotel was the most tense ride he'd ever been on. He said Elvis just kept fiddling with his pistols, cocking them and taking them apart and then reassembling them right there in the limo. He was saying he was gonna shoot someone in the face and he didn't care who it was. Jerry and Sonny got real nervous that Elvis might turn on them because he was acting so damn strange.

JERRY SCHILLING: Just when we thought it couldn't get any worse, a Beatles song came on the radio. It was "Yellow Submarine." Elvis got real ticked and he said, "I hate them goddamn Beatles, man." Then he whispered to us so the driver couldn't hear him. "They're part of the reason we're here, man." I said, "What does that mean?" Well, he didn't explain. He just said, "They're part of what's destroying these United States. They're part of the problem." Then he thought about it for a second and said, "No, they *are* the fucking problem, man." No one said anything else the rest of the ride back to the hotel. Elvis just kept mumbling about "fucking yellow submarine, my ass" under his breath. "I'll show you a fuckin' yellow submarine..."

SONNY WEST: We went back to the Washington Hotel and one of the hotel employees says, "Hello, Mr. Presley." Elvis reached for his pistol and said, "I'm Jon Burrows, goddammit. Look it up in your book there. I'm Jon fucking Burrows." And he pulled the pistol on the

ELVIS PRESLEY, CIA ASSASSIN

woman. She says, "I'm sorry. I guess I thought you were someone else," and he said, "You're goddamn right you did."

He was as mad as I'd ever seen him. Usually he would have tried to have sex with the woman, but he was just so damned mad about the way Krogh had treated him at the White House that he couldn't see straight.

We went up to the main room, and Elvis still had his gun out as we walked through the hotel. We went up to the room and turned on the TV. *Clambake* was on, and that made Elvis real happy. That was one of his favorite movies he'd worked on. He cheered up right away and he said, "You know, I screwed that chick right there, that Shelley Fabares." Of course we already knew he had, but we played along and acted like we were hearing about it for the first time. We just wanted a happy Elvis. A happy Elvis meant that we were gonna be happy. Then his cover of Jerry Reed's "Guitar Man" came on in the movie and Elvis perked right up. He just said, "Goddamn, that's a good song, man." Everything about the movie made him happy except Bill Bixby. He just said, "Bill Bixby's a damned Communist, man." Then he took some painkillers and went to sleep.

BUD KROGH: We didn't know what the hell to make out of Elvis Presley at the White House. Nixon didn't even know who he was. He actually said, "Now who is that Elvis Presley? Is he a foreign diplomat?" I had to explain to him all about Elvis and rock-and-roll music, and Nixon didn't care for that one bit.

Excerpt from a memo by Bud Krogh to White House Chief of Staff Bob Haldeman:

> Several people have mentioned over the past few months that Presley is very pro the president. Such a meeting with Mr. Presley would take very little of the president's time and could be beneficial for the president to build some rapport with him. In addition, if the president wants to meet with some bright young people outside of the Government, Presley might be a perfect one to start with.

BUD KROGH: Bob Haldeman almost laughed me out of the room. He called me and said, "Are you serious?" I said yes, I was. After all, this was an administration who still believed their relationship with Jack Webb, Billy Graham, and Art Linkletter might appeal to young people. Nixon really didn't have his hand on the pulse of America's youth. Haldeman and I argued about the matter for a few minutes before he finally said, "Tell you what. Let's flip a coin. Heads Presley goes home, tails he meets Nixon." So we flipped a coin and it came up tails.

JERRY SCHILLING: We got a call that afternoon from Bud Krogh. He said, "The president can see you in about twenty minutes. Get on over here." So the three of us—Elvis, myself, and Sonny—zipped across town to the White House. But the president didn't meet with us right away. First we had to go to Bud Krogh's office for a screening interview. Elvis didn't care much for that.

The official transcript of Elvis Presley's pre-screening with Bud Krogh:

>   PRESLEY: When am I gonna see the president?

>   KROGH: Soon. I just have to talk to you for a few minutes first to ascertain what your full intentions here are.

>   PRESLEY: Ascertain away, man.

>   KROGH: [Laughs.]

>   PRESLEY: What's so goddamn funny?

>   KROGH: Nothing. [Coughs.] So what made you decide to meet with the president?

>   PRESLEY: Everywhere I go people say to me, they say, "Elvis, this country of ours is going into the ground, man. It's going right into the ground." There's all this bad stuff out there. Hell, they killed

Sharon Tate before I even got a chance to have sex with her! Then there's Communists and Black Panthers and all this other crazy shit. It's scary out there, man.

KROGH: Right.

PRESLEY: I just want to do my part, man.

KROGH: And how do you intend to do that?

PRESLEY: That's a secret, man. That's just between Tricky Dick and me.

KROGH: If you wish to talk to the president, you'll have to tell me.

PRESLEY: Okay, I just want to be like an undercover agent out there. Out in the field, man. I figure I can live my life and whenever troublemakers and subversives come my way, I can help the government catch 'em.

KROGH: That's quite noble, Mr. Presley.

PRESLEY: You can say that again.

KROGH: So I understand you're a big fan of the president?

PRESLEY: Hell yeah. I voted for him, and I made all my boys vote for him. I said, "If you cocksuckers wanna live here anymore, you vote for that damned Nixon." I figure I got him about twenty extra votes there in Memphis.

KROGH: I see.

PRESLEY: We need to talk about [inaudible] hamburger with pickles, you know?

KROGH: Indeed.

BUD KROGH: Meeting Elvis Presley in person was really strange. He'd called me a cocksucker and a spy on the phone, so I wasn't sure what to make of him. He was quite a charming fellow in real life, but he was a little bit strange, to say the least. But the kids loved him, and that was all that mattered. We thought maybe Nixon could convince Elvis to record an anti-drug record called "Get High on Life" over at the federal narcotic rehabilitation and research facility in Lexington.

SONNY WEST: Elvis had on his black suede suit, a white shirt with high collars that opened down the chest, about five gold necklaces, and a huge belt from the International Hotel with a big gold belt buckle. He also had on a purple cape and his oversized sunglasses. Those people at the White House looked at him like he was some kind of alien.

JERRY SCHILLING: So they frisk Elvis after the meeting and they find the .45 he plans to give to the president. They're all like, "What is this shit?" And he says, "Oh, don't worry, I left my other five guns out in the car." So they took the gun and said they would make sure Nixon got it. You know, it was, "We can't let you carry a handgun into the Oval Office."
Elvis wasn't too happy with the guards.

BO WHITAKER: He told me later he shoulda killed those S.O.B.s with a couple of Karate chops.

BUD KROGH: I started to take Elvis and his friends into the Oval Office, but Elvis stopped me and said, "Only me. These guys stay outside." They looked at each other and one of them said, "But we want to meet the president." But Elvis said no. He said, "This is a top-secret mission." So I shrugged and led him into the Oval Office.

Transcript from the Oval Office recordings of the conversation between Elvis Presley and Nixon:

NIXON: I'm pleased to meet you, Evan.

PRESLEY: My name is Elvis, sir.

NIXON: Oh yes, oh, okay.

PRESLEY: Pleased to meet you, sir.

NIXON: Well, the feeling is mutual, son.

PRESLEY: I'm a big fan of yours, and I have been for a long, long time.

NIXON: Is that so?

PRESLEY: Yes, sir, Mr. President.

NIXON: Well, what is it you wanted to see me about?

PRESLEY: I'm concerned with the problems facing America today. I'm concerned about racism, and I'm concerned about the Black Panthers, and I'm concerned about the damn hippies. Mostly I'm concerned about Com-munism.

NIXON: I see.

PRESLEY: Do you know about the Beatles?

NIXON: Beetles?

PRESLEY: No disrespect, sir, but they're cocksuckers.

NIXON: Cock...suckers?

PRESLEY: Oh yeah, man. Big time cocksuckers.

NIXON: I'm not sure I follow you, son. What exactly are we talking about here?

PRESLEY: We're talkin' about freedom.

NIXON: [Inaudible.]

PRESLEY: I believe in America, sir. I believe in an America where little boys and girls can grow up and live without fear.

NIXON: Fear of what?

PRESLEY: You know, they fear all kinds of stuff, man. It's a real scary world out there.

NIXON: Oh.

PRESLEY: So what I want is to be a damn C.I.A. agent.

NIXON: What?

PRESLEY: I wanna be in the C.I.A. where I can help get this country back on track. Now I don't wanna go undercover, at least not yet. I wanna be kind of an agent out in the field, man. I wanna do good.

NIXON: Do good, I see.

PRESLEY: So yeah, I wanna be a damn C.I.A. operative.

NIXON: It's difficult to get into the Central Intelligence Agency, Alvin. At least that's what I'm told. I've never been in the C.I.A. myself. What makes you think you've got what it takes to be a C.I.A. operative?

PRESLEY: My name is Elvis Presley, sir, and my mama taught me that I could be any damned thing I wanted to be in this old country we call America.

NIXON: She did, did she? Hmmm.

PRESLEY: I been gettin' ready for this for a long time, sir. I'm a black belt in Karate. I could kill a man, sir.

NIXON: You could?

PRESLEY: Yeah, I was in the Army, too.

NIXON: Did you kill anybody in the Army?

PRESLEY: No, sir. Mostly I just cleaned latrines and worked on jeeps. That sort of thing.

NIXON: Oh, okay.

PRESLEY: And I can shoot a gun like nobody you ever saw. I can shoot like a damn Audie Murphy.

NIXON: You can, can you?

PRESLEY: I can shoot the pecker off a damn coon at a hundred yards. I believe in America, sir. I believe in freedom. I want to be in the C.I.A. or some other super-secret branch of the government if you got one. I'm not all that picky as long as I get to be a spy.

NIXON: I might be able to get you a meeting with the director of the C.I.A., but I can't promise you anything beyond that. Not many people make it, so I wouldn't get your hopes up too high.

PRESLEY: I'll make it, sir.

NIXON: Right. But I need you to do me a favor in exchange for my setting you up with this meeting.

PRESLEY: You want me to kill someone? I'll do it. Consider that fucker dead, man. You think I should shoot 'em or stab 'em or Karate 'em up?

NIXON: No, no, nothing like that.

PRESLEY: Just say the word and I snap into killer mode and become a damn killer robot.

NIXON: No, that won't be necessary. I just want you to record a song for me, son.

PRESLEY: Well, my name is Elvis Presley, sir, and that's what I do.

NIXON: It's a song about not doing drugs. Can you do that? Do you do drugs, son?

PRESLEY: No. Just painkillers and some other stuff.

NIXON: Good. Bud Krogh will fill you in about the song.

PRESLEY: And I'll meet with the C.I.A.?

NIXON: Yes, Albert. I'll make the call to Richard Helms this afternoon.

PRESLEY: Thank you, sir.

NIXON: It's good to meet a nice, upstanding young man such as yourself, son.

PRESLEY: Well, you know, T.C.B.

NIXON: T.C.B.?

PRESLEY: Takin' care of business, man.

NIXON: Thanks for coming by. Bud'll show you out.

BUD KROGH: Nixon sends for me, so I come in and get Elvis and take him back out to meet his friends. On the way back, Elvis turns to me and says, "You know something? I'm a damn cold-blooded killer, Mr. Krogh." I had no idea what the hell he was talking about, so I just nodded and kept walking.

SONNY WEST: Mr. Krogh brings Elvis back to us, and Elvis is smiling big as hell. He says, "I think I got it." I don't know what he's talking about, but I figured if it made Elvis happy, then it made me happy.

BUD KROGH: He says, "I got it." When he said that, I didn't know what the hell he was talking about. I just thought Nixon had given him one of the presidential lapel pins he kept on-hand for visitors and foreign dignitaries. It wasn't until later that I found out he wanted to be in the Central Intelligence Agency.

A memo from President Nixon to Central Intelligence Agency Director Richard Helms, dated December 20, 1970.

> I would like you to meet a young man I met today named Elvis Presley. I would like you to give him a tryout for your agency. He wants to be an operative. I know this isn't the way we normally handle this,

but I'm extremely impressed with him and I believe he has the credentials to be a good operative.

You're the director, not me. So if you give him a look-over and find that he's not suitable for the Central Intelligence Agency, feel free to pass. I'd just like you to look at this young man. I think he could do a very good job for you.

P.S.—Are we still on for a round of golf next Sunday? I'm doing *Meet the Press* that morning, but I can meet you at the country club at two. Call my secretary and let her know. Please give my regards to your wife.

A memo from Richard Helms to President Nixon, dated December 21, 1970:

Elvis Presley, the singer? Is this some kind of a joke? Please let me know. I'm not sure what to think about all this.

As for golf on Sunday, I'll be there. Be prepared to get your ass kicked for the fourth consecutive time, Dick.

A memo from President Nixon to Richard Helms, dated December 21, 1970:

No, it's no joke. I am indeed speaking of the troubadour Elvis Presley. We have done a full background check on him and he came up clean. Also, I believe he is a good young candidate for your program and I think he's got the mettle to do it. Just give the boy a look-see and let me know what you think.

P.S.—You will not be kicking my ass. I've been practicing. How about this? Sunday afternoon beers are on the loser. (It won't be me, I assure you.)

A memo from Richard Helms to President Nixon, dated December 21, 1970:

I'll check Mr. Presley out, but I'm not promising anything. He seems kind of dull to me, but you're the president.

And yes, beers will be on you this Sunday. I plan to consume several at your expense.

A memo from President Nixon to Richard Helms, dated December 21, 1970:

Do you remember that rash you had last summer? What did you do to get rid of that? I seem to be breaking out in a similar rash and it's all over the back of my calf and there's a little bit on my nut sack. Let me know. Thanks.

A memo from Richard Helms to President Nixon, dated December 21, 1970:

I tried that over the counter cream, but it didn't work. It was all over my back and on my legs and on my ass. Finally I had to go to the doctor. He gave me some kind of shot and it cleared right up.

CHAPTER THREE
CANDIDATE #452-H (1970)

BO WHITAKER: Elvis sat by the phone every day for a week, waiting for the C.I.A. to call. When they finally did call, Elvis was real irritated for having had to wait. Elvis was not a man who was used to waiting for things, man. The call came from Richard Helms, the big boss over there at the C.I.A. Elvis says, "What the hell took you so long, son?" I guess Helms just laughed uncomfortably and asked Elvis if he still wanted to apply to the C.I.A. Elvis said, "Does a bear shit in the woods and wipe his ass with a fluffy white rabbit?" I guess Helms didn't know what to make of that.

When Elvis got off the phone, he was happy as a lark. He said, "We gonna be in the C.I.A., Bo." And I said, "*We?*" 'Cause this was the first time I'd heard about my joining the C.I.A. with him. He said, "Hell yeah, Bo. You're comin' along with me, man." I wasn't sure I wanted to join the C.I.A., but I figured Elvis knew best so I just went along with it. He said, "I got me a tryout over there at the C.I.A. next week. At first it's just gonna be me, but after they hire me on I'm gonna make sure you get to go, too." This was big news. I had never even dreamed of graduating from high school, let alone joining the damn C.I.A. So I said, "Yeah, man, that sounds great," you know?

So Elvis flies out there to Langley for a couple of days. First they had to screen him before his testing began. I guess they hooked him up to a lie detector and asked him a bunch of questions.

Excerpt from transcription of Elvis Presley's Central Intelligence Agency screening with Chief Tester Russ Amplas, December 28, 1970:

AMPLAS: Elvis, I'm going to ask you a few questions. I'd like you to answer them as thoroughly and as honestly as possible.

PRESLEY: No problem, sir.

AMPLAS: Please state your full name.

PRESLEY: Elvis Aaron Presley.

AMPLAS: Where were you born, Mr. Presley?

PRESLEY: Tupelo, Mississippi.

AMPLAS: What were you like in high school?

PRESLEY: I was real outgoing. I had a lot of friends.

AMPLAS: What kind of grades did you get?

PRESLEY: I was a "B" student, man.

AMPLAS: Have you ever done anything that might be considered malicious or harmful to an animal?

PRESLEY: One time I strapped my dog Duke to the front of my Cadillac and drove it around town.

AMPLAS: Why did you do that?

PRESLEY: I guess I thought he might like it.

AMPLAS: Did he?

PRESLEY: He didn't really say, but I don't think so.

AMPLAS: Have you ever worked for a foreign government?

PRESLEY: Does New Jersey count?

AMPLAS: No. Why, have you worked for the New Jersey government?

PRESLEY: No, I was just wondering.

AMPLAS: How do you deal with anger?

PRESLEY: Sometimes I break stuff, shoot the TV, things like that.

AMPLAS: Why do you want to join the Central Intelligence Agency?

PRESLEY: I wanna give back to my country. I just wanna do my part, man. I wanna catch bad guys and fight crime.

AMPLAS: What is it you think we do at the C.I.A.?

PRESLEY: Y'all do spy stuff.

AMPLAS: And what do you think "spy stuff" entails?

PRESLEY: Super sneaky secret stuff, like James Bond.

AMPLAS: What special qualifications do you have that you think we might find resourceful here at the C.I.A.?

PRESLEY: Hell, I'm Elvis Presley, son.

AMPLAS: Meaning?

PRESLEY: Meaning I can get access to people and places that normal people can't.

AMPLAS: Such as?

PRESLEY: Such as an interview with the Central Intelligence Agency.

AMPLAS: *Touché.*

PRESLEY: Yeah, what you said, man.

AMPLAS: How do upsetting questions make you feel?

PRESLEY: I find that question to be upsetting.

AMPLAS: And how do you feel?

PRESLEY: I feel alright, man.

AMPLAS: Do you speak any languages besides English?

PRESLEY: I speak fluent pig latin. *Oday ouyay eakspay igpay atinlay?*

AMPLAS: *Esyay, iway oday.* What if you were asked to walk away from your friends and family for years at a time, maybe even forever?

PRESLEY: I guess I'd feel real bad about it, but I could do it. Whatever the job calls for, man.

AMPLAS: Anything? What if it entailed killing someone in the line of duty?

PRESLEY: I could do that. If you tell me to kill somebody, I'll kill that sumbitch deader than hell, man.

AMPLAS: What are your thoughts on the Cold War?

PRESLEY: I think they ought to let them boys wear coats so they won't be so damn cold.

Memo from Chief Tester Russ Amplas to Central Intelligence Agency Director Richard Helms, dated December 28, 1970:

I have just completed my screening test with candidate #452-H, Elvis Presley. I have found him to be honest, but completely unremarkable in every way. In truth, I find him to be a bit dull, but I could be wrong. I thought the same thing of Richard Nixon, and look where he's at.

BO WHITAKER: After the initial screening, they did a word association game with Elvis. He said he did real good on that one...

Excerpt from transcript of word association test with Elvis Presley conducted by Tester Garrison McCoy, December 28, 1970:

MCCOY: Mr. Presley, I am going to give you several words. When I give you a word, I'd like you to tell me the first thing that pops into your head. Okay?

PRESLEY: Sure thing, boss.

MCCOY: Okay, let's begin. The first word is "children."

PRESLEY: Airplanes.

MCCOY: "Submission."

PRESLEY: A spaceman with a green backpack on.

MCCOY: "Love."

PRESLEY: Air-conditioner.

MCCOY: "Society."

PRESLEY: Pickle.

MCCOY: "Honesty."

PRESLEY: Cow hooves.

MCCOY: "Religion."

PRESLEY: Chicken-fried steak with white gravy.

MCCOY: Okay...

PRESLEY: No, no, let me change that. Brown gravy, man. It's gotta be brown gravy.

MCCOY: "Mother."

PRESLEY: Fucker.

MCCOY: "Intelligence."

PRESLEY: Purple condoms.

MCCOY: "Death."

PRESLEY: Crusty ear wax. You know, just really crusty, man. Really nasty.

Memo from Tester Garrison McCoy to Central Intelligence Agency Director Richard Helms, dated December 28, 1970:

> I just gave the word association test to candidate #452-H. His answers were unlike any I have ever received before. Either he's the dumbest son of a bitch who's ever taken this test, or he's one of the most brilliant minds we've ever come across. I honestly don't know what to make of his responses. Either they're as stupid as they appear, or this young man is operating on a whole other plane we can't even begin to fathom.

Memo from Richard Helms to Garrison McCoy, dated December 28, 1970:

> If you were absolutely pressed to make an assessment, how would you assess this candidate?

Memo from Garrison McCoy to Richard Helms, dated December 28, 1970:

> I believe this man is so brilliant that he inadvertently circumvented traditional testing methods. I think he's the real deal. In my estimation, he's a keeper.

BO WHITAKER: I guess Elvis did real good on his tests, at least that's what he told me. He said they didn't know quite what to make of him on account of he was so smart and all. He said the word association game was real hard, but he was pretty sure he answered 'em right.

The next test they had him take was a physical training test to find out whether or not he was in shape. Because of his Army training, along with his Karate, he did real good on that, too.

Memo from Physical Tester Reginald Jacobs to Richard Helms, dated December 29, 1970:

> Candidate # 452-H, otherwise known as Elvis Presley, did quite well on his P.T. test. He did exceptionally on his 12-mile run and passed with flying colors on push-ups, pull-ups, and sit-ups. Physically, he is an above average specimen. His score was over 300.

BO WHITAKER: After they had him run and jump and do push-ups and all that nonsense, they had him take a 1,200 question written test about math, science, history, and a bunch of other stuff. Elvis was real nervous at first. He said there were questions he didn't quite understand and fancy two dollar words he'd never heard before. He said he looked at the test for a minute or so, said a quick prayer to Mr. Jesus, and just went through coloring in boxes at random.

Memo from Chief Tester Russ Amplas to Richard Helms, dated December 30, 1970:

> Candidate #452-H, Elvis Aaron Presley, finished his test in record time. He completed the entire test in an astonishing fifteen minutes. The previous record was three hours and forty-three minutes. At first I thought there could be no way he'd actually read the questions, but when we graded his test, we found that he missed only one question. This gives him the highest score in the history of this test by a considerable margin. I repeat, Presley not only finished the test in record time, but he also scored higher than anyone in the history of the Central Intelligence Agency.

> My conclusion: I was wrong. Elvis Presley may just be the most intelligent person on the face of the earth. Were he to become a part of the C.I.A. he would be the most intelligent man ever to do so.

Memo from Richard Helms to Russ Amplas, dated December 30, 1970:

Are you shitting me?

Memo from Russ Amplas to Richard Helms, dated December 30, 1970:

I shit you not. The man is a genius.

Memo from Richard Helms to Russ Amplas, dated December 30, 1970:

You've met the man. How is this possible?

Memo from Russ Amplas to Richard Helms, dated December 30, 1970:

It is my belief that Mr. Presley only appears to be stupid because his extremely high intelligence causes him to ignore or bypass normal social mores. We frequently find that highly intelligent people have little to no social skills and may come across as...well, retarded.

Memo from Richard Helms to Russ Amplas, dated December 30, 1970:

How sure of this are you?

Memo from Russ Amplas to Richard Helms, dated December 30, 1970:

In the words of Mr. Presley himself, I'd be willing to bet you a bucket of chicken and a Cadillac that this conclusion is correct.

BO WHITAKER: Just like that, the C.I.A. invited Elvis to train and become a special operative. Elvis said he just knew it was because of

Mr. Jesus that he passed that test as well as he had. That's what he always called him—"Mr. Jesus." He said, "Jesus needs to be shown more respect for the things he's done. That's why I call him Mr. Jesus." So I just said, "Okay, no problem, Elvis." He was the boss, and what the hell did I care if he wanted to call him Mr., or Dr., or even Jr. I didn't really give a shit one way or the other, man.

The guys at the C.I.A. told Elvis that he was special and they really wanted him to join them. They said, "If you pass the training course, we'll give you anything you want." Elvis just said, "If I pass the test, you make me a special operative. That's reward enough, man." So Elvis tells them, if you want me, you gotta take my friend, Bo Whitaker, too. They said, "Well, we'd be happy to take him if he passes the tests like you did." And Elvis says, "Hell no, man. We're a package deal. You want Elvis, you're taking Bo, too. He's gonna be my C.I.A. partner." They said, "C.I.A. operatives don't really have partners." But Elvis said, "Bullshit, Elvis Presley has a damn partner and his name is Bo." The thing was, Elvis hated being around people he didn't know. That's why he had all of us guys living up there with him at Graceland. Us and his family, we were his whole world, man. He didn't care about everyone else, and he didn't trust them. He told me that; he said, "I need to have someone else in the C.I.A. with me that I can trust." So finally they said, "Okay, you can take Bo along with you."

So Elvis asks them, "When does this training start? I gotta be home by six." They say, "Well, training lasts six to nine months." And Elvis said, "Not for Elvis Presley it doesn't." They didn't know what to do with him, but they wanted him in their C.I.A. so they said they'd make an exception for him. So while everyone else in the C.I.A. trained for six to nine months, me and Elvis just trained for a month. That was it.

So Elvis says, "Okay, when does this training start?" And they said it started immediately. Elvis was like, "I don't get to go back home first?" And they said no. They let him call me and Priscilla and that was it. I answer the phone and Elvis says, "You're coming with me to the damn C.I.A." And I said, "Okay, when?" He says, "Tomorrow." Then he tells me we gotta come up with an explanation as to why he's gonna be gone for the month. So I suggest maybe we say he went to rehab, but he says, "No, that's too far-fetched. We need something more realistic." Then he says, "Maybe we could tell 'em that NASA contacted me and I'm going out there to space in a rocket." But I convinced him that was a bad idea. Then Elvis came up with a few more ideas, like his being in prison for a month, or saying he became a pirate. Finally we came up with the idea that he would say he was taking a month-long vacation to get away, man.

PRISCILLA PRESLEY: Elvis called me and said, "I'm gonna be gone for a month or so, honey." I asked him where he was going and he said he was taking a break from everything. I asked him if I could come with him, but he said no. I asked him if everything was okay, and he said "sure." That's what he said, "sure." And that was it. I really think that was the beginning of the end of our relationship.

SONNY WEST: All the guys were real surprised when they found out Elvis was going on vacation without them. Everyone was all, "Where's Elvis?" And then we found out he went on a vacation without any of us. Just Bo. Bo was the only one who got to go with him. Everyone was real jealous. Everyone was saying, "Fuck Bo. What's so great about him?"

BO WHITAKER: So I go out there to Langley and they put me through the same tests they put Elvis through. They did the word association test with me, the physical training test, and the 1,200 question multiple choice test. Elvis said, "Ask Mr. Jesus for help," so I did. I really said that, too. I said, "Mr. Jesus, can you help me with these tests?"

Memo from Chief Tester Russ Amplas to Central Intelligence Agency Director Richard Helms, dated January 2, 1971:

> Candidate #955-D, Bo Whitaker, has completed all testing. If Elvis Presley is the smartest trainee we've ever had, Bo Whitaker will be the stupidest. He failed every test in dramatic fashion, and his physical prowess is as bad as I've ever seen.
>
> Why Presley wants this numskull to accompany him is beyond me. I know I shouldn't ask this, but are they gay lovers?

Memo from Richard Helms to Russ Amplas, dated January 2, 1971:

> I kind of wondered that myself, but our intel says Presley is a real ladies' man. Have you seen the ass on his wife? She's hotter than a two dollar pistol. I think he's his sidekick, like the Cisco Kid and Pancho. They always have dummies for sidekicks.

Memo from Russ Amplas to Richard Helms, dated January 2, 1971:

> Mrs. Presley is rather attractive. She has some great legs, which go up and make quite an ass out of themselves. Have you looked at the photograph of her in Presley's dossier? She's magnificent. I've probably looked at that ten or twelve times now. She's super hot.

Memo from Richard Helms to Russ Amplas, dated January 2, 1971:

> Russ, you are one sick bastard. It's you that's been masturbating all over the dossier photos, isn't it? And all this time I thought it was Terry Martinez from the Records Department. Hell, I almost fired him for that shit. No more, Russ. No more. I catch you doing it again, you'll be sacking groceries for a living.

BO WHITAKER: When I got to Langley that next day, they took us in a bus to their facility near Williamsburg. It's called Camp Peary, but everyone just calls it "The Farm." The senior instructor, his name was Samuels, told Elvis and me that we were gonna be taking a shortened version of the class since we had to be out of there in a month. He told us that most people washed out of the course, but Elvis said, "Nah, man, I'm gonna be a damn C.I.A. operative." In Elvis' mind, it was that cut and dried. There was absolutely no way he wasn't gonna make it, man. It was all he wanted, and Elvis always got whatever he wanted.

So we spent most of the time learning about demolition, guns, knives, disarming methods, surveillance, counter-surveillance, cryptography, photography, resistance to interrogation, you name it. We learned a lot during that month. We'd only been at The Farm for about two weeks when Elvis got kidnapped from a local C.I.A. bar called Teddy's Tavern. It was crazy.

What happened was, Elvis was outside the bar. He wasn't drunk. Hell, he didn't even have one drink. Well, he was standing out there when a bunch of guys drove up, jumped out of their truck wearing masks, and tossed him into the back and sped away. We later found out they were Russian operatives looking for information about The Farm. They didn't even know who the hell Elvis was.

They told Elvis they wanted the names of his instructors and any information about The Farm he could give them. He thought it was fake. Elvis thought the whole thing was a training exercise, so he made up his mind they weren't gonna break him. So I guess they beat the shit out of him for several days—just beat the living hell out of him. He said they kicked him in the balls so many times he was sure he'd never need to wear a rubber ever again after that. Then they put him in a cell with a bright blinding light in his face around the clock. He said it was unbearable. He said he would close his eyes and he could still see that light through his eyelids, man. And they kept asking him, "Who are your instructors? What do you know about The Farm?" And he wouldn't give them anything.

Then they turned out the lights and left him there for a few days without any food. They stripped him down naked and kept hitting him with a cattle prod. They hooked a car battery to his testicles, but he still didn't tell them anything. After all, he knew it was a training exercise. Of course it wasn't really, but he thought it was.

After a few days of all this, they brought in a man they said was a C.I.A. operative and they cut his throat in front of Elvis. Elvis thought it was fake, of course. He said, "I know that man's not really dead." Then they tried sleep deprivation for several days, and they just kept questioning him about his superiors. And Elvis gave them nothing. So then they turned on the stereo really, really loud and pumped it into his cell. It was the Beatles' "Strawberry Fields." He said the first few times he heard it was okay, but after a couple of days he was about to go out of his damn mind.

So then one day after Elvis had been gone for about a week and a half, he was real close to breaking. One of them got a little bit too close to him, and Elvis grabbed the guy's pistol and shot all of them.

After all, he thought the gun had blanks in it. He still believed this whole thing was fake. I guess he went crazy and just kept shooting at them until the clip was empty. He said he kept waiting for them to come in and turn off the music, but no one did. He waited for the men he'd shot to get up and tell him the exercise was over, but no one did. So Elvis ran to the nearest payphone and called the senior instructor.

Because of what he'd done, Elvis earned the Distinguished Intelligence Medal. He became the first man ever to be awarded the medal while still in classes at The Farm. Of course he didn't get an actual medal. Because this is all top secret, they just show you the medal and shake your hand. But he earned the damn thing, man.

After all that, they just let us go home. They told Elvis, "You're a NOC now." He said, "What the hell is a NOC?" They said it was a non-official cover operative. That meant that he was so secret he wasn't even on the books anywhere as an agent. If he was to get caught in another country, the United States wouldn't even recognize his existence.

Elvis just said, "Yeah, I'm a damn NOC now, man. Let's go home." So for a while we just went home. Sure, we went out on the occasional mission, but mostly we just sat around at Graceland. Elvis recorded some new music and we pretended like nothing out of the ordinary had happened.

CHAPTER FOUR
A MAN CALLED CLETUS (1971)

BO WHITAKER: When we were gone to Langley, a bunch of the guys had caught this show down in Knoxville by this fella named Cletus Monroe. By this time there were several guys out there imitating Elvis, but Cletus Monroe was just the spitting image of him. The S.O.B. looked just like Elvis. Hell, he could have been Elvis' twin brother Jesse if Jesse had lived. So Sonny and some of the other boys keep talking about this ol' boy, and they're trying like hell to get Elvis to go see his show. "I'll be damned, I thought I was watching you perform," Marty said to Elvis. "He looked just like you, man, and he's got all your moves down cold. I didn't tell him who I was, but I went up to him and shook his hand after the show. Shit, man, he looked *exactly* like you and I've known you forever and a day, Elvis. I almost thought you were playing some kind of joke on me. I thought maybe it was you."

Elvis doesn't like being made fun of, and he feels like this guy Cletus Monroe is out there making fun of him. We kept telling him that Cletus Monroe was just paying tribute to him and his work, but Elvis was real sore about the whole thing. Whenever one of the guys would ask him for some money, Elvis would say something like, "Why don't you go ask Cletus Monroe for the money." Shit, I remember asking Elvis what he wanted for dinner one night and he told me to go ask Cletus Monroe. He just didn't take things like that very well. It's like when he found out they were selling alcohol in decanters that looked like him. That made him mad as hell. He was yelling about how he didn't even drink alcohol, and I remember real well that he kicked a hole in the closet door in the south hallway at Graceland over that. Things like that just didn't sit well with him.

Then one night Elvis knocks on my door at three in the morning. I say, "Man, Elvis, it's three o'clock in the morning." He just looks at me all serious and says, "Can I come in?" I'm still half asleep and rubbing my eyes, but I say, "Well, shit, Elvis, you're the boss, now ain't you?" So I let him in and he locked the door behind him. He was acting real funny again and for a brief second I thought maybe he was gonna shoot me over the whole damn C.I.A. thing. I mean, I was the only one who knew about all that stuff.

He looks me right in the eyes and says, "I think I know how I can make this damn Cletus Monroe thing work in our favor, Bo." I didn't know what the hell he was talking about, so I asked him how. He says, "We don't want anyone to know we're in the C.I.A., right? But my life as Elvis Presley the entertainer has to continue. But the thing is, it can't continue because I got C.I.A. training to do. I don't think I can be Elvis the entertainer and Elvis the spy at the same time." I still don't know what the hell he's talking about, but I say, "Yeah, man, whatever you say, Elvis." And he says, "We're gonna drive up to Knoxville and see what this Cletus Monroe fella is all about. We're gonna see if he really looks and sounds like me. If he does, I'm gonna hire him to be my damn double." I'm still a little confused by all this. I say, "What exactly will he be doing?" Elvis says, "He'll be Elvis the entertainer. He'll do my live shows for me. We can teach him what to say in interviews. Hell, he can live here at Graceland when I'm off on C.I.A. business, man. That way the fellas won't even know I'm gone." It was nutty, but it sounded like a great idea if Elvis could really pull it off. So I ask him, "Are we going *now*?" I mean, it was still three in the morning. Elvis puts on his big sunglasses and says, "Put on your clothes, Bo. We're goin' to Knoxville, son."

LAMAR FIKE: Elvis walked into the living room at three in the morning. I'm sitting there watching some old monster movie on TV. I said, "Where the hell you going at this time of night, Elvis?" He just looks at me and says, "I'm going to Knoxville." I was like, "At three in the morning? What the hell is going on?" He just says, "I'm going to meet Cletus Monroe." So I asked him, "Do you want me to go with you?" He said, "No, it's just gonna be me and Bo." Things were weird with Elvis and Bo for a while. You couldn't separate them for a year or so there. It seemed like they had some kind of secret that the rest of us weren't in on.

BO WHITAKER: So Elvis and me drive down to Knoxville, and it's raining the whole way. Elvis keeps breaking into song, singing "Rainy Night in Georgia." It's a six-hour drive, but I think we made it in about four hours. Elvis was just real anxious to meet with this guy, Cletus Monroe. When we finally get to Knoxville, it's about seven, eight in the morning. Elvis tells me to pull up next to a payphone. I ask him what he's doing and he just says, "You stay put. I'm gonna go make a couple calls and find out where the hell this sucker lives, man."

DARNELL PINKLEMAN: Yeah, Elvis definitely called me at about seven-thirty in the morning. I'd been out drinking all night, and he says, "Darnell, is that you, man?" At first I didn't recognize his voice, so I was all, "Who wants to know," you know? And he says, "Darnell, this is Elvis." I hadn't spoken with him in a couple of years. He asks me, "You still running the bar?" I say, "Hell, yeah, Elvis. Business is booming, man. What do you need?" He says, "I hear you got a guy performing there named Cletus Monroe." I said yeah, and I'm starting to wonder if Elvis is pissed because we got a guy impersonating his act. He says, "I need to find Cletus Monroe. It's urgent." I say, "Goddamn, Elvis, it's seven-thirty in the morning. Can't this wait?" He just says, "No, man, I gotta find him ASAP." Then it occurs to me that Elvis might wanna hurt the guy, so I ask, "You ain't gonna shoot him or nothing like that, are you?" Elvis doesn't answer. Finally, after a minute or so, he just says, "I need you to introduce us, man."

So I figured shit, this was Elvis Presley. So I pushed the tranny hooker I was in bed with off me and got up and got dressed. I drove out to the bar to meet with him.

BO WHITAKER: Elvis knew this cat named Darnell who runs Pinky's there in Knoxville, where Cletus Monroe put on his show. Darnell says he'll take us to meet Cletus. It's still early in the morning, maybe eight or so, and it's pouring down rain. So we all go out to this rundown trailer park on the edge of the city. We go to one of the trailer houses—a real piece of shit—and it's Cletus Monroe's place. Darnell knocks on the door, and Cletus comes out in just a bathrobe, underwear, and those damned oversized sunglasses like Elvis had on. I'll be damned if he didn't look just like Elvis. He was the spittin' goddamn image. He says, "Who the fuck is it? It's only eight in the morning," or whatever time it was. Then he sees Elvis and he about shits himself.

We all go in and Darnell's trailer is absolutely covered with photographs and posters and dolls and figurines and collector's plates of Elvis. Elvis is looking around at the walls, and he's kind of stunned. He asks Cletus, "You don't wanna have sex with me or nothing like that, do you?" Cletus says no, he's straight, and Elvis looks relieved, man. Cletus is just in awe of Elvis, and I think Elvis is kind of in shock that this guy looks just like him. Elvis jokes with him and says something like, "You know, you're a pretty good lookin' man, Cletus." Cletus laughs and says the same back to Elvis. You know, it wasn't really that funny, but we all laughed anyway.

Then, finally, we got down to it. Elvis turns to Darnell and says, "Pinky, I need you to go outside." Darnell looks kind of sad about the whole deal, but he goes back outside into the rain. Elvis tells Cletus, "I can't explain it to you right now, but I might wanna hire you for a job." Cletus is in shock. "What kind of job?" Elvis just says, "Like I said, I can't tell you right now." So Cletus asks, "This gig you're talking about, does it pay?" This makes Elvis laugh, and he says, "More money that you can imagine, Cletus." Then Elvis tells him he wants to see his act. "Right here?" Cletus asks. Elvis says yeah, right there. So at eight in the morning, in his robe, right there in that tiny trailer, Cletus put on an impromptu version of his whole damn show. And it was amazing, man. It was just like watching Elvis perform. Cletus knew every single beat, every hip thrust, *everything*. Cletus was the real deal.

So Elvis says, "Cletus, you got yourself a job, son."

Excerpt from a letter written by Cletus Monroe to his father, Marty Monroe, dated February 19, 1971:

> I can't say much about it, mostly because I don't actually know any details yet, but Elvis Presley came to my trailer and offered me a job out in Memphis. I asked him how much the job paid, and he said, "More than you've ever made." Isn't that fantastic?

Excerpt from a letter written by Marty Monroe to Cletus Monroe, date unknown:

Are you out of your fucking mind? Your mother and I have been telling you for years to lay off the booze and go out and get a real job. You've been feeding us lies for years to make us believe you were doing okay. Yes, we knew the entire time that you were full of it. But how on earth do you expect us to believe that Elvis Presley actually came to your tiny shit hole of a trailer there in Knoxville and offered you a job? I've seen your act, son. You're not that good. What, is Elvis paying you to stop singing and giving him a bad name? It's seriously time for you to give up the alcohol and go out and get a respectable factory job. Why can't you be more like your older brother, Tim?

Excerpt from a letter written by Cletus Monroe to Marty Monroe, dated March 8, 1971:

Why can't you ever support anything I do? Why can't you just be proud of me, Dad? I've been trying for years to get your attention and make you proud of me, but nothing ever seems to work. That's it, Pop. You won't be hearing from me anymore. Now you'll have what you've always wanted—to just have Tim for a son.

BO WHITAKER: So Cletus comes out to Memphis and Elvis has a meeting with him. He tells him that he's working for the Central Intelligence Agency. "I could have you killed, man," he says. "Just like that," and he snaps his fingers. Then he explains that he wants Cletus to pretend to be him and do public appearances and shows. Elvis tells Cletus he will not be recording any of the new songs. "That's my job," Elvis said. "I'm the *real* Elvis." Then he says, "You ain't to tell no one about none of this. This is top secret spy stuff, man. You can't even tell any of the fellas that live here. They don't even know. Only Bo knows about all this shit." Then Cletus asks, "Am I gonna live here at Graceland?" Elvis says, "No, only when I'm gone away on spy business or training to be a damn killer, man."

A journal entry by Cletus Monroe, dated March 15, 1971:

> Elvis is a little bit of a prick. I guess that old thing about building up your heroes and then discovering what they're really like is true... Still, this is the gig of a lifetime if I can pull it off. I'd like to honor Elvis and his image by doing a really great job. Tomorrow is my first big day. Tomorrow I train with Elvis and Bo so that I'll be able to do interviews and TV appearances. They want me to make an appearance on *The Tonight Show* in a couple of weeks, so I have to be prepared by then.

BO WHITAKER: Elvis decided that the two of us should coach Cletus over what to say and what not to say in interviews. We knew that training him could take a while, but it was real important that he be prepared. Elvis wanted him to make his first appearance in his place on Johnny Carson's show, so time was of the essence here.

One thing we did was to have Cletus interview Elvis about important subjects that might come up. That way he could learn Elvis' beliefs on these things and would know what answers to give when he himself was asked those questions. We taped the interview with a tape recorder so Cletus could study it over in the weeks to come.

Transcript of taped interview between Cletus Monroe and Elvis Presley (with Bo Whitaker), March 18, 1971:

> MONROE: So what do you want me to do here?
>
> PRESLEY: We gotta turn the tape recorder on.
>
> MONROE: I think it is on.
>
> PRESLEY: No, it's not.
>
> MONROE: It's making a humming sound.
>
> PRESLEY: I don't know.

MONROE: The wheels are turning. It's taping now.

PRESLEY: Hey Bo, you know how to turn on this damn tape recorder, man?

WHITAKER: Hold on... Yeah, it's on. See those wheels turning there?

PRESLEY: You sure, man?

WHITAKER: Yeah.

PRESLEY: Okay, cool.

MONROE: So what do I do now?

PRESLEY: You just ask me questions that might come up in an interview.

MONROE: Then what?

PRESLEY: Then I'll answer them and you'll be able to study this tape and learn what your answers need to be when Johnny Carson asks 'em to you.

MONROE: Okay.

WHITAKER: Hold on a sec, man.

PRESLEY: Yeah?

WHITAKER: You forgot to take your pills, Elvis. Here they are.

PRESLEY: Thanks. [Takes a drink of water.] Okay, now where were we?

MONROE: I'm supposed to ask you questions.

PRESLEY: Okay, shoot, man.

MONROE: How are you doing?

PRESLEY: That's a shitty question.

MONROE: I'm supposed to say that?

PRESLEY: No. If they ask that question, which they won't, because it's kind of shitty, you just say, "I'm doing good, man. Real good."

MONROE: Okay. Are you working on any new material?

PRESLEY: Oh, yeah, man, I've got some great new material coming out soon. I think everyone's gonna love it. I really enjoyed recording it.

MONROE: Did you record those songs by yourself?

PRESLEY: I recorded them with the Jordanaires.

MONROE: I say that?

PRESLEY: Yeah.

MONROE: Every time?

PRESLEY: Yeah, it's usually the Jordanaires, so that's a safe answer.

MONROE: Are you making any new movies?

PRESLEY: No, I'm taking a break from the movies to focus on other things.

MONROE: Like what?

PRESLEY: Like being a damn C.I.A. operative.

MONROE: I say that? I thought that was a secret.

PRESLEY: Yeah.

WHITAKER: Elvis, you can't tell anybody about that. That's a secret, remember?

PRESLEY: Oh, yeah, don't tell nobody about that then.

MONROE: Then what do I say?

PRESLEY: What was the question?

MONROE: The movies.

PRESLEY: Oh yeah, don't answer that one.

MONROE: Why?

PRESLEY: 'Cause I don't feel like talking about that right now.

MONROE: Okay. Next question?

PRESLEY: Sure.

MONROE: How do you feel about Vietnam?

PRESLEY: The country or the war?

MONROE: The war.

PRESLEY: I don't have an answer for that one. Why don't you ask me about the country? I got a great answer for that one.

MONROE: [Inaudible.]

PRESLEY: Oh, Vietnam is a great little country. I'm a big fan of all those European countries. Especially France and, uh, Vietnam.

MONROE: So what do you think about the war?

PRESLEY: Which war?

MONROE: Vietnam.

PRESLEY: Just say something like this, "I think our boys are doing a great job over there defending our great nation against those damn Commie bastards." Something like that.

MONROE: Okay. What do you think about President Nixon?

PRESLEY: He's a great guy. I got to meet him a while back. We didn't talk about anything real important like, say, me becoming a spy or anything. We just talked about life and the problems facing this great nation of ours. I think he's got some real great ideas about fixing America, and I'm a big fan of his.

MONROE: What music do you listen to in your spare time?

PRESLEY: Besides my own?

MONROE: Yeah.

PRESLEY: I like Harry Nilsson a lot. I think he's about to be real big. You know, he's the guy who sang "Everybody's Talkin'" for *Midnight Cowboy*.

He's got a new album comin' out at the end of the year. I got to listen to a few tracks and it's great.

MONROE: What do you think about the Beatles' recent break up?

PRESLEY: I don't wanna talk about that.

MONROE: I should say that?

PRESLEY: No, just try to change the subject.

MONROE: Why?

PRESLEY: Because I fuckin' hate the Beatles, man. I hate those little foreign cocksuckers. I just look at 'em, I wanna punch 'em in their smug little faces, man. *Pow, pow, pow*, you know?

WHITAKER: There's four of 'em, Elvis.

PRESLEY: Okay, *pow*! That's four pows now, right?

MONROE: Okay. Will you be touring again soon?

PRESLEY: [Inaudible.]

WHITAKER: Are you guys hungry?

PRESLEY: Yeah.

WHITAKER: What are you in the mood for?

PRESLEY: Tacos. I'd definitely like some damn tacos, man.

MONROE: You think I'm gonna be ready for the *Tonight Show*?

PRESLEY: I'm gonna get some sour cream on my tacos.

BO WHITAKER: So we worked with Cletus for weeks, prepping him for that interview. We taught him to really *be* Elvis Presley, man. We even had him talk to Elvis' daddy, Vernon, just to see if Vernon had any idea something was wrong there. Vernon didn't know at all, man. He saw Cletus and just started yelling at him like he was Elvis. Cletus came back and said, "That old man was yelling at me about some damn peanut butter. What do I say back to him?" Elvis just says, "You just yell back at the fucker. Tell him to stick that peanut butter up his ass. That's what I do." So Cletus goes back in there and looks at Vernon, who's reading his newspaper, and just says, "You can stick that peanut butter right up your ass, old man." Elvis just grinned in the next room and said, "That's my boy." Then when some of the fellas came up to Cletus and asked him for some money, Elvis just had him give 'em a few hundred apiece, and no one had a clue it wasn't him. As long as he was givin' the fellas money, they weren't gonna notice anything out of the ordinary.

So a couple of weeks go by and it's time for Cletus to go on Johnny Carson. Elvis tells me, "I never liked going on that show anyway." I asked him why, and he just said Carson asked too many questions. Elvis hated to be asked questions, but it turned out Cletus loved the attention, man. He was the exact opposite of Elvis. Cletus really thrived in that kinda situation.

Excerpt from Cletus Monroe's first appearance as Elvis on The Tonight Show, April 5, 1971:

> CARSON: We haven't seen you in a while. How have things been?
>
> MONROE: Things have been great. I'm not doing any new spy stuff or anything like that. You know, I've just been working on some new material, doing my thing, being Elvis Presley.
>
> CARSON: That's good. What can we expect from the new material?

MONROE: It's good, real good. I think everyone's gonna be real happy with it. I recorded it with the Jordanaires. It's some of the best stuff I've ever done.

CARSON: Why don't you sing some of it for us?

MONROE: No, I can't. You'll hear it soon enough.

CARSON: Sing anything for us.

MONROE: What would you like me to sing?

CARSON: Anything. How about "Suspicious Minds"? That's a pretty good one.

BO WHITAKER: So Cletus stands up on his chair, and he's wiggling his hips a little, and he starts singing "Suspicious Minds" real slow and sexy-like. And he's doing great. He's got Carson and that audience in the palm of his hand. Elvis turns to me and says, "He's doin' it all wrong. No one is gonna believe that's me. Sloppy, man, just sloppy." Meanwhile, the crowd is just happy as hell and Carson's got this great big damn grin on his face. And when Cletus finishes, everyone in the audience stands up and claps. I looked over at Elvis and I could see this wasn't a good thing. Then Carson says, "I think that's the best I've ever heard you sound live. That was amazing." Then he looks at the audience and says, "Wasn't that amazing?" And everyone cheered.

Elvis turned beet fucking red, man. He was pissed. He didn't say anything, he just sat there at first. Then, out of the blue, he jumps to his feet, picks up the TV set, and throws it out the window. By this time I was pretty used to that, so I just went down the hall to the room filled with TVs and brought another one back. But Elvis hated it that Cletus was getting such a great response. To him, it was like he was being upstaged, and he didn't like that one bit.

But he didn't say much else, not for a while. And Elvis didn't fire Cletus, because he still had stuff to do.

CHAPTER FIVE
ELVIS MEETS YOJIMBO (1971)

BO WHITAKER: What happened was, Charlie Bronson invited Elvis to the premiere of *Red Sun*. Elvis didn't care much for movie premieres. Hell, sometimes he didn't even go to his own movie premieres. But Elvis liked Charlie Bronson a lot. He used to say, "Charlie's a man's man" or "That's one tough S.O.B. right there." I think he also hung out with Charlie because he wanted to sleep with Charlie's wife, Jill. So Elvis goes to this premiere, and he's really diggin' the movie, man. It's a Western with Charlie as the cowboy and a Japanese actor, Toshiro Mifune, as a samurai. Elvis liked that. He leaned over to me during the movie and said, "I shoulda had a damn samurai in *Flaming Star*. Why didn't we think of that?"

Elvis really admired Toshiro Mifune in the movie. He kept telling me, "That little guy with the funny name is one bad S.O.B." Then he asked me who I thought would win in a fight between Mifune and Muhammad Ali. I said, "I don't know. Does Mifune get to use a sword?" Elvis said yeah, so I said Mifune then. Obviously the guy with the samurai sword is gonna win that fight. I mean, fists can only do so much damage, even if they're Muhammad Ali's. I'm pretty sure Sonny Liston woulda whupped Ali if he'd been allowed to use a samurai sword. That wouldn't even be fair, man.

So after the movie, Elvis goes to Charlie and tells him how much he liked the movie. He kept telling Charlie how much he had liked him ever since *Machine Gun Kelly*. Charlie just kept saying yeah, he knew, because Elvis always told him that. Then Elvis pulled him to the side and whispered something to him. I thought Elvis was telling him he wanted to make a movie with him, but it turned out he was asking Charlie to introduce him to Toshiro Mifune.

So Charlie goes off and gets Mifune and brings him over to us. Mifune says he knows who Elvis is, and Elvis keeps saying Mifune has a funny name. "I sure liked you in *Hell in the Pacific* and *Yojimbo*," he says. And then he adds, "And *The Seven Samurai* was pretty damn good too, man."

Bronson later detailed this meeting in a July 9, 1982 interview with Charlie Rose:

> One of the funniest Hollywood meetings I ever saw was Elvis Presley and Toshiro Mifune. It was really awkward. It was one of those great matches made in movie heaven. ... Mifune was trying to understand everything Elvis was saying because his English wasn't so good, and Elvis just kept talking about *Hell in the Pacific*. He kept saying, "That part where Lee Marvin pissed in your face was really great, man." Then he would say something else about Mifune being pissed on. Mifune looked real irritated, but Elvis didn't seem to notice. I guess he might have been high at the time. I don't know. So the topic shifts, and Elvis asks Mifune, "Did Lee Marvin really piss in your face?" Elvis told him he was a big fan of method acting, but he wasn't about to let anybody piss in his face. Mifune just looked at me and we both kind of smiled knowingly.

BO WHITAKER: Elvis told Toshiro Mifune that he liked the scene in *Hell in the Pacific* where the other guy took a piss on him. Mifune looked happy as hell that Elvis was interested in his movie, so Elvis just kept talking about it. Then he told Mifune, "You're Japanese, right? Not Chinese or Korean? I get all you guys mixed up. Anyway, you'll get a kick out of this—I'm a damned black belt in Karate." Mifune kind of nodded and said, "Oh yeah?" Elvis got real happy and started bragging about all the boards and bricks he had broken with his fists. Then he said, "You know, I could kill a man with my bare hands, Toe-shee-rah." That's how he pronounced his name, "Toe-shee-rah." Mifune seemed really happy about the way Elvis said his name. I could tell Mifune was real impressed by Elvis.

Excerpt from a letter written by Toshiro Mifune to his wife, Sachiko, date unknown [translated by Soko Fukimoto]:

> Last night I met the American singer named Elvis Presley. I did not tell him about how we saw his movies in Japan and laughed and laughed at the idiot. He was very rude in person. He said over and over again he liked watching Lee Marvin take a pee on my face in *Hell in the Pacific*. Then he said he can't tell the difference between Japanese, Chinese, and lowly Korean dogs. He just kept saying he liked to watch Lee Marvin take a pee on my face. I think maybe something is wrong with Elvis Presley. You know, like that boy Ichiro that lives down the street from your mother and eats his own feces.

BO WHITAKER: So then, out of the blue, Elvis says, "I wanna make you an offer, man." Mifune looked real confused by this. Then Elvis took Mifune for a walk outside and left me standing there with Charlie Bronson, his wife Jill, and his manager. I think his name was Ted or something like that. I tried to make conversation with Charlie, but Charlie just laughed and walked away.

Excerpt from a letter written by Toshiro Mifune to his wife, Sachiko, date unknown [translated by Soko Fukimoto]:

> Elvis says he wants to take me for a walk outside. At first I think maybe he wants to kiss me. These Hollywood people are very strange. Like I said, he reminds me very much of little Ichiro. You never know what he will say or do. Elvis keeps talking to me, but sometimes I didn't know what the hell he was saying. It was not because my English was bad, but because Elvis just says stupid things. He kept saying "T.C.B." Finally I said, "What is T.C.B.?" He says, "To take care of some business." Do you know what this means? I do not.

So I say, "What do you want from me, Elvis?" And he looks around and he says, "I want you to teach me to be a killer like you, man." I say, "I do not kill, Elvis. I'm an actor." He says don't tell anyone that he works for C.I.A. I don't know what C.I.A. means either, but I think it must be like T.C.B. But Elvis just kept saying he wanted me to teach him to kill people...to train him to be a samurai.

At least six times I said, "Elvis, I am an actor. I do not kill people. When I kill in a movie it is not real and is because I am an actor." He says to me, "I'll give you two million U.S. dollars if you teach me how to be damn killer." I said, "Two million dollars?" He says, "Two million dollars." I say, "For two million dollars I'll train you to do anything you want. I'll train you to be an astronaut for that much money. So I accepted the job to train Elvis for a few months.

Something is very wrong with Elvis. Please ask Buddha for guidance because I think spending so much time with him is going to be bad. But for two million U.S. dollars I'll do it. I will make him the greatest killer who ever walked the earth.

BO WHITAKER: Elvis convinces the greatest samurai of all time to train him to be a killer. How badass is that, man? When they come back in the damn theater, Mifune just keeps laughing. Man, he's laughing his ass off. Charlie says, "What the hell are you laughing about, Toshiro?" And Mifune's laughing so hard his little face is turning beet red and he has tears in his slanty eyes. Charlie says again, "Toshiro, what the hell is so damned funny?" Mifune looks at Elvis and just keeps cracking up. He's laughing so hard he can't even breathe. Finally he got his shit together and just walked away.

Later Elvis said it was because Mifune was so damn happy about his offer that he kept laughing. "Them Japs laugh a lot when they get happy," Elvis says. I nod like I know all about it. Elvis says, "We had a little foreign guy in our outfit over in Germany and he used to laugh all the time. That's just how they are." I say, "The guy in your unit, was he from Japan, too?" Elvis says, "No, he was from Canada."

Then Elvis says, "I'm gonna buy a damn island, man." This is a big surprise to me, because I never heard Elvis talk about buying no damn island before. I say, "Elvis, what the hell do you need with an island?" He says, "I'm gonna go live there for a while and train with Toshiro. You and me are gonna go out there, just us, and we're gonna learn to be killers, man." I say, "What are you gonna name the island?" He says, "Freedom Land, son."

Excerpt from a letter written by Dale Pimiento to Sandy Curtis, dated September 16, 1971:

> You won't believe this. I finally managed to unload that stupid island. As you know, I've been trying to sell that hunk of mud for the past decade. Now I will have the money to retire and move to Minnesota to be with my father, who's sick and in the hospital. But that's not even the funny part. You won't believe who I sold the island to. It was Elvis Presley! I'm not even joking. He asked me to take him out to the island to look around, so I did. He kept running up and down the beach and doing some kind of karate kicks.
>
> Finally he said, "This is a damn nice island, man. How much you want for it?" So I think about it for a minute, knowing full well in the back of my mind I would like to get at least $20,000 out of it. But before I can say anything, Elvis says, "I'll give you a million bucks." I just look at him and say, "Sold." On the ride back he says, "What name did you give the island?" I didn't want to tell him that we used to call it Hunk of Shit, so I said it didn't have a name. Then he says, "I'm gonna name it Freedom Land." I try not to laugh and I say, "As long as your check clears, I don't give a damn what you call it."

BO WHITAKER: So Elvis and I pack a few jumpsuits and gold chains and we go out to live on Freedom Land. About two days after we got there, Mifune shows up. I can tell right away he's not really diggin' the island. He keeps talking about how nasty it is, talking about all the bugs and weeds and mud. So I say, "Screw this guy, man." Elvis gets real pissed at me and says, "He's our master now. You have to respect him, no matter what he says or does. Don't you know anything about being a damn samurai?"

A journal entry by Toshiro Mifune, dated October 2, 1971 [translated by Soko Fukimoto]:

> I do not enjoy this island and I do not enjoy Elvis and Bo. What kind of name is Bo anyway? It's a dumb name if you ask me. Anyway, Elvis keeps bowing before me and calling me "master." Something is really wrong with this guy. He keeps asking me if he can break things with his fist and sword fight with Bo. Sounds good to me. If he's doing that, I don't have to deal with him as much.
>
> Today Elvis and Bo had a sword fight. Elvis had a stick and Bo had a rotten piece of an oar. They fight and fight each other all day like samurai warriors who have brain damage. Elvis smacked Bo in the face with the stick and Bo started to weep very loudly. It was all very funny, but like with small children, you cannot allow them to see you laughing. I bit my tongue to keep from smiling and scolded them very badly. I told them to run laps around the island for the rest of the day. As they did that, I sat on a rock and read *The Tale of Genji*. I sure am glad I brought some books to read while these dummies do their silly things.

BO WHITAKER: Mifune was impressed with us right from the beginning. Elvis asked him if we looked like true samurai warriors and Mifune said, "Sure." That made us both very proud to know that the greatest samurai in history thought we were a couple of tough hombres.

A journal entry by Toshiro Mifune, dated October 8, 1971 [translated by Soko Fukimoto]:

> Elvis and Bo are the two weakest men I have ever met in my life. Elvis says all the time he is a killer and he brags about being in the American Army. Bo doesn't say much, which is a good contrast to Elvis. I am thankful that Bo doesn't speak much, but I wonder if it is because Bo is mentally challenged.
>
> Today I let them shoot at turtles all day. Elvis says to me, "I bet you a car and some chicken I can hit that turtle. I can hit a pecker off a raccoon at one hundred yards." Then of course he missed the turtle six times in a row. Then he got mad and kicked a tree and threw some rocks at the turtle. The turtle just sat there in the water staring at him like he was not very smart. Come to think of it, I look at him the same way. Who says man and turtle do not have much in common?

BO WHITAKER: Elvis must have taken thirty, forty guns to Freedom Land. He said, "You can't be too careful. What if we get stranded out there like *Gilligan's Island*, man? You gotta have some guns. Can you imagine if Gilligan and the Skipper had each had six or seven guns on 'em, man?" I'm not sure how things would have been different if they had guns. I mean, they'd still be stuck on that island, but that's what he said.

A journal entry by Toshiro Mifune, dated October 12, 1971 [translated by Soko Fukimoto]:

> Today I watched as Bo and Elvis built sandcastles on the shore. Every time Bo would get his sandcastle built, Elvis would pretend to be Godzilla and stomp around on Bo's construction. This made Bo weep like a baby and Elvis asked me, "How do I make Bo feel better, master?" I tell him I don't know and don't really care.
>
> I am extremely tired of these two dumb Americans. I had hoped to work in Hollywood more extensively in the future, but Elvis and Bo make me not want to be around Americans. Today I instructed them to swim out into the ocean as far as they could until their arms got tired. I told them to then swim for another five minutes after that. I told them this is the test of a true samurai warrior. Of course this is nonsense, but I told them this anyway, hoping they might drown.

BO WHITAKER: Mifune told us to swim as far out as we could. Elvis said, "What if we die out there, Toe-shee-rah?" Mifune just laughed and said he knew we'd survive because this was the true test of a samurai warrior. I was real scared, and I think Elvis was, too, but we did what he told us. After all, he was our master and we wanted to learn how to be killin' machines. So we swam way out there, man, and my whole life was passing before my eyes. I was gettin' more and more tired and I could hardly breathe. I looked over at Elvis, and damned if he wasn't starting to sink. I had water in my mouth, but I said, "Just five more minutes now, Elvis." Elvis looked at me and gurgled something, but I couldn't make it out 'cause there was too much water in his mouth.

Then, all of a sudden, as I'm starting to drown, my feet touch the bottom of the ocean. I stood up, and the water only came to my waist. It turned out there was a sandbar there and the water was shallow. I yelled to Elvis and told him about it. He looked at me and gurgled something, but I don't know what. Then he stood up, and the water just came to the top of his sequined swim trunks.

Elvis spit out the water and said, "Holy shit. It's a miracle, son. Mr. Jesus saved our lives today." I said I wasn't sure it was a miracle, but Elvis said, "Don't blaspheme, man. This was the work of Mr. Jesus. Our holy father reached down outta heaven and saved our lives today, Bo. And even better than that, we're goddamn samurai warriors."

A journal entry by Toshiro Mifune, dated October 12, 1971 [translated by Soko Fukimoto]:

Fuck my life.

BO WHITAKER: At that point Elvis became real obsessed with God and religion. He had always gone through cycles where he was real religious, but this one was big for him. After we survived out there in the ocean, Elvis became convinced of two things—that God was watching over him, and that he couldn't die. He just didn't think it was possible. "I'm like a damn Superman," he said. He even asked me to shoot him to find out if he was a Superman.

A journal entry by Toshiro Mifune, dated October 17, 1971 [translated by Soko Fukimoto]:

Today Elvis asked me if I thought he was a super man. I told him I did not. Then he became angry and started kicking sand all over the beach and he punched a rock, injuring himself in the process. He started to scream obscenities at me. Then he said, "I'll prove to you I'm a damn super man, son." I had no clue what the hell he was doing, but he went and got Bo and brought him to where I was standing.

"Shoot me in the damn face, Bo," he said. Bo did not want to do it, but Elvis kept saying, "Shoot me in my face, man." Bo said, "You will die, Elvis. If I shoot you in the face you will die." Elvis just kept saying, "Do it, cocksucker. Shoot me." After arguing for thirty minutes, Bo gave in and said he would shoot Elvis in the leg. Elvis says, "I do not want you to shoot me in the leg. Shoot me in the face. I am a super man, Bo."

Finally Bo shot Elvis in the leg. Elvis fell down and wept on the beach. I looked at him, shook my head, and went back to reading my book.

BO WHITAKER: I just shot Elvis with the .22 because I knew he wasn't a Superman. I didn't wanna do it at all, but he just kept insisting. He called my mother a whore, slapped me across my face, and threatened to fire me from both his entourage and the C.I.A. I didn't really have a choice. So, like I said, I shot him.

Elvis fell to the sand, and the water is washing up over him, and he's crying. He's saying, "I'm hurt real bad, man. I'm fuckin' hurt." The blood is washing back out into the ocean in small red waves, and Elvis is screaming like a madman. "Help me, Bo. Help me, Toe-shee-rah. I'm fuckin' hurt, man."

That was the last time Elvis ever spoke about being a Superman.

GEORGE C. NICHOPOULOS: As Elvis' doctor, I was on call 24/7 while he was training on Freedom Land. I probably made eight or nine trips out there to see him and fix his ailments, be it hemorrhoids or gunshots. It became a big joke. As my boat would approach the island, Elvis and Bo would say, "Well, Dr. Nick is here for his daily visit." Elvis was injured that frequently.

Excerpt from a journal entry by Toshiro Mifune, dated October 18, 1971 [translated by Soko Fukimoto]:

Well, Elvis didn't die yesterday and I'm really depressed about it. I miss my wife and I miss Japan. I miss conversation with intelligent people. I miss the days of my life that did not have Elvis in them. I miss not hearing about Jesus, Communists, and cocksuckers. This is not a happy life. The only way I manage to continue is by dreaming of all the things I will do with the two million dollars Elvis is giving me. I have also started making a game of trying to get Elvis to injure himself.

Today he came to me and apologized for swearing at me and calling me names yesterday. He said he now realized that I was correct, and that he was not a super man. He was hobbling very badly. He had a piece of purple cape tied around the wound and was walking with a stick as a cane. He said, "What can I do to make it up to you, master?" I thought about it for a moment and told him to climb up the five highest trees on the island and to jump out of the tops of each of them.

Bo got jealous and asked me what he could do, so I told him to stand beneath the trees and attempt to catch Elvis.

BO WHITAKER: I think I cracked my ribs when Elvis jumped on top of me out of the third tree. It never did heal properly, man. In fact, it still hurts sometimes when I breathe. But it was worth it, because we were on the path to enlightenment as true samurai warriors. When Elvis jumped out of one of those trees—I think it was just the first or second one—he busted his leg up real good, and this was the *other* leg. So now he had two busted up legs and he had to walk around with these great big sticks for crutches. But even with his legs busted up like that, he still climbed up those other three or four trees and jumped out onto the ground. I think he jumped down onto rocks once, sand once, and onto me the last three times.

When we got finished with the whole damn tree business, we went to Mifune. He was just reading a book and he said, "Are you done?" And we was just as proud as some peacocks and Elvis said, "You're damn right we are, man."

Excerpt from a journal entry by Toshiro Mifune, dated October 18, 1971 [translated by Soko Fukimoto]:

Bo and Elvis came walking up to me. I was reading Izumi's *The Operating Room*, and it was a really good part, and they interrupted me. They looked terrible. They were bloody and I think Elvis may have broken his other leg. Elvis was extremely happy to have accomplished the task I assigned him. Bo was, too. Elvis asked me what he needed to do next.

BO WHITAKER: I really wanted to rest after having Elvis jump on me all those times, but Elvis went back to Mifune and asked, "Now what, master?" And Mifune says he wants us to walk over burning coals. Elvis says, "We ain't got no coal," so Mifune takes a bunch of rocks and puts them in the campfire. He lets them get real hot and then he has us walk over them barefoot.

Excerpt from a journal entry by Toshiro Mifune, dated October 18, 1971 [translated by Soko Fukimoto]:

> I made Elvis and Bo walk over hot coals today. I didn't really want to make Bo do it since he isn't really as big a pain in the ass as Elvis is, but they insisted. Elvis went first. He walked very slowly over the hot coals with tears in his eyes. He screamed rather loudly before losing his balance and falling onto the coals. He burned the palms of his hands badly, and his black sequined jumpsuit caught on fire. Bo jumped up and ran to help his friend. Bo then tripped and fell onto the coals and his jumpsuit caught on fire. Finally one of them got the bright idea to run the ten feet to the water and jump in to put out the fire. The other followed and soon both of them were okay.

> Then Elvis says, "God saved us today, Bo. He came down out of the sky and put that ocean there and saved us, man. Just as sure as shit, god and Mr. Jesus saved us." Then Bo started talking about god, too. The whole thing irritated me—the insistence that their silly man-made god came and saved them— that I decided to put them through more hell.

Bo looked at me and said, "We survived, master." I looked him in the eyes and reminded him that he still had to walk over the coals himself. Bo wept a little bit, but then did his own walk of ignorance.

BO WHITAKER: Elvis kept telling me that God saved us. I wasn't sure about that, but I went along with it, man. I mean, I got nothing against God, and me and him are cool and all, but that ocean was already there before we started walking over those damn coals. So I said, "Yeah, God saved us, Elvis." Then Mifune looks at me and says, "You haven't walked across the coals yet, Bo." I pleaded with him that I had already burned my feet and shouldn't have to do it, but he said it was an ancient samurai rule and could not be broken. So I shrugged and figured what the hell. I told him that my jumpsuit burned all to hell and now all I had on was my boxer shorts. "You don't want to do it in your boxer shorts?" he asks. I say, "Hell no, Mifune." So he says, "Then do it naked."

So I did.

Excerpt from a journal entry by Toshiro Mifune, dated October 18, 1971 [translated by Soko Fukimoto]:

Honestly a part of me had hoped that Bo would fall again and burn his private parts on the coals. Anyway, it didn't happen. Bo walked across the coals, weeping as he did. Then when he got to the end, Elvis made him turn and walk back through the coals one more time. He said, "Do it one more time, man. If you wanna stay employed by me, you'll do it again." Bo asked him why he wanted him to do this again, and Elvis said, "I just wanna see it again, man. I thought it was pretty good stuff." So Bo walked across those coals in the nude again. It was really quite funny.

GEORGE C. NICHOPOULOS: Both Elvis and Bo had third-degree burns all over their feet. I gave them creams and painkillers and advised them to stay off their feet, but they kept saying, "We can't stay off our feet. We're training to be samurai warriors."

BO WHITAKER: I didn't mind walking across those coals naked because I knew—I mean, I hate to brag, but I *knew*—that my penis was pretty good sized. I ain't got nothing to be embarrassed of down there. One time I looked over at Elvis' dick when we was at a urinal taking a piss, and I saw that his dick was only about an inch bigger than mine. So, you know, we both had pretty good-sized dicks.

Excerpt from a journal entry by Toshiro Mifune, dated October 18, 1971 [translated by Soko Fukimoto]:

> Bo had the smallest penis I have ever seen. People
> say that Asians have small male parts, but Bo's penis
> was infinitesimal. No wonder he isn't married. The
> whole incident with Bo and his tiny penis made me
> laugh uncontrollably.

GEORGE C. NICHOPOULOS: Bo has what we in the medical field refer to as a "micro-penis." It works just like a regular penis, but it's smaller. It's about as big as a Vienna sausage but with a tiny head.

BO WHITAKER: When I walked across those coals, Mifune just kept laughing and laughing. At first I thought he was enjoying my pain, but then I remembered what Elvis had told me about foreigners laughing when they're happy. So then I knew that Mifune was just happy to have such excellent students as Elvis and me. It really made me proud, man.

Our training on Freedom Land went on that way for a while. One day Mifune had us stack ten thousand rocks. The next day he told us to move the pile of rocks. Then, after we had moved it, he told us to move it back. Samurai work was hard as hell, man. Another day Mifune told us to take turns punching each other in the face for several hours. We both lost a couple of teeth and were bloody as hell.

The training was supposed to last somewhere between six months to a year. That's what Elvis told me, anyway. But then one day, after we'd been there for about a month and a half, Mifune told us our training was finished. We had accomplished so much in such a little time that he said we were ready to go out in the world as trained samurai.

Excerpt from a journal entry by Toshiro Mifune, dated November 20, 1971 [translated by Soko Fukimoto]:

> I am sick of these guys and I want to go home. I have devised a plan to make that happen and still get the two million dollars Elvis promised me. I decided to tell them that they have graduated and are now true samurai warriors. Of course it's only been six weeks, but I really need off this island and I need to get away from these idiots. I will tell them no pupil of mine had ever graduated as quickly as them, which is true since I've never taught anyone to be a samurai before, and that they are finished.

BO WHITAKER: When Mifune told us we were finished with our samurai training, Elvis was as happy as I had ever seen him. He hugged Mifune and me both, and kept saying that Mr. Jesus was responsible for our now being trained killers. We packed our bags and headed back to Graceland.

GEORGE C. NICHOPOULOS: The guys looked terrible when they got off that island. I couldn't help but think that Mifune was getting some kind of perverse pleasure from watching these men injure themselves. They just looked terrible, with cuts and bruises from head to toe. But I guess it was worth it, since they told me they were now official samurai warriors.

CHAPTER SIX
PROJECT GEMSTONE (1972)

CHUCK COLSON: President Nixon was freaking out. There had been several leaks to the press about various goings on within the administration, and Nixon wanted to stop those leaks. By this time, he had already started recording conversations inside the White House, and he had attempted to implement a secret executive order that would have given the C.I.A. and F.B.I. the right to spy on Americans in their own homes. He even had a private investigator named Tony Ulasewicz who was digging up information on supposed enemies to the administration, such as the Kennedy family.

Then he hired a "special investigations unit" headed by former C.I.A. operatives Gordon Liddy and Howard Hunt to do his bidding. His paranoia was becoming more and more of a concern to us by the day. He saw betrayals and potential enemies everywhere in his midst. He wanted widespread polygraph testing done within the administration, from the C.I.A. to the members of his own cabinet.

He then became increasingly paranoid of a Democratic plot to defeat him in the election. He believed they had damaging evidence against him that would reveal some sort of illicit dealings with Howard Hughes, and he also suspected they were funding or helping to fund the anti-war protest movement.

When he was told that the Brookings Institute—a big Hollywood think tank—had documents that could be damaging to him, he actually suggesting starting a fire in their building and stealing the documents.

These were uneasy times in the Nixon administration.

Memo from President Richard Nixon to Intelligence Chief Gordon Liddy, dated April 15, 1972:

> The more I think about it, the more I'm convinced that the Democratic National Committee is funding the anti-war protesters. If this is true, this is complete bullshit since the Democrats are the ones who got us into this fucking war in the first place. I'll be damned if they're gonna use this war as a means by which to defeat me.
>
> I have reason to believe that Larry O'Brien, the chairman of the DNC, is in possession of documents that would be compromising to this administration. What would you advise me to do in this situation? I don't feel comfortable just sitting back and waiting to take the hit.

Memo from Gordon Liddy to Richard Nixon, dated April 15, 1972:

> Do you want O'Brien "taken care of"? If you do, just say the word and I'll make it happen. It can be made to look like an accident. No one would ever have to know.

Memo from Richard Nixon to Gordon Liddy, dated April 15, 1972:

> No, nothing so dramatic as that. I just want to find out what O'Brien has on me so steps can be made to at least soften the blow before that information is released to the public.
>
> Do you have any other suggestions?

Memo from Gordon Liddy to Richard Nixon, dated April 15, 1972:

> Well, when I was still in the C.I.A. we would have conducted a black bag operation and simply broken

into the building and stolen the documents. That is still an option here, Mr. President.

Memo from Richard Nixon to Gordon Liddy, dated April 15, 1972:

That sounds promising, Gordo. Let's do it.

GORDON LIDDY: Nixon wanted me to go forward with the plan. We called it Project Gemstone. The plan was to break into Larry O'Brien's sixth floor Democratic National Committee office in the Watergate building. Nixon wanted the rooms and telephones bugged, and he wanted us to look through his documents to see if there was anything that could harm him politically.

I knew immediately that I wanted some Bay of Pigs veterans on the job to handle the break-in. I told Nixon I would personally oversee the break-in myself, but he said no, that he wanted an additional firewall between the robbers and the White House. That's when he suggested C.I.A. operative #67357, Jon Burrows, to oversee the robbery. With all the media leaks, Nixon didn't trust anyone in the C.I.A., but he said he believed he could trust that particular operative. "He's the only person in the C.I.A. that I trust right now," he told me. "I personally got him his position."

So I called operative #67357 in for a meeting.

Transcript of White House recording of a meeting between Gordon Liddy, Chuck Colson, and Elvis Presley (a.k.a. Jon Burrows), April 27, 1972:

PRESLEY: Jon Burrows reporting for duty, man.

COLSON: A pleasure to meet you, Mr. Burrows.

LIDDY: I have an extracurricular mission for you.

PRESLEY: Under whose authority?

LIDDY: This comes straight from the top.

PRESLEY: Helms?

LIDDY: Higher.

PRESLEY: Nixon?

LIDDY: Yes.

PRESLEY: Well, hell, why didn't you say so? Ol' Tricky Dick is my buddy. He's the one that got me this job in the first place.

LIDDY: It's a black bag operation.

PRESLEY: What can you tell me about it?

LIDDY: We need you to lead a six man operation—a break-in.

PRESLEY: Where?

LIDDY: The Democratic National Committee office at the Watergate building.

PRESLEY: What's the security like?

LIDDY: Weak.

PRESLEY: Who are the men I'll be working with?

LIDDY: One of my former C.I.A. operatives, Bernard Barker. He'll be your number two on the job.

PRESLEY: No, I come with my own number two man. His name is Bo.

LIDDY: Bo?

PRESLEY: He's my assistant, man. He goes with me on every mission.

LIDDY: That's rather unorthodox.

PRESLEY: No, he's a Methodist.

LIDDY: Okay... Besides this Bo fella, you'll have Bernard Barker, James McCord, Rolando Martinez, Frank Sturgis, and Virgilio Gonzales.

PRESLEY: Martinez and Gonzales—are they Mexicans?

LIDDY: Cubans.

PRESLEY: Okay, good, I can't work with Mexicans. They steal.

LIDDY: Well, this is a burglary, so why would that matter?

PRESLEY: They might try to steal what we're stealing before we can steal it.

LIDDY: Uh...

PRESLEY: You just can't be too careful, man. So what's the time frame for this job? How long will we be in that office?

LIDDY: Fifteen, twenty minutes tops.

PRESLEY: What are we stealing?

LIDDY: You'll be looking for important documents. Mainly you'll just be photographing documents and bugging the place.

PRESLEY: That's a lot to do in twenty minutes.

LIDDY: It's an easy in, easy out.

PRESLEY: What kind of documents?

LIDDY: Documents and photographs that could potentially hurt the administration.

PRESLEY: Like what? Like Nixon having sex with barnyard animals? Like maybe a goat...

LIDDY: Nothing like that—

PRESLEY: Cows...sheep...

LIDDY: We don't really know what they might have in there, so just use your best judgment. If it looks important, photograph it.

PRESLEY: [Breaks into song] "It's a rainy night in Georgia..."

LIDDY: So you'll take the job?

PRESLEY: Yeah, man. I'll take it.

LIDDY: Good. Now let's have lunch.

PRESLEY: What do you have?

LIDDY: Sandwiches. I've got tuna and roast beef.

PRESLEY: I'll take the tuna fish sandwich, man. Roast beef gives me gas.

GORDON LIDDY: Burrows was a real strange guy. In all my years working for the C.I.A. I had never seen an operative like him. Usually they were all the same—looked the same, spoke the same, dressed the same. But this guy, he had high collars and gold chains around his neck and a great big gold belt buckle. He reminded me of a blond-haired Elvis Presley. I told him that and he just laughed. Then he said if I ever said that again he'd kill me. I didn't usually let people talk to me like that, but I had a sense that Burrows meant business.

CHUCK COLSON: Neither of us knew what to make of Burrows. He came in wearing these great big gaudy sunglasses. He had a black shirt open to his belly button. He kept breaking into songs at awkward points in the conversation. And that hair—it was blond, obviously bleached blond... He looked really strange. And that mustache looked like something straight out of a porno movie.

BO WHITAKER: So Elvis calls me to come and pick him up in Washington. He was in full Jon Burrows mode with the slicked-back blond hair and the blond mustache. He always thought he looked like Robert Redford, but he didn't. He wasn't a bad-looking guy with the blond hair, but he didn't look like Robert Redford. The whitish hair made him kind of look like an albino. I guess maybe he looked like an albino Robert Redford.

Elvis says, "We got a job to do that goes beyond the normal call of duty." I asked him what it was, and he says, "We're gonna be working for the president himself. We're gonna be breaking into the Democratic National Committee offices." I asked him what for, and he said, "We gotta find some documents and photographs that make the president look bad." I said, "Like what? Is he screwing a goat?" Elvis just said, "Aw, man, I dunno. They said we'll know 'em if we see 'em."

Transcript from White House recording of a conversation between President Nixon and Gordon Liddy, April 28, 1972:

>NIXON: Where do we stand on this Project Gemstone thing?

>LIDDY: Everything's in place.

>NIXON: You talked to operative Burrows?

>LIDDY: He's agreed to help us. He's gonna oversee the whole thing.

NIXON: He'll be in there, with the Cubans?

LIDDY: Yes, sir.

NIXON: What did he say?

LIDDY: He asked if they had photographs of you with a goat.

NIXON: Why does everyone always assume that? I've never even come into contact with a damned goat in my entire life.

LIDDY: How about a sheep?

NIXON: Well, that's another story, Gordo. I mean, who amongst us has never screwed a damn sheep, am I right? I mean, we're in politics for Christ's sake. We screw *everybody*.

LIDDY: Are you sure we can trust Burrows?

NIXON: I trust him like I trust you.

LIDDY: What do we do with him afterward?

NIXON: What do you mean?

LIDDY: Should I have him killed?

NIXON: No, we might need him again. He's one of us... He's one of the good guys.

BO WHITAKER: So we all watched from the window of a room at the Howard Johnson's across the street. Gordon Liddy was there with us, but Elvis was clearly running the show. We waited until everyone had gone home for the night at the DNC. One hard-working S.O.B. didn't leave until a quarter to one, so we weren't able to get in there until late that night.

O'Brien's door was supposed to be unlocked for us, but it wasn't. Luckily Elvis had his pick set, so he went to work on the door. It took him about ten minutes to get the door unlocked, man. We were all standing there around him, sweating bullets. We just knew Joe the Janitor or some asshole nightwatchman was gonna show up at any moment, but no one did.

Elvis said, "We're supposed to be out of here in less than twenty minutes total. We've already wasted half of that on the damn lock." Because of the limited time we had, we just put a bug on the secretary's switchboard and another on a secondary phone. I remember Elvis saying, "Hey, you Cubans go and photograph some documents."

But they didn't find anything of any value.

GORDON LIDDY: The whole damn fiasco turned up nothing useful. Even the wiretaps got us nothing. It was a colossal mess from start to finish.

Sample transcript from Democratic National Committee office telephone, May 30, 1972:

> SECRETARY: I heard Harold is cheating on his wife with that slut, Barbara.
>
> WOMAN: Really? That bastard. He's the worst.
>
> SECRETARY: Right. It's just unconscionable.
>
> WOMAN: I really hate that lying, cheating bastard.
>
> SECRETARY: Me too.
>
> WOMAN: That Barbara is just a sleazy whore. Who would sleep with a married man?
>
> WOMAN: I'd sleep with Harold, though.
>
> SECRETARY: Me too, but that would be different.
>
> WOMAN: Exactly.

Sample transcript from Democratic National Committee office telephone, June 6, 1972:

O'BRIEN: Hello?

WOMAN: Hello, Super Happy Time Chinese Restaurant.

O'BRIEN: I'd like some kung pow chicken. Is that good?

WOMAN: Huh?

O'BRIEN: Is that good?

WOMAN: Oh yes, very good.

O'BRIEN: Okay, I'd like some of those yellow noodles with that. You know, the fat ones.

WOMAN: The fat ones, yes.

O'BRIEN: I'd like a side of rice. The white rice, not the brown.

WOMAN: Okay, white rice.

O'BRIEN: I'd also like some crab rangoon.

WOMAN: Crab rangoon?

O'BRIEN: Yes. And could you include some chopsticks. I like playing with those.

WOMAN: Sure thing.

CHUCK COLSON: The tapes turned up jack shit. There was nothing useful on them whatsoever. The whole thing was a wash. Needless to say, Nixon was not impressed with these tapes containing nothing but brownie recipes and women complaining about their hairdressers.

GORDON LIDDY: I just wanted to kill someone. I always wanted to kill people, but they never let me. They never let me do anything fun.

Memo from Richard Nixon to Gordon Liddy, dated June 9, 1972:

> Project Gemstone has failed to yield results. The photographs turned up nothing useful, and one of the Cubans took a picture of his penis, for God's sake.
>
> I know Larry O'Brien has something on me. I just know it. Do you have any other clever ideas, Gordo? Sometimes I wonder what the hell I'm paying you for...

Memo from Gordon Liddy to Richard Nixon, dated June 9, 1972:

> I realize the project has as yet yielded absolutely no results, and I am willing to take the blame for that. I would recommend that we send those guys back in there again. This time we'll send them to take photographs of virtually every document in there and we'll put so many bugs in there they'll need a damn exterminator. What do you say?
>
> As for the photograph of the guy's dick, it does look Cuban, but you can't be sure because of the dark lighting. That could be anyone's dick.

Memo from Richard Nixon to Gordon Liddy, dated June 9, 1972:

> All right, we'll try it again. We can call this Project Gemstone Two. What do you think of that name? I came up with that myself.

As for the penis, I'm pretty sure it's Cuban. I've seen a Cuban penis or two in my day, and I'm completely certain it's Cuban. I even had Pat and Tricia look at it, and they both think it's Cuban, too.

GORDON LIDDY: We called operative #67357, Jon Burrows, back to Washington to discuss his leading a second break-in at the DNC headquarters. He came in that second time and was dressed just as strangely as he had been the first. He had a cape on this time.

Transcript from White House recording of a conversation between Gordon Liddy and Elvis Presley (a.k.a. Jon Burrows), June 12, 1972:

PRESLEY: What seems to be the problem, son?

LIDDY: The operation was a failure. We didn't get much of anything out of it.

PRESLEY: Not even on the wiretaps?

LIDDY: I'm afraid not.

PRESLEY: Damn. So now what do we do?

LIDDY: We gotta go back in there.

PRESLEY: Into the Democratic National Committee headquarters?

LIDDY: Yes.

PRESLEY: Are we sure they don't know they've already been compromised?

LIDDY: We're certain.

PRESLEY: Nothing on the tapes suggests—

LIDDY: No. The most juicy thing that turned up on those tapes was a phone sex conversation between a volunteer and some woman in Connecticut.

PRESLEY: What kind of phone sex?

LIDDY: Water sports.

PRESLEY: Like piss?

LIDDY: Yeah.

PRESLEY: Aw, man, that's just gross. Pissin' and sex don't go together, man.

LIDDY: I want you to lead the second break-in. This time I assure you the door will be unlocked. Jim McCord has access to the building. He's gonna go in there ahead of us and put a piece of tape over the bolt so the door will open.

PRESLEY: That easy?

LIDDY: It should be.

PRESLEY: Will I have the same guys this time?

LIDDY: It'll be you, your guy Bo, McCord, and four Cubans.

PRESLEY: *Four* Cubans? I heard they multiply fast, but this is friggin' ridiculous.

LIDDY: They're good guys. I can vouch for all of them. I worked with them on the Bay of Pigs.

PRESLEY: Yeah, and look how well that turned out.

LIDDY: So you'll do it?

PRESLEY: Yeah. Anything for Tricky Dick.

LIDDY: Good.

PRESLEY: What's our objective, man?

LIDDY: Same objective, but this time you guys are gonna photograph every single document in there and you're gonna put listening devices everywhere.

PRESLEY: Everywhere?

LIDDY: If someone takes a shit in that building, I wanna be able to hear how many turds hit the water.

PRESLEY: [Breaks into song] "How great Thou art..."

LIDDY: Can I ask you a question?

PRESLEY: Yes, sir. Anything.

LIDDY: Why do you do that? Why do you suddenly break into song in the middle of important conversations?

PRESLEY: Old habit, I guess.

BO WHITAKER: Before we went in there that second time, Elvis warned those guys that if anyone got caught and said a single word about him or me, he would kill every member of their families in a very brutal fashion. That seemed to get them all shook up, no pun intended.

CHUCK COLSON: I had my doubts about returning to the scene of the crime. We didn't find anything the first time, so I doubted we would find anything this time. And doing all of this bugging and taking all these pictures was going to take a great deal of time. What had begun as a ten or fifteen minute burglary was now turning into an hour or two operation. It just seemed like a really bad idea to me, but I held my tongue. In retrospect, maybe I shouldn't have, but I did.

GORDON LIDDY: I thought going back in there was a solid plan. I mean, the last place you expect lightning to strike is in the same place it struck last time. Statistically, any other building in Washington had a better chance of being robbed that night, so I felt pretty good about the whole thing.

BO WHITAKER: So we all go up to the sixth floor, and lo and behold the damn door is locked. McCord says, "I swear to you I put tape in the door. Someone must have removed it." My first thought was that if someone removed it, then they might have some idea that someone was trying to get in there. We called Liddy on our walkie-talkies and told him that, but he said to go ahead with the mission. Elvis kept saying, "I don't like this, man. I don't like this one damn bit."

So Elvis picked the lock again. And I'll never forget the last words he said to me before we went into that office. He said, "Bo, don't take any pictures of your dick this time."

GORDON LIDDY: I was watching the whole thing through binoculars from across the street. I saw the office lights come on, and I saw three men in suits enter through the front door. My first conclusion was that this was probably a bad thing.

BO WHITAKER: These guys come in and yell, "This is the police. Whoever's in here, come out!" We were all hiding under the desks, and I thought that was a pretty safe hiding place myself. I really think we could have just stayed under those desks and no one would have ever found us. But those damned Cubans, they got up from under their desks one by one. The police were talking to them, and they were jibber-jabbering away in Cubanese. I don't know what the hell they were saying. Me, Elvis, and McCord stayed under the desks as long as we could, but finally the cops came over and ordered us out of there.

The cops said, "What the hell are you guys doing here?" Elvis tried to tell them we were there to check the meters, but the cops didn't believe him. So they sent for reinforcements and they took us all to jail.

GORDON LIDDY: The president was out of town. I wanted to call him and tell him firsthand what had happened. I needed a secure line to call him on, so I went to the Situation Room and called him from the KYX scrambler phone. I thought it was a secure line, but it turned out that Nixon had bugged that phone, too.

Transcript from White House recording of a telephone conversation between President Nixon and Gordon Liddy, June 17, 1972:

> NIXON: Hello?
>
> LIDDY: Dick, it's me, Gordon Liddy.
>
> NIXON: Goddamn it, Gordo. Do you have any idea what time it is?
>
> LIDDY: They got caught, sir.
>
> NIXON: Who got caught?
>
> LIDDY: The guys from Project Gemstone.
>
> NIXON: You mean Project Gemstone Two.
>
> LIDDY: Right. They got caught.
>
> NIXON: Got caught by who?
>
> LIDDY: The police.
>
> NIXON: Jesus Christ, Gordo. What are you telling me?
>
> LIDDY: I think we could be in trouble.
>
> NIXON: Why do you say that?

LIDDY: The Cubans won't say a word. Burrows and the other guy won't say anything. They can't be traced back to us.

NIXON: Then what?

LIDDY: McCord, sir.

NIXON: McCord was there?

LIDDY: Yes.

NIXON: You mean to tell me you sent an employee of the administration in there?

LIDDY: Would you like me to have someone killed, sir?

NIXON: Please. Go kill yourself.

BO WHITAKER: A team of C.I.A. agents got us out of there before the squad car even reached the station. They warned the cops driving the car that if they told anyone what had happened, they would be killed.

GORDON LIDDY: When all hell broke loose, the guys started giving everyone else up. At first there were mentions of Burrows and the other guy. McCord didn't mention them, but the Cubans gave them up right away.

Transcript of police interrogation of Rolando Martinez, date June 17, 1972:

COP: You said there was another man.

MARTINEZ: Yes, another man. Two men, actually.

COP: Two men? Who are they?

MARTINEZ: A weird guy named Burrows who sings all the time.

COP: What does he sing?

MARTINEZ: Mostly hymns. It was really strange. He was talking about someone being a cocksucker, and then he broke into "When the Saints Go Marching In."

COP: Can you describe what this man looks like?

MARTINEZ: He's a blond guy with big sideburns and a mustache. He had a big gold belt and a couple of gold chains.

COP: Did you ever hear his name?

MARTINEZ: Burrows. They called him Mr. Burrows.

COP: What about the other guy?

MARTINEZ: His name was Bo. He was real stupid.

COP: He was stupid?

MARTINEZ: Yes. They were both stupid.

BO WHITAKER: Elvis and me had messages sent to those boys in lock up telling them that their families would be slaughtered and fed to wild hogs if they didn't recant their stories immediately. That seemed to do the trick.

Transcript of police interrogation of Rolando Martinez, date June 19, 1972:

COP: Now you said there were two other men.

MARTINEZ: No. No, I didn't.

COP: Yes you did. You said they were stupid white men.

MARTINEZ: No, I must have misunderstood the question. My English isn't always that great, you know.

COP: Bullshit.

MARTINEZ: No, is not bullshit. I don't know about no two white men. The only white man who was there was McCord.

COP: If you don't stop lying to me, I'll deport your ass quicker than you can say burrito supreme.

MARTINEZ: *No hablo.*

COP: So the other guy, the one with the sideburns. Tell me about his songs.

MARTINEZ: I don't know what you're talking about.

BO WHITAKER: The whole Watergate scandal went on for quite some time. Everyone else involved with the break-ins eventually went to jail and, well, you know, Nixon resigned when they was gonna impeach him. I've heard there were whispers about Elvis and me being there, but no one ever came after us. We were like ghosts. It was like we were never even there. Everyone was too damned afraid to mention us, and we just went on with our lives.

CHAPTER SEVEN
THE CLETUS SITUATION (1972)

BO WHITAKER: While Elvis and me were out on missions for the Central Intelligence Agency, things were gettin' crazy back home. Cletus was still working as Elvis' double, and he was really making a mess of things. First of all, he was starting to get fat, which was really stressing Elvis out. People on television were starting to make jokes about Elvis' weight, not knowing it was really Cletus they were talking about.

MARTY LACKER: Elvis put on the pounds really quickly. It just wasn't like him to, you know, be fat and overindulgent. Suddenly here he was eating entire turkeys and these nasty little fried peanut butter and banana sandwiches. I would get up to go to the bathroom at three or four in the morning and Elvis would be in the kitchen eating these huge meals. He called them "late night snacks," but there was enough food there to feed a damn army.

RED WEST: Man, he just blew up like a balloon. I never saw him working out or doing Karate anymore. Instead he just ate. I mean, that's all he was doing these days was eat. He was putting on weight so fast you could almost hear his skin expanding when you were hanging out with him. And he'd just be there eating some really nasty concoction, like anchovy pizza dipped in Neapolitan ice cream.

RAY WALKER: I didn't see Elvis for a while there. It was probably three months or so, and we were taking a break from recording and doing shows. And man, I didn't even recognize Elvis. He was just huge. I was like, "Where's Elvis and who is this fat guy?" I'm serious. I didn't have a clue who the hell he was.

BO WHITAKER: We'd been on this mission in Bangladesh for quite some time, and the truth is that Elvis was in the shape of his life. He was lean and mean. He had six-pack abs. But no one knew, because that asshole Cletus had gone and put on all that weight.

It just broke Elvis' heart to see what was happening to his image. We'd turn on the TV and there'd be someone on there making jokes about Elvis being fat. He just couldn't take it. He'd just mutter, "Fucking Cletus" under his breath. He was really pissed about the whole thing.

Then Cletus did an interview on *The Dick Cavett Show*. On that interview he promised that the new album would have "a lot more banjo." Why he said that, we had no idea. Elvis had never recorded any banjo-heavy tracks before and he wasn't about to start now. But Cavett was real interested in that, and he kept asking questions about banjo music, and Cletus just kept laying it on thicker and thicker. Then he said, "Hell, the whole damn album is gonna be banjo. It's gonna be a fusion album, like Miles Davis and the jazz guys are doing. Only it's gonna be banjo/rock-and-roll fusion." When Elvis heard that, he went through the roof. And that wasn't all Cletus said...

Excerpt from an article in Rolling Stone *magazine, December 21, 1972:*

> Elvis Presley recently told celebrity interviewer Dick Cavett that his new album, *Elvis Gets Banjo Fever!*, will feature fourteen new songs, all containing lots of banjo. "We're gonna have all the top banjo players on there," Presley told Cavett. When pressed to provide further details, Presley revealed that one of the banjo-laden tracks will be a love story about two male sailors. "It's gonna be titled 'Two Gay Guys and a Banjo," explained Presley. "It's a real love ballad. It'll be a duet with another famous male singer." Presley refused to give further details regarding his duet partner. "You'll just have to wait and see," Presley said.

The singer also revealed that several of the tracks will be produced by Slim Whitman. Presley explains, "This is my attempt to develop a more contemporary sound. With cutting-edge groups like Pink Floyd and Led Zeppelin out there, I have to incorporate lots and lots of banjo into my songs to maintain my place in the current music scene."

BO WHITAKER: Elvis went fucking ballistic. "Why would he say that shit?" he asked me. I had no answer. I didn't know Cletus as well as the other guys did since I was usually away on missions with Elvis, but he'd always seemed like a rational guy. This kind of behavior was completely unexpected. "This is my fucking image at stake here, man," Elvis said. He was so mad he actually broke down and cried. He said, "I've spent the past twenty years building up this image and this no-talent ass clown is gonna destroy that in the blink of an eye." We were still in Bangladesh, and Elvis got so mad he couldn't even decide how to destroy the television. So he shot the damn thing twice, then threw it on the floor of our hotel room, and then chucked the fucker out the window. I had never, ever seen Elvis this angry, and I had known him since we was just runts.

RED WEST: We were all watching this interview, and then Elvis said he was gonna make a gay record with lots of banjo on it. We were all kind of in shock. He had never mentioned any of this before. It was just nuts. And Col. Tom Parker, Elvis' manager, almost had a coronary right then and there.

SONNY WEST: The gay thing didn't shock me as much as the banjo thing. Elvis was kind of homophobic, but he fucking *hated* banjos. I remember when we saw *Deliverance* and Elvis said somebody should shoot the little retarded kid playing the banjo. I asked him why and he just said, "Fucking banjos, man. Fucking banjos."

BO WHITAKER: Elvis called our C.I.A. handler—a guy named Boots Peltier—and told him he had to get back home to Memphis right away. Peltier asked him what the problem was, and Elvis told him about Cletus. The guy was real understanding, but he said there was nothing he could do. He said we had to stay in Bangladesh until our job was over, and that was still at least six weeks away.

BOOTS PELTIER: I really wanted to help him, but our mission was way too important to compromise. Besides, every C.I.A. operative knows the dangers the job presents to our personal lives from day one.

BO WHITAKER: The next thing we knew, Cletus was giving a damn interview to a group of reporters outside the gates of Graceland. You just had no idea what the hell was gonna come out of that man's mouth. Meanwhile, everyone else thought it was really Elvis saying all this weird shit.

Excerpt from Associated Press interview, December 22, 1972:

REPORTER: What are you doing these days?

PRESLEY: Having lots and lots of wild orgy sex.

REPORTER: Aren't you still married to Priscilla?

PRESLEY: Oh, yeah, but she don't mind. She's at home taking care of our daughter while I'm out having all this wild orgy sex.

REPORTER: With whom are you having all this orgy sex?

PRESLEY: Not just orgy sex. *Wild* orgy sex.

REPORTER: Uh, sorry. With whom are you having all this wild orgy sex?

PRESLEY: Anyone and everyone. Elvis is taking all comers, if you know what I mean.

REPORTER: That's gross.

PRESLEY: If you think that's gross, you should see all the wild orgy sex I'm having.

REPORTER: Aren't you afraid this will damage your image as a wholesome clean-cut young man?

PRESLEY: Hell no, man. I'm just a wholesome clean-cut young man who loves to have sex. Wild orgy sex.

BO WHITAKER: Elvis almost committed suicide after that interview went public. He just sat on the edge of the bed with his .45 in his mouth. He had tears streaming down his cheeks. I was really scared. I just knew he was gonna take his own life that night. I had to talk him back down. It took several hours. Finally he took the gun out of his mouth and said, "Bo, why is that cocksucker doin' all this?" I said I didn't know, and that was the God's honest truth. I had no clue why a man would do something like that to a guy who was as nice and kind as Elvis was. It just didn't make any damn sense.

SONNY WEST: When the guys heard that interview, they were real pissed. Everyone was like, "Why aren't we getting invited to these wild orgies?" Things were real tense around Graceland for a while, and everyone was steamed about it.

BO WHITAKER: We didn't know about it at the time, but I guess Cletus was doing a lot of cocaine. Elvis hated drugs—except for all the ones he took—and he was really pissed about that. He said, "Cocaine? Cletus is doing cocaine? Man, Elvis doesn't do no fucking cocaine!"

MARTY LACKER: Elvis would just have these mountains of coke around him like Tony Montana from *Scarface*. And he would look at you with all that white powder on his nose and he looked kind of like a puppy. I dunno why exactly I thought that, but I did. I thought he looked like a white-nosed puppy. I guess it's because I used to have a puppy that looked kind of like that when I was a kid. His name was Spanky.

SONNY WEST: It wasn't like Elvis to do coke, but man he was doing it every day. Everyone was kind of making jokes about it in private, but the truth was it was real scary. Between his weight and the coke, we all thought he was gonna die.

BO WHITAKER: Then Cletus made an appearance on the religious program *The 700 Club* with Pat Robertson, and things went south real quick.

Transcript from Presley's appearance on The 700 Club, *December 24, 1972:*

ROBERTSON: Praise be unto Jesus.

PRESLEY: Go fuck yourself.

BO WHITAKER: Elvis got really, really upset after Cletus said those nasty things to Pat Robertson. He said, "You know I would never disrespect Mr. Jesus or any of his leaders like that." I just kept saying, "I know, Elvis. I know." And again Elvis broke down into tears. He stayed up all night praying and crying. "Why have you forsaken me, Mr. Jesus? Why are you letting that bad man do all of this to me? Have I not been your humble servant, Mr. Jesus?"

MARTY LACKER: Things were really strange there for a while. It was bad enough that Elvis was getting so damned fat, but now he was saying terrible things on TV just about every other day. None of us knew quite what to make of it. We were real depressed about it all, but no one dared mention it to Elvis.

PRISCILLA PRESLEY: I asked Elvis why he said those terrible things to Pat Robertson. I said, "I thought you loved Mr. Jesus," and he said, "Well, sometimes I do and sometimes I don't. You just gotta catch me on the right day." I thought that was a really strange thing for him to say.

RED WEST: The crazy part wasn't even the comment he made to Pat Robertson. The really crazy part, I thought, was when he leaned over and snorted a rail of coke off Pat's desk. That was just downright crazy, man.

BO WHITAKER: Things only got worse from there when Cletus showed up on *60 Minutes* to promote an upcoming concert from Hawaii that was being televised the following week. Elvis and I just kind of held our breath as we watched that interview. Who knew what kind of horseshit would come out of Cletus' damn fool mouth?

Transcript of interview with Mike Wallace on 60 Minutes, January 1, 1973:

> WALLACE: How will this new concert be different from televised concerts you've had in the past?
>
> PRESLEY: This time I'm gonna come out and piss all over the audience.
>
> WALLACE: Off the stage?
>
> PRESLEY: Yeah.
>
> WALLACE: Lately you've been saying a lot of things that seem out of character for you. How do you explain that?
>
> PRESLEY: I'm the same me I've always been. I just didn't have the balls to say what I really felt like saying.
>
> WALLACE: What do you feel like saying right now?
>
> PRESLEY. I just want everyone to know that I'm a damn Communist. Always have been.
>
> WALLACE: Really?
>
> PRESLEY: Hell yeah, man. I'm a big ol' Commie.

WALLACE: What would you say to people who say they think you're on drugs?

PRESLEY: I would tell them to mind their own damn business.

WALLACE: Are you on drugs?

PRESLEY: Define drugs.

WALLACE: Cocaine, pills, grass, LSD...

PRESLEY: Yeah, I'm on all that stuff, man.

BO WHITAKER: Elvis was getting more and more frustrated by the day. Here he was stuck in Bangladesh, and Cletus was doing everything he could to destroy his image. It just wasn't fair, man. Elvis never did nothing to nobody, and he didn't deserve to have that little bastard do all this stuff to him. Elvis just kept telling me, "I ain't no Commie, man. They can think whatever else they want about me, but I ain't no damn pinko." Then he added, "And I love Mr. Jesus, too."

Elvis was really concerned about the mood back at Graceland. He just kept saying, "What are the guys gonna think of me?"

RED WEST: We all thought, wow, what a dick. Then we started thinking that maybe all that cocaine was starting to have an effect on Elvis. We were real scared because we thought we might not have a place to live. And, well, yeah, we were afraid Elvis might hurt himself, too, but mostly we were just afraid of losing our home at Graceland.

BO WHITAKER: Elvis called Boots Peltier again and asked to go home. I even got on the phone and told him I could handle the Bangladesh problem myself. For some reason he laughed for a minute or so after I said that. Then he made me put Elvis back on the phone and he said we both had to stay until after our mission had been completed.

BOOTS PELTIER: Operative #67357 just kept calling me over and over again, asking me if he could go home. I said, "Suck it up. You're a fucking NOC now. Act like it."

BO WHITAKER: Elvis got really scared because Cletus was performing in a big sold-out Hawaiian show that was being televised all over the world. I think Elvis really just wondered what in the hell Cletus was gonna do next.

RED WEST: That Hawaii show was probably the best show Elvis ever did in his entire career. He was just magical that night. His moves were better than ever, and his voice just sounded golden. It was amazing.

BO WHITAKER: Cletus did everything right that night. He didn't say anything racist or attack the church or anything. He just sang those songs like they'd never been sung before. It was one hell of a performance, man. As soon as I saw that, I knew I was gonna have to go downstairs to the front desk of our hotel and pay for another damn TV set. And sure enough, Elvis was beside himself. He kept trying to tell me that Cletus did everything wrong, but deep down we both knew the truth. "Cletus moved his hips out too far when he swayed there," Elvis would say. Or "I think he missed the note right there. Did you hear that?"

Before the show was over I excused myself to go to the restroom. When I did, I made sure to hide Elvis' pistol because I'm pretty sure he would have killed himself that night. I just kept trying to reassure Elvis by telling him that at least things couldn't get any worse.

PRISCILLA PRESLEY: I flew all the way to Hawaii that night to be with Elvis. After the show, we made sweet love in ways that we'd never done it before. It was beautiful, and Elvis was sweeter than he'd ever been to me. It was easily the best night of my life up until that point. I really thought we were gonna get back together.

JERRY SCHILLING: Bo telephoned that night. He said he was out in Phoenix. We asked him if he wanted to speak to Elvis, but he said no. He just kept asking how all the guys were doing. I told him we were all doing great. Then I told him that Priscilla had flown out to see Elvis and that we were all real surprised. "They're having sex so hard in that room that the damn headboard is about to break through the wall!" I thought that was really funny, but Bo just hung up the phone.

BO WHITAKER: I didn't tell Elvis about Priscilla right away. They had been separated since February. Elvis had been holding onto this idea that he and Priscilla would get back together one day, and now she was trying to—*only it was with Cletus!* If I had told Elvis that night, I think he would have killed us both. Forget the TV set, I would have been the one going out the window!

SONNY WEST: First Elvis had that great show in Hawaii. Then he and Priscilla hooked up, and we were all hoping they'd get back together again. Then RCA called up and said they wanted to put the concert out as an album. Everyone was real happy about that.

BO WHITAKER: Elvis was not happy about it one damn bit. Elvis just kept saying, "Cletus wasn't supposed to appear on any of the albums. That was the deal. He would just be the face of Elvis Presley, and I would be the voice." I kept saying, "I know, Elvis. I know." I felt like a broken record, but I didn't know what else to say.

So Elvis called Boots Peltier again and asked for permission to go home. Of course Peltier said no, but Elvis had to try.

MARTY LACKER: The reviews for the *Aloha from Hawaii: Via Satellite* album were some of the best Elvis had ever received.

Review from Billboard *magazine, February 10, 1973:*

> Elvis Presley's new concert album, *Aloha from Hawaii: Via Satellite* is one of the greatest records the singer has ever recorded. His vocals have a richness to them that somehow sounds new and fresh. To listen to the record, you would have no idea that Presley was a veteran performer who'd been doing this since the early 1950s. This is one of the greatest concert albums ever recorded.

ELVIS PRESLEY, CIA ASSASSIN

Review from Rolling Stone *magazine, February 12, 1973:*

> Guess who's back? Elvis Presley has just unleashed a monster of a new album this week. A concert recording, *Aloha from Hawaii: Via Satellite*, is pure unadulterated genius through and through. Elvis hasn't sounded this great since...well, ever. Every great singer with longevity eventually puts out an album that will stand the test of time. This just may be the one for Elvis.

BO WHITAKER: The entire world thought Elvis was making a successful comeback, and he was as sad a man as I had ever seen. He was just really broken up, man. The concert album shipped gold, and wound up knocking Pink Floyd out of the top spot on the *Billboard* chart. Sure, Elvis had scored a minor hit a few years before with "The Wonder of You"—I mean, it did hit number one in England—but that was nothing like this. *Aloha from Hawaii: Via Satellite* became the first Elvis Presley record to hit number one in the U.S. in several years, and the damn thing wasn't even him.

He got real down one night and said, "I'm gonna call Priscilla." I tried to talk him out of it, but he said she was the only person who could cheer him up.

PRISCILLA PRESLEY: Elvis called me up one night and started talking to me like we hadn't spoken in months. It was really strange. I asked him if he was drunk, but he said he still wasn't drinking. I reminded him that he was drinking just about every day and doing lots and lots of coke. Then I reminded him of all the nights we'd had crazy monkey sex over the past month and he just sat there silently. I said, "Don't you remember that wild thing we did with the Vaseline, the porcelain rhino, and the box of fishing lures?" He acted like he couldn't remember any of it. Then I reminded him about all the nights I had complimented him for becoming a better lover and somehow having a bigger penis. Elvis started crying uncontrollably and hung up on me. I think that was the last civil conversation we ever had until we were divorced later that year.

119

BO WHITAKER: I knew what Priscilla was telling Elvis, and there was nothing I could do to soften the blow for him. He hung up on her and just sat there staring at the phone. Then, after a moment or two, he grabbed the telephone and threw it into the wall. He turned and looked at me and, I swear, his eyes were red like a demon. He growled at me and said, "Get that fucking Cletus on the phone and find out what he's up to." Of course I had to go to the office and pay to get a new phone, but I did it. Then, after hooking up the new phone, I called Graceland. Vernon answered the phone, and I told him I needed to talk with Elvis.

Cletus got on the phone and we got into it real quick-like. I said, "What the fuck are you doing, Cletus?" He said something like, "I don't know what you're talking about, man." And I said, "Listen to me, you little piss ant, you'd better stop whatever the hell it is you're doing right now." And he said, "What? Don't you know I'm Elvis Presley?" Then he said, "Look, Bo, I have all the leverage. I can do anything I want. You tell Elvis I will destroy his life and his image unless he gives me five million dollars up front and half of everything he makes from now on. I deserve it, Bo." I politely reminded Cletus of our agreement, but he said, "Fuck our agreement. Your golden boy is either gonna pay me five million dollars or I'm gonna destroy everything he loves." Then the bastard threatened to sign away parental rights to Lisa Marie if Elvis didn't give him the money. That's when I knew I was speaking to a dead man.

BOOTS PELTIER: Operative #67357 didn't call in one day. Something in my gut told me he had gone back home. I sent someone over to the hotel, and neither he nor his buddy, Bo, were there. Operative #67357 had gone off the reservation.

BO WHITAKER: Elvis and me took a plane back to the United States using fake identification papers. I kept asking Elvis what exactly we was gonna do, but he wouldn't answer me. He just sat there staring out the window of the plane, hour after hour, man. He was so mad he wouldn't even talk to me, and I was literally the one person at that moment who was on his side.

TOBY WONG: Elvis called me early in the morning, and he sounded different. I asked him if he was calling from a secure line, but he told me not to worry about it. He said I should meet him at the airport with a trunk full of weapons. He also said he needed me to call one of my contacts and obtain the use of a helicopter for an hour or so. I had no idea what the hell was going on, but I did what Elvis asked.

BO WHITAKER: When we landed at Memphis International Airport, Toby was waiting for us there in a stolen Dodge Charger with a trunk full of guns, knives, and Chinese throwing stars. He hadn't seen us since Elvis had started bleaching his hair blond and had grown a mustache. He said, "You look different." Elvis just laughed and told Toby that he looked the same.

Toby took us to a vacant house in North Memphis. We went in and devised the plan to kill Cletus, and Elvis and me chose our weapons for the mission. I really wanted to take the AK-47, but Elvis said we should get .45s with silencers on them. So that's what we did.

That night at 2300 hours we hovered over Graceland in the chopper. Toby was flying it. We dropped a rope out the cargo door and slid down onto the roof of the house. We entered through a window there on the East side and snuck down the hall towards Elvis' room. I asked Elvis, "What do you we do if Cletus has someone else in there with him?" Elvis whispered back that we'd have to kill them, too.

Elvis tried the door and it was unlocked. He opened it, and Cletus was there by himself, asleep in the bed with the TV on. Some gangster movie with Paul Muni was on, but I don't know which one it was. It might have been *Angel on My Shoulder*... So we go inside and shut the door behind us. We walk over to where we're standing over Cletus, and he's just snoring away. Elvis tells me, "No matter what happens, you let me handle it. This cocksucker's mine."

So Elvis kicks the bed, but Cletus just keeps on sleepin'. Elvis kicks it again. This time Cletus starts waking up. He opens his eyes and looks at us. He says, "What the fuck?" Elvis says, "Are you surprised?" Cletus starts begging Elvis to let him live. "I was just playin' around, Elvis," he says. Elvis isn't buying it. He says, "You got any last words?" Cletus just cries. Elvis raises the gun and squeezes the trigger, but the gun jams. Cletus hears the gun click and dives for his .38 on the nightstand. Just before he can reach it, Elvis pulls out a Chinese throwing star and hurls it at him. It catches Cletus right in the eye and sticks there in his eye socket. So Cletus starts to scream, but his screams are kind of muffled by the loud TV. Elvis says, "I'll be damned if I didn't always wanna do that, man." Then he asks me for my gun, so I hand it to him. He aims the .45 at Cletus' head and pulls the trigger. This time there's no misfire, and Cletus' brains blow out all over the headboard.

Elvis says, "We need to clean all this shit up quick." So we cleaned the room and Elvis called Toby on his walkie-talkie. Toby came back and lowered the rope down to the window again. We tied Cletus' body to the end of the rope and then climbed up to the helicopter. We went back to that abandoned house and buried Cletus deep beneath the floor boards.

Elvis had to dye his hair black and shave his mustache to go back to Graceland. He went back, stuck a pillow in his shirt so he'd look fat, and told the guys he'd be out of town for a few weeks. Then we went back to Bangladesh. Elvis called Boots Peltier and apologized, and that was that.

CHAPTER EIGHT
OPERATION BUNNY HOP (1973)

BO WHITAKER: By 1973, the war in Vietnam was pretty much over for the United States. Operation Homecoming had brought most of the prisoners home, but there were still P.O.W.s over there.

One of the last U.S.O. choppers brought in to entertain the troops was shot down by the Viet Cong at the end of 1972. The Partridge Family and three Playboy bunnies were on board. This was all kept hush hush because the U.S.O. wanted to keep their perfect record intact. I mean, how would they have gotten other groups to fly into combat zones had they known about that?

C.I.A. intel said that the bunnies and The Partridge Family were being held in a tiny prison village just outside Hanoi.

Memo from President Richard Nixon to Central Intelligence Agency Director Richard Helms, April 8, 1973:

> I would like you to put together a mission to go in and extract those three Playboy bunnies. They are a national treasure and we cannot allow the enemy to keep them. Freeing those girls is also quite important to the future of The United Service Organizations (U.S.O.) cause to maintain troop morale during wartime.
>
> Please bring those Playboy bunnies home alive and unharmed. Should The Partridge Family be injured or killed, well, so be it. These things happen.

Please put your best man on this, and by best man,
you know who I mean...

BOOTS PELTIER: I got the call to send operative #67357 into
Vietnam to extract the civilians. I was told that the order came all the
way down from the president himself. When I spoke with operative
#67357 he said, "Playboy bunnies? Shit yes, man. I'm the man for the
job." I told him the mission was to extract them out of the country,
not to have sex with them. He just said, "Well, you've got your
priorities, son, and I've got mine."

BO WHITAKER: Elvis was happier than a pig in shit when he found
out we were going in there to extract those Playboy bunnies. I
reminded him about The Partridge Family, but he just kept talking
about those Playboy bunnies. He said he'd already slept with six or
seven Playboy bunnies already, but he was always up to sleep with
more. As for me, I just wanted to meet David Cassidy. I was a real big
David Cassidy fan back then. I had a great big poster of him hanging
up over my bed back at Graceland. The guys used to make fun of me
for it, but I was like, "Screw you, man. That's David fucking Cassidy,
man. You show some goddamn respect," you know?

SGT. RUDY RANDOLPH: I flew these two cats in to base camp.
Neither one of them was very smart, and the blond one, Capt.
Burrows, looked a lot like Elvis. He had these big dumb sideburns and
he wore the collar of his BDU jacket open so you could see his
necklaces. He had two pendants on. One was a crucifix and the other
a star of David. I asked him why he wore both and he said, "I wanna
be sure I'm on the right side." During the flight I said, "Do you know
you look just like Elvis Presley with blond hair and a mustache?" He
just laughed and said, "You're funny. You're a funny guy." But he was
saying it in this weird way that made me think he was crazy or
something. He took out his pistol and told me never to say anything
like that again or he'd have to shoot me. Then he laughed. I just said,
"Fine, man. I won't mention it again." I guess he wasn't a fan of Elvis
or something.

Then he asked me who the hottest woman I ever slept with was.
I told him my wife, Loretta, and I showed him her picture. He just
laughed and said she was "maybe a six." Then he said, "You ever see

a damn Playboy bunny? Those women are tens, easy. I'm gonna nail me a few of them." The guy was really nuts, but I kept my mouth shut. People got shot for saying the wrong shit to the wrong people over there in 'Nam, and I didn't wanna be one of 'em.

BO WHITAKER: Elvis just kept talking about wanting to bang those Playboy bunnies. I loved Elvis, but I got kind of tired of hearing about it. But then I suppose Elvis got tired of hearing me blabber on and on about wanting to meet David Cassidy.

So they flew us into Bravo Company base camp. We had a briefing that lasted about two hours, and they told us all about the captives and the layout of the prison camp. Then they assigned a small squad of grunts to us. There were six of them in all—Sgt. Davenport, Tex, Russo, Junior, Conard, and Doc, the medic. They were going with us to extract those captives.

PVT. TYRELL "JUNIOR" REDDING: Them white boys was crazy as shit. The one with the big blond sideburns kept calling people cocksuckers and talking about "Mr. Jesus." I wanted to give them shit, but I knew they was C.I.A., and you didn't fuck with the C.I.A. At least not if you wanted to go home when your tour was up. I wasn't about to get fragged out there in the middle of nowhere.

The funny thing was, the weird blond guy kept acting real funny. I think he thought he was actin' black, but I've never known any brothers that acted like that cat. He was just real fuckin' weird, man.

BO WHITAKER: We stayed that night at base camp and played poker with the soldiers. Then we pitched quarters in the sand. I was pretty good at that. I think I won maybe ten or twelve dollars. Elvis did okay, too, I think, but I don't remember specifically how well he did. What I do remember is that none of us slept very well that night. I think everyone was just kind of worried about what the extraction mission was gonna bring.

We all got up at zero dark thirty the next morning and got our gear together. We each had a ruck on our backs, an M-16, an entrenching tool, and...well, that was about it. Elvis and me were packing .45s on our hips and Pvt. Conard was carrying the big .50 cal machine gun. We left base camp around 0600 hours in a chopper. He took us several clicks down the river, where we were just a couple of days away from that prison camp. Since I'd never been in war before, I was scared shitless. Elvis had never been to war either, but he was just as cool as ice, man. He wasn't scared at all. Maybe it was the adrenaline coursing through his veins, maybe it was the thought of banging those damn Playboy bunnies, but he wasn't afraid one bit.

SGT. LARRY DAVENPORT: This was my third tour of the 'Nam, so I knew a thing or two about soldiering. These two new guys—the C.I.A. spooks—didn't know shit. But Capt. Burrows kept trying to give the orders. He'd look at the map and say, "We need to go over here, and we need to do this and that." Finally I just looked at him and said, "Request permission to speak." He said, "Permission granted, man." And I told him he didn't have a fucking clue what he was talking about. He acted real pissed and he punched a tree, but eventually he let me lead the damn squad. I wasn't trying to be the alpha dog or anything like that, but this was a matter of life and death and I wasn't about to let those soldiers die because of that stupid motherfucker.

BO WHITAKER: We'd only been in the jungle for a couple of hours before Elvis got into an argument with Sgt. Davenport. "I really wanna frag this cocksucker, man," Elvis told me. I talked him into letting the guy live, though, so he could get us home. Frankly Sgt. Davenport knew way more about Vietnam than Elvis and me put together.

PVT. TYRELL "JUNIOR" REDDING: I was like, is this dude for real? That blond dude was just crazy as hell, man. He kept trying to tell Sarge what to do and how to do it. Finally Sarge got fed up and just let him have it. He said, "Do you want to lead and die or let me lead you and live?" Then the blond guy went nuts and started kicking the trees and he tried to Karate chop a snake. I said, "Shit, nigger, that snake is poisonous, man. You can't be doing that shit." And that dude, I shit you not, said, "I'm a damn black belt in Karate. I could Karate chop a damn snake in half. Fucking snake better not mess with me, man."

BO WHITAKER: I think those soldiers all respected Elvis from the beginning. I could tell they really wanted him to be the leader, but it just wasn't a good idea.

CPL. TOMMY "DOC" MARCUM: We were all relieved when Sarge took control back from that crazy fucker Burrows. We *hated* that guy. We'd dealt with some crazy ass officers by this point, but this C.I.A. cat was the worst. There wasn't a one of us in the squad who didn't seriously consider shooting him and leaving him out there in the bush.

BO WHITAKER: Elvis looked just like a seasoned veteran out there. He really knew his shit.

PVT. TYRELL "JUNIOR" REDDING: That guy didn't know shit. I mean it. He didn't know anything about soldiering. I think a motherfucker could learn more from watching old war movies than that cat knew. If he'd have led that squad, either we'd have been dead in an hour, or he'd have been dead in an hour. Something had to give.

BO WHITAKER: I could tell they really liked me, too. I felt like I was one of them, and I think they felt the same way.

PVT. TYRELL "JUNIOR" REDDING: I'm pretty sure Bo was gay. He just kept talking about David Cassidy. I got nothing against gay dudes, but he seemed like a damn stalker. It was real creepy. I was like, "Man, why you talk about David Cassidy all the time? Shit, talk about *something* else. Anything."

BO WHITAKER: One of the guys, I think it was Tex, said, "Hey, buddy, you look just like Elvis Presley." Elvis just laughed and said, "You know, I've heard that before. But I got a mustache and blond hair, so I can't be him. He has black hair and no mustache." Then he thought about it for a moment and said, "What do you guys think about Elvis Presley?"

PVT. TYRELL "JUNIOR" REDDING: I said, "I can't stand that motherfucker Elvis." And that dude Burrows says, "Why?" And I said, "He stole all of his shit—his songs, his sound, his moves—from black people. He got rich. Do you know what those old blues cats he ripped off got? Not a damn thing."

BO WHITAKER: I was pretty sure Elvis was gonna kill Junior before we got out of the bush. Junior just kept talking about how Elvis stole his sound from black people. I tried to defend him by saying that Elvis probably only did it out of respect, but Junior told me to go fuck a picture of David Cassidy. I thought that was kind of rude, man.

SGT. LARRY DAVENPORT: We stopped and ate c-rats at an old monastery around 1500 hours. The blond guy was really driving everyone crazy. He just kept telling us how he'd take on a whole company of gooks with just his Karate skills. Then Junior asked him, and I know he was trying to be an asshole, if he thought he could beat Bruce Lee in a fight. The blond guy said, "Oh yeah, I could beat him in a heartbeat, son." Then he said something about his sensei knowing a guy who defeated the cousin of Bruce Lee's sensei twenty years ago or some nonsense. Then Junior went nuts.

PVT. TYRELL "JUNIOR" REDDING: Hell yeah, I yelled at that dude. He was stone cold full of shit. I don't care if he was C.I.A. Fuck that dude. He was trying to say he could beat Bruce Lee and shit. Man, that dude was so full of shit. Seriously, fuck that guy. Please print that.

BO WHITAKER: Those guys were all real impressed with Elvis' Karate skills. They were just hanging on his every word.

CPL. TOMMY "DOC" MARCUM: I wanted to punch him in the face. I just sat there listening to this crap, thinking about how much I wanted to punch him.

BO WHITAKER: I think we all bonded over that first meal. We were like a team now.

SGT. LARRY DAVENPORT: I wanted to shoot both of them. They were both creepy, and they were both stupid. But they were C.I.A. and you just didn't fuck with the C.I.A.

BO WHITAKER: I kept hoping Elvis would stop talking about music, but he just wouldn't do it. He asked everyone who their favorite musicians were.

SGT. LARRY DAVENPORT: Tex gets all animated and starts talking about the Beatles. I'd never even heard Tex speak before. He talked about how much he loved the Beatles for a good half an hour.

CPL. TOMMY "DOC" MARCUM: Right after that conversation, Tex left the camp to take a piss. That was the last time any of us ever saw him. We didn't even find his body. Funny thing was, there were no signs of gooks anywhere around. We just found Tex's weapon and helmet, and that was it.

BO WHITAKER: So after everyone finally stopped hunting for Tex's body, we started back on our journey. We were still a day or so away from the village where the captives were being held.

Late that night we set up camp deep in the jungle. Elvis volunteered for first guard duty. He said he'd always wanted to do that. So he sat alone in a foxhole with a poncho over his head while everyone else slept. There were claymore mines set up all around the perimeter, and Elvis had the detonation device. The deal was, if he saw anyone entering the perimeter, he was to set off those claymores and wake everyone up. Well, Elvis fell asleep that night and the gooks entered the perimeter. He woke up and they were right on top of us. So he detonated the claymores and all hell broke loose. There was fire coming from all sides, and bright red tracers lit up the night sky. It was chaotic as hell, man, and I was afraid I'd shoot the wrong damn person in the dark.

In all the confusion, Conard got tagged. He died before Doc could even get to him. Elvis was feeling real bad about falling asleep there and letting the Charlies into the perimeter, so he mustered up all the courage he could and ran for Conard's big .50 caliber machine gun. He tossed the chain of bullets over his back and picked up that machine gun like some kind of 1970s Rambo. Somehow he hefted that heavy sumbitch with one hand, and he fired and fired and fired until every last one of those goddamn Victor Charlies was dead.

CPL. TOMMY "DOC" MARCUM: I was rushing towards Conard. I didn't know he had already checked out, and Burrows jumps in there and grabs that big .50 cal. machine gun and just starts mowing the gooks down all around us. It would have been an incredible sight if he hadn't been the reason Conard was dead.

SGT. LARRY DAVENPORT: I think it would be an understatement to say I wasn't too keen on Capt. Burrows. First he let the enemy into the perimeter... I'd bet you dollars to doughnuts he was asleep, although he denied it. Then, he jumped up with the .50 cal machine gun and went ape shit. That kind of thing looks good in the movies when Audie Murphy or John Wayne does it, but in real life it endangers the lives of other soldiers. I never fragged anyone in the 'Nam, but I came damn close to putting a bullet in Burrows' head.

BO WHITAKER: Everything got real heated real quick. First Elvis says, "Don't think of me as no hero. Anyone would have done what I did." Then Sgt. Davenport started screaming at him, saying he was responsible for Conard's death. He said Elvis could have gotten everyone in the squad killed. Then, before Elvis could respond, Junior sucker punched him in the side of the head. Everyone gathered around, and I think they were all rooting for Junior for some reason. Then Junior pulled a knife on Elvis, but Elvis just used his Karate to knock the knife to the ground. The he delivered a perfect roundhouse kick to Junior's head, and Junior was down for the count.

Elvis just stands up, shakes his head, and says, "What the hell was all that about?" In Elvis' eyes, he was a hero, plain and simple, and nothing those guys had to say could change that.

SGT. LARRY DAVENPORT: I told Burrows that I was going to write him up when we got back to base camp. He just sneered and broke into a song. "If you're lookin' for trouble, you came to the right place..."

PVT. TYRELL "JUNIOR" REDDING: That cracker Burrows never would have beat me in the daytime. The truth was, I was still groggy and shit from having just been asleep. That sucker got lucky. That's all that was. Man, if I was to see him again, I'd stomp a mud hole in his dumb cracker ass.

BO WHITAKER: Things were real tense after that. I think everyone started losing respect for Elvis then, since he'd fallen asleep on guard duty. Of course Elvis would never admit it. He told me, "Man, I just mistook those Victor Charlies for trees was all. If I had known they was Charlies, I would have squeezed off those damn claymores sooner." In Elvis' mind, he didn't kill Conard—he saved the rest of us.

SGT. LARRY DAVENPORT: We spotted the enemy village around 1500 hours that second day. Burrows took over the operation at that point. I didn't mind so much then. After all, I'd assumed that the C.I.A. would take over things once we actually reached the village. What I hadn't counted on was how stupid Burrows was.

BO WHITAKER: Elvis' first idea maybe wasn't so good. I mean, I'll defend him to the day I die, but I'm not so sure that was his best idea.

PVT. TYRELL "JUNIOR" REDDING: Burrows came up with this brilliant idea. First he asked for a volunteer. I wasn't about to volunteer for shit with this stupid motherfucker. So Russo raises his hand and volunteers. I'm like, "Stupid move, newbie." So Burrows takes a big tree and ties it to the top of Russo's helmet. Then he tells him to walk in through the front gates and they'll think he's a tree. Then he can save the prisoners. Russo doesn't look too sure about all this. Sarge tries to convince Burrows that this idea won't work, but Burrows says he saw it in a movie once. He tells Russo, "Just act like a tree. If you need to do anything, just do it the way a tree would do it." So Russo says, "But how do I walk?" And Burrows says, "Walk like a damn tree, man."

BO WHITAKER: So Russo walks real slow, like a tree would walk. He gets about five feet from the front gate and they gun him down. Sgt. Davenport and the others immediately get upset about Elvis' idea. Elvis just says, "He did it all wrong, man. He was supposed to do it like a tree." Then he says, "We'll just have to try it again. Any volunteers?" This time no one volunteers, so Elvis says, "My buddy Bo will do it, won't you, Bo?"

CPL. TOMMY "DOC" MARCUM: I never laughed so hard in my life. The look on Bo's face was priceless. He knew it was a shitty idea.

So he starts trying to talk to Burrows, but Burrows is tearing down another small tree to tie on Bo's head.

BO WHITAKER: I said, "Elvis, me and you go a long ways back, but this is a bad idea." Elvis just looks at me and says, "You think so, huh?" He says, "Let me clear my head for a minute and mull this over." So he takes a handful of painkillers and walks off by himself for a few minutes. Then he comes back and asks, "What if you disguised yourself as a rock instead of a tree? You think that might work?"

PVT. TYRELL "JUNIOR" REDDING: I knew it was a terrible idea, but I just kept rooting him on. I was like, "Hell, yeah, be a fucking rock, Bo. You could be a rock and they would never see your ass going in there." Truth is, I just thought it would be funny to see Bo get shot. Then, maybe, Burrows would see that this was a stupid ass idea.

BO WHITAKER: I said, "I don't think disguising ourselves as anything and walking through the front gate is gonna work." So Elvis says, "Are you sure, man? I think you could be a really great rock, Bo." But I said, "Please, Elvis, this isn't gonna work, and I'll be gunned down like Russo was." So Elvis says, "Yeah? Well, shit, man, let's come up with a new plan."

SGT. LARRY DAVENPORT: After hearing Burrows just mentioning various things people could disguise themselves as, I finally spoke up. I said, "Look, there's an opening over there on the west side of the village. If the four of us soldiers lay down cover fire at the front gate and keep the guards busy, then maybe you guys could sneak in through that opening and free the prisoners."

But Burrows wasn't too sure.

BO WHITAKER: Elvis said, "What if Bo ties a snake on top of his head and pretends to be a damn snake, man?"

CPL. TOMMY "DOC" MARCUM: I reached for my pistol during that conversation. I was a damn conscientious objector—I was a pacifist who wasn't about to shoot anybody—but I was really gonna shoot Burrows in order to save everyone else's lives. I looked at Sarge and he looked back at me. He knew what I was thinking.

SGT. LARRY DAVENPORT: Doc was about to frag Burrows. Our eyes locked and I pleaded with him not to do it. I saw him start to pull the pistol out of its holster, but then he stopped.

CPL. TOMMY "DOC" MARCUM: Burrows will never know how close he came to dying right at that moment.

SGT. LARRY DAVENPORT: Then, at that exact moment, Burrows says, "Sarge, I like your idea. Let's do it."

BO WHITAKER: Elvis and me climbed down the hillside and snuck around to the west side of the village. There was a twenty-foot section where there was no fence. We moved slowly towards the village perimeter, dug in, and waited.

Finally, Sgt. Davenport and the others started firing on the village gates. About fifty V.C. just came out of nowhere, man, and they're all shooting back. It was just intense as hell. And Elvis says, "Come on, man. Let's go." So we make our way up to that open area. We see a V.C. guard right inside there, so Elvis sneaks up on him and cuts his throat. He turns and says, "T.C.B., baby. T.C.B." Then we creep into the enemy perimeter and sneak from one bamboo hut to the next. Several times we came close to getting caught, but we made it to the prison area. There were three big bamboo cages, and guards all around. There were five of them, I think.

So Elvis says, "You take the two on the right, and I'll take the three on the left." He was always cocky that way. So we both came running in at them, our .45s out and firing. I dropped my two guys with three shots. I think Elvis dropped his three in three straight shots. Then we took the AK-47s off the dead guards and opened those cages. Well, Elvis opened the cages while I watched his back. A couple of Charlies came running out at us, but I mowed 'em down.

Elvis freed the captives. "Look at these hot damn women," he says. And the three Playboy bunnies and Susan Dey look sexy as hell. They're a little bit dirty and their clothes are torn and tattered. They looked kind of like sexy cave women. Then I saw David Cassidy. I ran over to him and told him I was a big fan. I could hear Elvis gunning down some more V.C. behind me, but I really wanted David Cassidy's autograph. David Cassidy looked at me kind of funny and said, "I'd be happy to sign an autograph for you when we get out of here." I told him it was okay, that I had an ink pen on me, but he still said we should wait.

DAVID CASSIDY: I was really uncomfortable around that Bo guy. I was happy to be getting out of that prison alive, but Bo really creeped me out. He kept looking at me in this weird way. I swear he was undressing me with his eyes.

BO WHITAKER: So Elvis led the way and I ran just behind the captives. That way the two of us could protect them from both sides. Elvis and me both gunned down a couple more V.C. each, and then we finally made it back to the hole in the fence. We all ran out and escaped back into the jungle. Elvis called Sgt. Davenport on his walkie-talkie and told him we were out. Then we all met up back up on the hillside.

SGT. DAVENPORT: The two C.I.A. spooks came back with the captives. I looked at them for a moment and I said, "Is that the fuckin' Partridge Family?" I thought I had somehow lost my mind out there. I had to be seeing things.

PVT. TYRELL "JUNIOR" REDDING: I looked at those captives and I said, "Is that Miss January, 1972?"

DAVID CASSIDY: Bo followed me everywhere I went. I had to take a leak in the bushes and Bo came with me. He said he needed to protect me from enemy combatants. While I was urinating, he walked around in front of me and looked at my penis. He said, "Yeah, mine's pretty big, too." Frankly, Bo kind of scared me.

BO WHITAKER: Elvis threatened everyone that if anybody told anyone they'd been kidnapped by Charlie that they'd be dead as hell. He held up his gun to show them he meant business. Then he pointed it at Danny Bonaduce. He said, "I just know you're gonna be the one that says something. I promise you, if you make me come after you, I will bury you in a hole so deep no one will ever find your remains." Danny Bonaduce pissed his pants, I think.

DANNY BONADUCE: What are you talking about? I was never kidnapped by anyone. I have nothing to comment on any of this. Just leave me alone. Please.

BO WHITAKER: We hiked for several hours before setting up bivouac. Elvis made all the women sleep inside his tiny pup tent. He said he needed to keep them safe.

DAVID CASSIDY: Bo made me sleep inside his tent. He said it was to keep me safe. He...never mind. I don't want to talk about it. I don't even want to think about it.

BO WHITAKER: I don't know if it was true or not, but Elvis said he had a six-way with those Playboy bunnies, Shirley Jones, and Susan Dey. I asked him who was the best and he said, "Shirley Jones, man. Shirley fuckin' Jones."

The next day Elvis and me delivered the four soldiers, the three Playboy bunnies, and all the members of The Partridge Family back to base camp in one piece. When we were flying back home, Elvis said, "You know, Bo, Vietnam is a nice place to visit, but I don't ever wanna go there again."

CHAPTER NINE
AREA 51 (1975)

BO WHITAKER: It was around August, I think, when Elvis and me got called down to Nevada. We were temporarily stationed at a secret military installation known as Area 51, just outside Edwards Air Force Base. The C.I.A. sent a military chopper for us, and we flew all the way from Memphis to Nevada. It was hotter than hell out there in the desert, and we both wondered what all this was about. Anytime we'd ask, we'd get told we were gonna be briefed once we arrived wherever it was were going. Hell, they wouldn't even tell us what state we were flying to.

We landed at Area 51 around four in the afternoon, and we were both hungry as hell. So as soon as we put away our gear in our barracks, we were led to the cafeteria. I remember Elvis was real mad they didn't have corn dogs. He kept saying, "I flew all this way, now I want a damn corn dog." The lady at the cafeteria said she didn't have any corn dogs, but she had some beanie-weenies. She said that was as close as she could get to corn dogs. So Elvis ate the damn beanie-weenies, but he was still mad. He took the little weenies and wrapped 'em in Wonder Bread and stuck a straw in them, but that still wasn't good enough. He kept grumbling about how he wanted corn dogs. He said, "What I'm really in the mood for is one of those honey-batter corn dogs like you get at the state fair. Them sumbitches are good as hell, man." I agreed. You know one time I ate seven corn dogs? And they were those big long John Holmes corn dogs.

Anyway, after our meal we were taken to an underground room where we were briefed by an Air Force officer named Lt. Col. Holcum. He told us that Area 51 was a top secret military base where aliens had been kept in a cryogenic freezer since they was discovered back in the 1950s.

Excerpt from transcript of briefing between Lt. Col. Demney Holcum, Elvis Presley (a.k.a. Jon Burrows), and Bo Whitaker, August 10, 1975:

> PRESLEY: Aliens, sir?

> HOLCUM: Yes, Mr. Burrows. Aliens.

> PRESLEY: What kind of aliens are we talking about? You mean the illegal kind? Like Mexicans and Hawaiians?

> HOLCUM: I mean aliens from outer space.

> PRESLEY: You mean they's Mexicans in outer space?

BO WHITAKER: Elvis just couldn't wrap his head around it. He couldn't understand that these were real space aliens. I kept telling him, you know, like *Star Trek*. But he didn't understand. So finally I reminded him of an old *Twilight Zone* episode we had seen where there was this alien on the wing of an airplane. That episode had scared the hell out of Elvis, and he'd slept with the lights on for a week after that. So when he realized what I meant, he said, "Holy shit, Bo! You mean there's one of those wing guys *here*?" Finally Lt. Col. Holcum and me got Elvis calmed down, but there for a while he was scared out of his wits.

LT. COL. DEMNEY HOLCUM, RET.: Briefing operative Burrows was one of the most difficult jobs the Air Force had ever given me, and I'd been through two wars. The guy really wasn't too bright. I thought, if this is the best the Central Intelligence Agency has to offer, then we're all in big trouble.

BO WHITAKER: Lt. Col. Holcum kept trying to talk, but Elvis just kept interrupting and asking him questions about the aliens.

Excerpt from transcript of briefing between Lt. Col. Demney Holcum, Elvis Presley (a.k.a. Jon Burrows), and Bo Whitaker, August 10, 1975:

PRESLEY: So we're talking about spacemen?

HOLCUM: Yes, spacemen.

PRESLEY: I didn't think those S.O.B.s were real, man. I always just figured that was some gobbledy-gook silly shit for the movies.

HOLCUM: That's what most of the world believes, and it's been our job since 1956 to make sure the world keeps on believing that it's all—

PRESLEY: Gobbledy-gook.

HOLCUM: Precisely.

PRESLEY: So where are the little bastards?

HOLCUM: Who?

PRESLEY: The spacemen.

HOLCUM: The aliens are being kept frozen in a laboratory several floors beneath us. I'll take you there in a little while, Mr. Burrows.

PRESLEY: What color are they? I'll bet they're black. Or brown. Do they look like Jamaicans? I'll bet they look like Jamaicans.

HOLCUM: The aliens are green, Mr. Burrows.

PRESLEY: Well, holy shit! They're green, huh?

HOLCUM: Yes.

PRESLEY: All of them?

HOLCUM: What do you mean?

PRESLEY: Are they green from head to toe?

HOLCUM: Yes.

PRESLEY: So they have little green wangs?

HOLCUM: What do you mean?

PRESLEY: Do they got green cocks, man?

HOLCUM: [Inaudible...] green balls.

PRESLEY: Man, I'll bet that's something to see, them little green cocks and balls.

HOLCUM: They are interesting specimens.

PRESLEY: Where did they come from?

HOLCUM: Our scientists believe they came from another solar system altogether.

PRESLEY: What's the name of their planet?

HOLCUM: We don't know.

PRESLEY: I'll bet it's got some crazy name like jibbyjobowokkywokko...

HOLCUM: They—

PRESLEY: Booboobobocondo.

HOLCUM: Are you finished, Mr. Burrows?

PRESLEY: Kakkidakowdicobbo.

HOLCUM: You men are probably wondering why you're here, and why you're being briefed by an Air Force officer rather than Central Intelligence Agency officials.

PRESLEY: Bokkybokkowokky.

HOLCUM: [Sighs.] Does he do this all the time?

WHITAKER: Nah. Just when he's trying to figure out the name of an alien planet. I've seen this one other time.

HOLCUM: Are you finished, Mr. Burrows?

PRESLEY: Yes, sir. Go on, man. I didn't mean to interrupt you.

HOLCUM: I appreciate that.

PRESLEY: I have a question though. I was just wondering how we managed to capture these spacemen.

HOLCUM: They crash landed on earth about twenty miles east of here. They were all cryogenically frozen in the same capsules they're frozen in now.

PRESLEY: All of them?

HOLCUM: All but one. We believe he was the pilot of the spacecraft.

PRESLEY: And no one thawed them out or tried to cut 'em open?

HOLCUM: We did. There used to be twenty-seven of them in all.

PRESLEY: How many are there now?

HOLCUM: Three.

BO WHITAKER: Elvis was just in awe of the whole thing. I hadn't seen him this excited since the Beatles broke up. He was like a damn kid at a zoo, just looking around at everything with wide eyes and asking all kinds of questions.

Lt. Col. Holcum told us we were there because the C.I.A. was taking over Area 51 and they wanted Elvis to oversee the transition.

LT. COL. DEMNEY HOLCUM, RET.: The Central Intelligence Agency had told us that their top men would be on this project. But this guy Burrows... I don't know if he was just stupid or if he was playing dumb for me, but I didn't know quite what to make out of him. At least he was more intelligent than the other guy, Bo.

I informed them that the operation was now going to be run by the C.I.A. with cooperation from the United States Air Force. I also informed them that Burrows and I would be heading up the operation jointly.

BO WHITAKER: Lt. Col. Holcum said a bunch of stuff I didn't understand. I could tell Elvis didn't know what the hell he was talking about either. So we both just nodded our heads a lot and said, "Right." Then, after our initial briefing, we met up with a couple of C.I.A. honchos.

Excerpt from transcript of briefing between Lt. Col. Demney Holcum, Elvis Presley (a.k.a. Jon Burrows), Bo Whitaker and Central Intelligence Agency operatives Sam Gould and Edward LaFontaine, August 10, 1975:

GOULD: It's a real pleasure meeting you, Mr. Burrows. You're a legend in the agency.

LAFONTAINE: We'll help show you around and make sure you get accustomed to things here at Groom Lake.

PRESLEY: Groom Lake? What the hell is Groom Lake, man?

LAFONTAINE: Sorry. Groom Lake is another name for Area 51.

PRESLEY: How many names does this sumbitch have?

GOULD: Just a couple, Mr. Burrows.

PRESLEY: Okay, cool. I was afraid I was gonna get confused with too many names to remember. It's like when we had to memorize the presidents in school. There were so many of them I kept gettin' confused. I kept thinking Col. Sanders was a president. I kept getting him and Roosevelt mixed up.

LAFONTAINE: Which one?

PRESLEY: You mean there was more than one Col. Sanders?

GOULD: We're going to accompany Lt. Col. Holcum here in showing you around and filling you in on all the day to day details of what goes on here. We're still kind of new to this ourselves.

LAFONTAINE: The agency only just got involved with Area 51.

WHITAKER: How long have you boys been here?

GOULD: About two weeks.

PRESLEY: And how long will *we* be here?

LAFONTAINE: As long as it takes to get everything transitioned over.

PRESLEY: When will we get to see the damn spacemen?

LAFONTAINE: We can take you there now, if you'd like.

SAM GOULD: Meeting operative #67357, Jon Burrows, was one of the biggest days of my life. When I was a kid I always wanted to meet Mickey Mantle. I never did get to meet him, though. But I did get to meet Jon Burrows, possibly the greatest C.I.A. operative of all time. It was a real honor. I tried to act as professional as I could around him, but secretly I was thrilled.

EDWARD LAFONTAINE: Operative #67357 was a hero to us all. It was truly an honor just to breathe the same air as him. In the agency, people used to whisper about him in hushed voices. He was as big a legend as the agency had ever had. I swore never to divulge any top secret information about the agency or Area 51, but since we're talking about Burrows, fuck it. He was and is one of my top heroes, right up there with Johnny Unitas and John Denver.

BO WHITAKER: Those guys were just falling all over Elvis. They kept asking him for his autograph and asking him about missions he'd been on. But Elvis refused to talk about that stuff. "That's top secret, man," he'd say. They told him they had security clearance, but Elvis wouldn't budge. For him, top secret meant top secret. Hell, he didn't even like talking to me about the missions, and I'd been on the damn things with him!

LT. COL. DEMNEY HOLCUM, RET.: I don't know what was up with those C.I.A. guys. They acted like they wanted to blow the guy or something. I don't know what exactly Burrows had done to become such a legend in the Central Intelligence Agency, but they couldn't take their eyes off of him. He just had this magnetism that seemed to suck them in. He could have easily been a famous star of some sort. Anyway, those C.I.A. guys treated him like he was a star already.

BO WHITAKER: They took us six or seven floors down to a huge room filled with all kinds of gadgets and electronic wickerdoos. There were about a dozen scientists working in there. Then the C.I.A. guys led us to another room where there were these big glass capsules with little green spacemen inside them. They were about four feet tall and naked, with all their little spaceman goodies hanging out. They had great big heads with these big ol' eyes with little white goatees. They were real creepy. But Elvis didn't mind. He just leaned over and said, "They ain't as scary as that furry wing bastard on *The Twilight Zone*, man." I think he was a little bit relieved by that.

Excerpt from transcript of briefing between Lt. Col. Demney Holcum, Elvis Presley (a.k.a. Jon Burrows), Bo Whitaker, Sam Gould, and Edward LaFontaine, August 10, 1975:

PRESLEY: Sure enough, they got little green peckers on 'em. Just as clear as day, there they are.

GOULD: They're tiny little things, aren't they?

PRESLEY: They aren't too tiny. Hell, them things are bigger than Bo's dick.

WHITAKER: That ain't true. I got a great big dick.

PRESLEY: Nah, Bo's hung like an infant.

WHITAKER: [Inaudible.]

PRESLEY: Why you think they don't wear clothes?

HOLCUM: We don't have any answers for that.

PRESLEY: How old are these little bastards?

HOLCUM: We don't know that either. Our scientists say they could be anywhere between fifty and a thousand years old.

PRESLEY: They really got it narrowed down, huh?

HOLCUM: There really isn't any way for us to know for sure.

PRESLEY: I know. I was just messin' with ya, man. So are these little cocksuckers dangerous? I'll bet they can make laser beams come out of their eyes. I'll bet they can start fires with their minds.

HOLCUM: They're not dangerous in this state.

PRESLEY: Nevada?

HOLCUM: No, I mean they're not dangerous when they're frozen in these capsules. They had some incidents when they thawed them out where they went ape shit and started tearing up the place. But that was back before I worked here.

PRESLEY: What did they do? Make atomic bombs by snapping their fingers?

HOLCUM: Nothing like that.

PRESLEY: I'll bet they can fly like Superman.

HOLCUM: We don't think so.

PRESLEY: I wonder if they can read our thoughts. I'll bet they can.

HOLCUM: That's been discussed, but we've never been able to verify whether or not that's true.

PRESLEY: I don't want them little cocksuckers reading my mind. I think about dirty stuff a lot. You know, titties.

WHITAKER: Yeah, I think about that a lot, too.

EDWARD LAFONTAINE: Those guys sure thought a lot about titties. That was all they talked about. And Burrows kept calling everybody cocksuckers. I thought that was a little bit strange, but hell, he was our hero, so we didn't mind if he called us that.

SAM GOULD: I started using that phrase a lot after I met operative #67357. But one time I screwed up and accidentally called John the Baptist a cocksucker in a conversation with my pastor, so my wife made me stop using that word. But no one could use it quite like Burrows did.

EDWARD LAFONTAINE: Yeah, Burrows was a master at using that phrase. Over the couple of months we worked together, he probably said cocksucker about a million times. Sam and I both started using that word a lot after that. It was because, you know, he was our hero.

BO WHITAKER: Then the C.I.A. guys took us back up to the surface and we all walked to an airplane hangar that was surrounded by armed guards. When we went in, we couldn't believe what we saw.

Excerpt from transcript of briefing between Lt. Col. Demney Holcum, Elvis Presley (a.k.a. Jon Burrows), Bo Whitaker, Sam Gould, and Edward LaFontaine, August 10, 1975:

PRESLEY: Holy shit!

WHITAKER: That's amazing!

PRESLEY: What is that?

HOLCUM: That's our reproduction of their spacecraft. It's a beaut, huh?

PRESLEY: It looks like a sideways taco.

HOLCUM: The government calls it X9736, but we all refer to it as Big Blue.

PRESLEY: Yeah, it is blue. You know, it would look pretty sweet if it was all pink like one of my Cadillacs.

LAFONTAINE: It can fly about five hundred miles an hour.

PRESLEY: And it'll fly to space?

HOLCUM: We haven't flown it into space much, but yeah, it will fly into outer space. We're trying to duplicate the alien construction perfectly and then learn exactly how it works. We're still a little bit confused about some components of it.

PRESLEY: Will it go through time?

HOLCUM: No.

PRESLEY: It goes five hundred miles an hour? That's fast as hell, man. You'd get one hell of a speeding ticket if you were going that fast.

GOULD: Could you imagine moving that fast?

HOLCUM: The pilots say you can't even tell you're moving when you're inside it.

PRESLEY: It looks awfully big for such little spacemen.

HOLCUM: Well, that's because we've enlarged everything to human-size.

PRESLEY: That's great. Mind if Bo and me go inside and take a look around?

HOLCUM: That shouldn't be a problem. Just don't touch anything.

PRESLEY: Okay, cool, man.

LT. COL. DEMNEY HOLCUM, RET.: I never should have let those morons get onboard Big Blue. It was one of those mistakes that you kind of know you're making at the time you're making it. But I figured, what could it hurt?

BO WHITAKER Elvis and me went up in that big blue spaceship and looked around a little bit. I kind of wondered where the toilet was, you know? What if you were up there in space and you had to take a shit? I figured that was gonna be the first thing I asked Lt. Col. Holcum when we got back out of there. It was crazy though. There were TV screens everywhere. Man, there must have been ten of them in there. I was kind of afraid Elvis was gonna get mad and shoot the damn TV screen just out of habit, but he didn't do that.

Elvis sat down in one of the two seats at the control panel. He said, "Sit down, man. We'll pretend like we're flying this sumbitch. I always did want to fly a spaceship." So I sat down next to him and we started pushing all the buttons and pulling all the levers. Then the console started making these crazy sounds, like boop-beep-boop, you know? Then this big green rock on the console lit up and got all bright. Then Big Blue started shaking and vibrating like one of those motel beds that you put the change in.

Neither one of us knew what was happening. I asked Elvis what we should do, and he said we should hit the buttons and pull the levers some more. So that's what we did.

LT. COL. DEMNEY HOLCUM, RET.: They accidentally activated the force field and the whole thing started vibrating really, really hard. It just kept shaking and shaking, and making this loud whirring sound. And then it lifted up about ten feet off the ground and hovered there for a moment. Then the shaking became more intense and Big Blue shot out through the aluminum wall of the hangar and they were gone.

SAM GOULD: They were there one second, and the next they were gone. We all just stood there with our mouths hanging open, wondering what in the hell we should be doing.

EDWARD LAFONTAINE: Man, I almost lost it. I couldn't believe what I was seeing. Operative #67357 and operative Bo just shot out of that hangar so fast it was like they disappeared. If it hadn't been for them tearing the front wall out of the hangar, I would have thought they had just disappeared. That was probably the craziest thing I've ever seen in my life. It was amazing.

BO WHITAKER: Elvis and I was kind of in shock for the first few moments. Then Elvis got real into it and started yelling, "Yee-haw!" He just kept pulling those levers and pushing those buttons. He said, "I think this one is the cigarette lighter." Then he pushed it and the spacecraft changed directions. I guess we were probably going five hundred miles an hour or so, but the thing turned as smoothly as anything I had ever seen. Even a damn Buick doesn't turn that smoothly.

Elvis hit some more buttons and kicked the console a couple of times. "We're flyin', man," he kept saying. "We're fucking flying!" Every so often he would hit a new button and the ship would tilt or fly straight up into the sky or turn or zig zag. It was just crazy. A lot of people have asked me if I felt like throwing up when all that was happening, but the truth is that I couldn't even feel it. I could see it happening, but it was the smoothest ride I'd ever experienced. Even when Elvis made the damn thing spiral, we stayed in our seats. It was really wild.

EARL DUNLEAVY: Me and Sharon Jean were just driving down the highway and I saw something flying across the sky. It looked sort of like a sideways taco, only it was blue. Then it turned real sharply and shot off in another direction. That's when I knew I had seen a real flying saucer. And from that day on I vowed to devote the rest of my life to studying UFOs and proving to the world that they were real.

SHARON JEAN DUNLEAVY: Yeah, I saw the spaceship. It was bright blue and it went faster than any airplane I had ever seen. And when it turned, it turned really sharply in a way that I've never seen anything else turn. Yeah, I'm pretty sure it was a spacecraft. The truth is, I wish we'd never seen the damn thing. That was when Earl became obsessed with UFOs. He started wearing an aluminum foil hat and trying to call UFOs on his CB radio. He kept documentation and started a UFO watchers club. My life has really been shit ever since that day.

EARL DUNLEAVY: Sharon Jean never has understood me. She thinks I ignore her all the time and that I only think about UFOs and spacemen. Well, hell, if she'd put out once in a while I might be more inclined to think about her.

SHARON JEAN DUNLEAVY: Earl said that? He can be a real shithead sometimes. If he thinks I haven't been putting out enough now, just wait until he sees what happens thanks to that stupid comment.

Front page article from the Beaumont Times Daily, *Beaumont, Nevada, August 11, 1975:*

> The Beaumont Sheriff's Department received nearly thirty calls Sunday afternoon when local residents claimed they saw an unidentified flying object over our fair city.
>
> "It was blue and it looked kind of like a sideways taco," said Eunice Gatewood. "I was just sitting out on the porch, drinking a little brandy when I saw that thing go shooting across the sky. It about scared the bejeezus out of me."
>
> The descriptions provided by other witnesses seem to match Eunice's story.
>
> "Truth be told, I was taking a leak behind Greeley's Market when I saw the thing," said Tom Watkins of Watkins Television and Stereo Repair. "I've never seen anything like it in my entire life, and I know all about electronics. It was a flying saucer for

sure. People keep saying it looked like a sideways taco, but I'm not real sure what that means. But it was bright blue and it moved faster than anything I've ever seen before."

Beaumont Sheriff Ed Masters believes it was just a weather balloon. "We've been getting reports of flying saucers for years in this area, and the government always says it's weather balloons," said Masters. "It's nothing to worry about."

Locals were so frightened that Sunday bingo at the First Presbyterian Church was cancelled. According to Esther Robinson, bingo will commence this coming Sunday.

BO WHITAKER: Elvis just kept hitting buttons and that sucker kept zipping around all over the place. Then, finally, the damn thing crashed into the desert. Thankfully neither of us was hurt. Elvis just laughed and said, "Damn, that was fun!" It took about two hours before the Air Force came and saved us.

LT. COL. DEMNEY HOLCUM, RET.: I really didn't think Burrows was as much of a hero as everyone else did, but what the hell do I know? I mean, sure, he managed to maneuver Big Blue in ways that no one before him had, but I really think it was an accident. Nevertheless, everyone went and made a big damn deal about the whole thing and Burrows just became more of a hero to his fellow C.I.A. operatives.

SAM GOULD: It was really impressive how operative #67357 figured out how to fly and maneuver that spacecraft without any instruction whatsoever. He even figured out how to land the thing perfectly during that first flight. There wasn't so much as a ding on that spacecraft after he landed it in the desert.

EDWARD LAFONTAINE: We chalked that up as a huge victory for the C.I.A. I mean, the Air Force had been fiddling around with that craft for years, and they still knew very little about it. Here one of our guys just climbs onboard and flies it all over the place without so much as a single lesson. Jon Burrows really was a hero to all of us at Area 51. It seemed like there was nothing that guy couldn't do.

BO WHITAKER: Elvis and me stayed there at Area 51 for another couple of months, man. We never did know what exactly we were doing, but everyone just kept saying we were doing a great job.

About a month after we flew Big Blue out into the desert, Elvis was messing around in the laboratory late one night. He always said he did his best thinking there around those spacemen. So one night, Elvis is poking around and he pushes a couple of buttons, and one of the spacemen immediately thawed out inside its capsule. It was awake in there and looking out at him. And to Elvis' surprise, the little green bastard was able to speak perfect American. No one knows how that was possible, but he did.

LT. COL. DEMNEY HOLCUM, RET.: No one knows what Burrows did to make that alien thaw out. For all we know, it just happened by chance when he was there. Either way, we do know that he was the first human to have conversational contact with one of the aliens.

Transcript from laboratory recordings of conversation between Specimen Twenty-Six and Elvis Presley (a.k.a. Jon Burrows), September 18, 1975:

> ALIEN: You there, standing over there.

> PRESLEY: Me?

> ALIEN: Yes, you. Can you tell me what planet this is?

> PRESLEY: This is earth.

> ALIEN: The blue planet?

> PRESLEY: Yeah, mostly.

ALIEN: Shit. We must have made a wrong turn somewhere. What is your name?

PRESLEY: Jon Burrows.

ALIEN: My name is Tenndack. I mean you no harm.

PRESLEY: What is the name of your planet?

ALIEN: Booboobobocondo.

PRESLEY: I knew it, man! I just knew it.

ALIEN: We're just going around the galaxy finding out what life on other planets is like. What kind of creature are you?

PRESLEY: I'm a damn human, man.

ALIEN: What are damn humans like?

PRESLEY: We're pretty nice folks. We don't do much to hurt nobody.

ALIEN: What happened to the rest of my crew?

PRESLEY: They were cut into tiny pieces and killed.

ALIEN: No shit?

PRESLEY: No shit.

ALIEN: Tell me, sir, are all of the damn humans about as intelligent as you are?

PRESLEY: Shit no, Tenndack. I'm one of the smartest around. Hardly anyone here is as smart as I am.

ALIEN: [Chuckles.] Are you serious?

PRESLEY: Hell yes I am.

ALIEN: Do you think you could do me a favor?

PRESLEY: Anything.

ALIEN: You see that green button down there beneath this window? The sixth one down, in the middle column of buttons?

PRESLEY: Yeah.

ALIEN: Could you hit that button nine times in a row, then pause for a moment, and hit it another six times?

PRESLEY: No problem, Tenndack.

LT. COL. DEMNEY HOLCUM, RET.: None of us at Area 51 knew quite what to make of that. It made us look like shit. I mean, we'd been experimenting with those specimens for years, and then this Burrows guy just comes along and has the first known conversation with one of them. The downside is that the alien, Specimen Twenty-Six, escaped. After Burrows hit that sequence of buttons, the window slid down and the creature jumped out of the capsule and disappeared.

The government wasn't unhappy about this at all. They figured, hey, we had two more aliens to experiment with, and Burrows had made a huge breakthrough by actually having a conversation with one of them.

SAM GOULD: This guy Burrows was incredible. He just walked in and schooled those Air Force boys. It was really something to see.

EDWARD LAFONTAINE: I'm not gay, but I totally would have had sex with Jon Burrows. That guy is amazing. He's like a blond-haired Jesus. He's seriously my own personal role model. If I could be just a little bit like him—as a C.I.A. operative and as a man—I could die happy. Jon Burrows is a goddamn hero. That's just all there is to it.

BO WHITAKER: About a month after Elvis spoke to the spaceman, we were relieved from our post at Area 51 and allowed to go home. Between flying Big Blue and Elvis talking to that little green fucker, it was one of the greatest times of our lives.

After that, we went back to Graceland and it was business as usual. Elvis went back on tour and our lives went right back to normal.

CHAPTER TEN
THE DECISION (1977)

CAROLYN MERRILL: This was a really sad time in Elvis Presley's life. I think he was trying very hard to stay afloat. Maybe it was drugs, I don't know. I always figured he kept doing all those shows throughout the seventies because he wanted to stay relevant. New sounds and styles of music had come into the picture, and to some people his brand of rock-and-roll seemed archaic. It's no secret that the kids weren't really buying his records anymore by 1977. The kids who had been buying his records in the fifties were still buying his records, but now they were middle-aged parents with jobs and mortgages.

I suppose we all knew deep down inside that we were witnessing his decline, but most of us were just happy to still have him out there making music, even if it was mostly crappy music. Sure, he was fat and sweaty now, but most of us just overlooked that and chose to consider him as simply being more mature as both a sex symbol and as a musician.

JOE ESPOSITO: Elvis was unraveling right before our eyes. The toll fame was taking on him just seemed to be too much for him to bear. He couldn't go out anywhere in public. He was touring constantly. He just seemed worn out. Some of us would suggest that he take a break, but Elvis being Elvis, he just said no and kept going at the expense of his own mental and physical health. Sometimes I think maybe things would have ended differently if we had been more stern with him about his weight and the touring, but the fact of the matter is that nothing would have changed him. He was very much an independent man—very stubborn—and by God he was gonna do whatever the hell he wanted to do.

LAMAR FIKE: Elvis did literally thousands of shows between 1970 and 1977. He was really tired, to say the least. He couldn't remember what city we were in, and sometimes he couldn't remember the words to his own songs. He would just get frustrated and walk off the stage after fifteen or twenty minutes. The audiences were disappointed, but I don't think anyone was more disappointed than Elvis himself. He had always lived a certain way... He had always maintained very strict goals and ideals for himself and his image, and I think he saw it all slowly fading away. We were all kind of scared about it, and I know there were many conversations held quietly behind closed doors, but we didn't want to piss him off. I mean, this wasn't just his life—it was all of ours, too. I think maybe we needed him even more than he needed us. There at the end, he became very distant from most of us. It wasn't all happy-go-lucky like in the old days. Something was different about Elvis as a person. He just wasn't right.

BILLY SMITH: We knew something was wrong with Elvis. He was taking more and more drugs beyond just the normal painkillers. He had drugs to get him up before a show, and he had drugs to get him back down.

Elvis' behavior was really crazy in his final years. I remember one day when Jimmy Gambill, Patsy Presley's son, was playing shoot 'em up with all of our kids. They were out in the yard there at Graceland. The kids had built a fort and Jimmy climbed up on top of the fence with a toy gun, pretending like he was going to shoot them. Elvis just happened to be looking out the window, and he saw Jimmy there. He thought Jimmy was an assassin sent to murder him. Elvis grabbed an M-16 machine gun and ran outside. He forced Jimmy down on the ground and put the barrel of the M-16 in his mouth. Even when he realized who he had there, he just kept going on and on about how he should kill him. He said, "I'll blow your brains out, you cocksucker!" And that happened in front of all our children. It was really scary. But luckily Elvis didn't pull the trigger.

On another occasion, one of the guys told Elvis he saw a snake going up a tree out behind the house. This was at about seven in the morning, and Elvis was zonked out of his mind on painkillers. Well, he decided it was time to go on a snake hunt. So he went outside, wobbling around like a damn drunkard, and kept firing his .45 automatic pistol at the tree. None of us could see a snake, but Elvis kept insisting he could see it. He reloaded the gun several times, but he never hit a snake. Elvis was just out of his damn-fool mind.

BO WHITAKER: Everyone thought Elvis was exhausted because of all the fame and the touring, but really it was just him trying to balance two lives. He was tired of being Elvis Presley the entertainer. It was just wearing him down. He wanted to be a full-time C.I.A. operative. He wanted to be Jon Burrows all the time. He talked about this quite a bit. And having to constantly switch between the blond-haired Jon Burrows and the black-haired Elvis was becoming real tiresome. Once he even walked through the house as Elvis, but had forgotten to remove his blond mustache. Everyone looked at him like, What in the hell? When Elvis realized what he'd done, he just joked and said it was a fake moustache. Then he went back to his bathroom and shaved it off.

Also, Elvis had decided way back after killing Cletus that he was gonna wear a fat suit whenever he was in character as himself. He thought that would make him look more like Cletus had looked. Then he just kept wearing it so no one could tell that they both were the same person. With Elvis being fat, people stopped commenting about Jon Burrows looking like Elvis Presley. But man, Elvis *hated* that fat suit—hated it with a fucking passion. That was part of the reason he stopped going out. And he really hated wearing it on the stage. He'd say, "Do you know how fucking hard it is to do Karate kicks and swivel your hips when you're wearing that sumbitch?" And because we never knew when he would have to go to work on a C.I.A. operation, he had to wear a big black wig over his slicked-back blond hair. Life had just become a huge pain in the ass for the King.

Elvis hated his life. The only time he was happy was when we were out on those C.I.A. missions. We did quite a few of them between 1973 and 1977, and a lot of them were really memorable. One time we went undercover in the Klu Klux Klan. Another time Elvis helped stop Squeaky Fromme from assassinating President Ford. Another time we went undercover and stopped a huge drug cartel. Then there was the time we went undercover in the Mafia... It was all just so crazy. All of those missions went pretty well except for the time

Elvis and me tried to go undercover as Black Panthers. That didn't go over so well. Somehow they knew we weren't really black, despite the brown paint we put on our faces and all the cool handshakes we learned.

Elvis really enjoyed the C.I.A. work, man. He loved being Jon Burrows. Instead of being Elvis Presley pretending to be Jon Burrows, he had become Jon Burrows pretending to be Elvis Presley. No, he liked the C.I.A. stuff a lot. It was everything else that made him sick. "Bo," he'd say, "I just want out of this life, man." And I'd say, "Yeah, I know, Elvis." I mean, what else could I say?

Then one night real late, maybe four in the morning, Elvis came and knocked on my door. I remember it real well. I was watching *The Creature from the Black Lagoon* and jacking off to Julie Adams. I got up, wiped off my hand, and answered the door, and Elvis was standing there with this shit-eating grin. I said, "What's going on, Elvis? It's four in the morning." And he said, "I'm gonna die, Bo." I said, *"What?"* I really thought he might try to off himself. But then he said, "No, nothing like that. You and me, we're gonna stage a fake death— the death of Elvis Presley." So I asked, "Why?" And he said, "So we can become full-time C.I.A. operatives." That sounded pretty good to me. Then I said, "Should I fake my death, too?" And Elvis said, "Nah, no one cares about you, Bo. No one will even notice you're gone."

BOOTS PELTIER: I got a call from operative #67357 late one night. I remember I was watching *The Creature from the Black Lagoon* when he called. He said, "Boots, old boy, I wanna fake my own death, but I need your help, man." He asked me if we could assist him with that so he could become a full-time operative. Since he was one of the best operatives the agency had ever had, I said that could probably be arranged. I mean, I knew this was going to make our superiors extremely happy. This was what they had always wanted.

Memo from operative "Boots Peltier" to Central Intelligence Agency Director Stansfield Turner, dated June 25, 1977:

> I am writing to inform you that field operative #67357, Elvis Presley, wishes to publicly fake his death in order to become a full-time Central Intelligence Agency operative under his

pseudonym, Jon Burrows. He asked me if it would be possible for the agency to assist him in orchestrating this public death and faking the medical records. I told him I couldn't say for sure, but I would get back to him.

What are your thoughts on this?

Memo from Stansfield Turner to "Boots Peltier," dated June 26, 1977:

This is a most irregular request. However, given that this operative is one of our finest assets, and given his high-profile persona, I believe we must assist him in this endeavor. Tell him yes, we will take over the entire thing. Make sure he knows that no one besides his lackey, that dumb Bo guy, can know anything about any of this. This means his friends and family. If he is to "die," he must literally become dead to them—even to his daughter.

If he is to do this, however, I have one request. Would you please ask this operative if he would be interested in becoming an assassin rather than a regular field operative. We are in desperate need of someone of his caliber in that capacity right now, and he has always done fine work killing for us whenever the need has arisen. Whether or not he says yes, tell him we will assist him with his death.

BOOTS PELTIER: After receiving the go-ahead from Chief Turner, I telephoned operative #67357 and informed him that the Central Intelligence Agency would do anything and everything in their power to assist him with his death. He was extremely happy to hear this. Then I told him Chief Turner wanted to know if he might be interested in becoming an assassin rather than a field operative. He said, and I'll never forget this, "T.C.B., man." I asked him what that meant, and he said, "Sure, I'll do it, Boots. Tell Turner I'm on board and that I would be glad to kill enemies of the United States any time I am asked to do so. I love killin' Commies, man."

JOE ESPOSITO: I don't know what it was, but something in Elvis' demeanor changed dramatically in the weeks before his death. He finally seemed happy again. I don't know if he'd gotten ahold of some real good drugs or was just getting some really great sex, but he was happy in a way I hadn't seen him a long time. It was really something to see.

BO WHITAKER: Elvis really wanted to be an assassin. He said, "You know, Bo, this is what I joined the C.I.A. for in the first place. I want to kill people so I can help make this country great again. I'm gonna kill for Mr. Jesus." Man, I had never seen him so damned happy and pumped up. He would look at himself in the mirror and talk to himself like Bobby De Niro in *Taxi Driver*. He would say, you know, "Come on, you punk. You want a piece of me? I'll fucking kill you, you Commie S.O.B.," or "I'll flush your fucking head down the toilet, you turd." You know, things like that.

Elvis told me, "The first thing we gotta do is figure out how I'm gonna die. It's gotta be something heroic." Elvis thought maybe he could be killed rescuing a baby, or maybe even a bald eagle. Then he said, "What if I rescued a baby bald eagle, man? Wouldn't that be something?" He wanted his death to mean something to people, to continue the legacy he'd always wanted as a national hero. I mean, he'd already saved President Ford's life, but no one knew anything about it. It was all top secret. He just kept saying, "However I die, it's gotta be real special. It's gotta be heroic, man."

Memo from "Boots Peltier" to Stansfield Turner, dated July 7, 1977:

> Operative #67357 has requested that his fake death be something memorable and "important." He would like to die a hero.

Memo from Stansfield Turner to "Boots Peltier," dated July 7, 1977:

What exactly does he mean by "hero"?

Memo from "Boots Peltier" to Stansfield Turner, dated July 8, 1977:

> He would like his death to be a high-profile one with him perhaps doing something heroic like saving a baby bald eagle or shooting a Communist spy. He wants very much to preserve what he perceives as being a noble image. He wants his death to be remembered for many years to come.

Memo from Stansfield Turner to "Boots Peltier," dated July 8, 1977:

> Tell him we will come up with something heroic, and that he need not worry about it. I'll put my finest men on the job.

BOOTS PELTIER: I telephoned operative #67357 and told him what Chief Turner had said. He kept asking, "How am I gonna die? Am I gonna die rescuing a baby from a burning building? What if I rescued the president's baby from Russian kidnappers and then killed all of 'em on top of Mount Rushmore? That would be something. That would be memorable as hell, man." I told him that the chief was very secretive about the whole thing and that even I didn't know what the method of death would be. Considering how great an operative #67357 had been over the past seven years, I believed the C.I.A. would devise an extremely honorable death for him.

BO WHITAKER: Elvis had never been happier than when Boots Peltier informed him that his death would be an honorable one. Elvis just kept saying, "I'm gonna save the president's baby from Russian spies and I'm gonna kill 'em all." I remember the number of Russian spies in Elvis' story kept increasing. At first he said there would be three spies, then it was four or five, and then I remember him finally saying he would be killing probably eighteen or nineteen Russian spies with his bare hands. "I'll just Karate the hell out of 'em, man." He asked me if I thought that was too far over the top. I said, "Hell, no, Elvis. That's why you're the King."

Memo from C.I.A. Assistant to the Assistant Director Roger Kimball to Executive in Charge of Fake Deaths Peter Cleaverman, dated July 20, 1977:

> You know we always have a good time devising fake deaths for operatives. Remember that time we said operative #36552 died from choking on a chili cheese dog? Let's try to come up with something funny like that for operative #67357.

Memo from Peter Cleaverman to Roger Kimball, dated July 20, 1977:

> Let's make a little contest out of this. Let's say whichever of us comes up with the funniest death for Presley wins a free steak dinner on behalf of the other. What do you think of that, Rog?

Memo from Roger Kimball to Peter Cleaverman, dated July 20, 1977:

> Deal. May the best man win.

BOOTS PELTIER: I was the one who had to tell operative #67357 how he would die. Needless to say, he was really angry.

BO WHITAKER: When Elvis got off the phone with Boots, he was beet red. He immediately pulled out his pistol and unloaded the entire clip into my television set. I asked him why he was so mad. I had absolutely no idea what the hell was happening.

BOOTS PELTIER: I prefaced the whole thing by apologizing and saying that I had never heard of an operative dying in such a manner. I thought maybe that would soften the blow a little bit.

BO WHITAKER: Elvis had come close to committing suicide on a number of occasions, but I was pretty sure he was really gonna do it this time. He just couldn't believe what Boots Peltier had said to him.

BOOTS PELTIER: He just kept saying, "Am I gonna die rescuing a baby from angry negroes? Am I gonna save the First Lady from the burning White House?" So I took a breath and then I told him the truth. "You're gonna have a heart attack while you're taking a shit and then you're gonna die." He was really upset. He screamed at me for several minutes, calling me everything from a cocksucking Commie to someone who has sex with their dead uncle Morty. I don't even have an Uncle Morty. I understood why he was angry, but it was still difficult to take all those insults. It really hurt my feelings.

BO WHITAKER: Elvis had tears just streaming down his face, man. Then he started to hyperventilate, so I put a bag over his head. And there he was, sitting there with that plastic bag over his head, crying and waving around his pistol and singing "My Way." Frankly, I was scared for my life. I figured he was gonna shoot us both. I mean, I didn't want him to die, man, but if he wanted to die, then so be it. But I wasn't ready to go yet.

Finally he said, "Bo, they're gonna have me die while I'm taking a shit." I was real surprised by that. I said, "How exactly does that happen? Do you get shot by the Russian spies while you're taking a shit, or what?" He just kept crying and repeating that the C.I.A. were some damn cocksuckers.

BOOTS PELTIER: He was really in denial about the whole thing. He kept calling and suggesting different ways he could die. He'd call up and say, "What if I pulled an elderly woman out from under a burning AMC Gremlin. Then, after she's safe, the Gremlin blows up and kills me? That would be okay." He just couldn't accept the method of death the C.I.A. had selected for him. He'd say, "Level with me, Boots. How am I gonna die?" And I would repeat the story to him about his dying on the toilet. Then he'd curse for a few minutes and say, "What if it was a burning Pinto? That could work, too, you know."

BO WHITAKER: Elvis had a real hard time dealing with the death they had come up with. Apparently they said it would be more believable than Elvis saving twenty-six children from a burning school bus. I don't know all the specifics. But Elvis was just really upset about the whole thing. He would alternate between being upset and then convincing himself that he could die a different death.

BOOTS PELTIER: He called me every single day, maybe twice a day. I'd answer the phone and he would just start talking. No hello, no nothing. Just "how about if I died trying to save the planet from a fiery meteor?"

BO WHITAKER: Elvis just kept saying, "Elvis Presley doesn't die while taking a shit, man. That just doesn't happen. I'm the goddamn King. Could you imagine what would happen to this world if Elvis Presley died while taking a shit? It could be like a black hole, man. It could just destroy the whole damn planet. Elvis Presley is that damned important, son."

BOOTS PELTIER: Finally I had to tell him that it was the only way; if he wanted the Central Intelligence Agency to assist him with his death, then he'd have to agree to their terms. I remember he kept sobbing into the telephone, calling me a pinko fuckhead. Then he broke into a song—I think it was "In the Ghetto." But finally he accepted the terms as they were and said, "If I gotta die taking a shit, I'll die taking the greatest shit the world has ever known." I'm not sure what exactly he meant by that, but he sounded really proud of himself for having said it.

BO WHITAKER: It took a while, but finally he came to terms with the whole thing. It was a real blow to his pride, but he wanted desperately to be a damn full-time C.I.A. assassin. He told me, "Bo, dying by taking a shit is the only way they're gonna let me do this. I need their help. I have to die. So what if Elvis Presley dies an embarrassing death? What do I care? I'm not gonna be him anymore. I'm gonna be Jonny fucking Burrows, son. Maybe he can die an honorable death." Then Elvis took a handful of painkillers, and shot my TV.

CHAPTER ELEVEN
THE DEATH OF A KING (1977)

JOE ESPOSITO: I don't know if Elvis had just resigned himself to dying, but I think he knew he was about to die. About three weeks before he passed away he started giving all the guys his most prized possessions. He gave me a motorcycle that said T.C.B. on the side and his 14-karat gold pill dispenser. He loved both of those things, and when he gave them to me, I knew something was really wrong.

BO WHITAKER: About three weeks before Elvis was supposed to die, Sonny and Red came out with their book [*Elvis: What Happened?*]. It was a tell-all book that focused on the negative side of Elvis, and it was all lies. For instance, they talked in-depth about Elvis taking drugs and aiming weapons at people and threatening to shoot them. It was all, you know, lies. They were just steamed because Elvis had fired them. He and Vernon told them it was because money was tight, but really there were other reasons.

SONNY WEST: It was terrible the way Elvis and Vernon fired us. We didn't do nothing wrong. They told us that money was short, but hell, we both knew better. Elvis was still buying everyone cars and diamond rings. We knew there had to be other reasons for him firing us, but for the life of us we couldn't figure out what they might be.

BO WHITAKER: Sonny would always clog up the toilets in the house, the bus, the airplane, and the hotel rooms. He would just take these monster dumps, and Elvis got real tired of having to deal with that. It seemed like someone was always saying, "Who the hell shit in here and left the toilet clogged up?" Everyone acted like they didn't know who did it, but Elvis was pretty sure it was Sonny. One night he told me, "Sonny's the one who's been breaking all the toilets with them huge shits. I'm tired of it, man. Just real tired. I'm the most famous man in the world. I'm Elvis Presley, man. I shouldn't have to deal with shit like this." Then he realized he'd said "shit" there and that really cracked him up. Then he fired Sonny.

RED WEST: Vernon just called us in and said, "Boys, pack your bags. You're going home." When we asked him why we were being sent home, he wouldn't give us a straight answer. He just said money was tight, but that was a damn lie. I wanted to go and talk to Elvis, but I wasn't allowed to talk directly with him about the matter. It was all bullshit.

BO WHITAKER: The real reason Red got fired was because he had this annoying way of opening cereal boxes. He would open the top and cut out a huge chunk of the plastic bag inside. Then no one could seal the damned things, and the cereal would get stale. I remember Elvis telling me, "Shoot, man, I'm out on the road doing all these damn shows, and I come home and I wanna sit down, watch *M*A*S*H*, and eat a bowl of Count Chocula. I should be able to do that. But some asshole keeps cutting the damn bag open and then the little chocolate pieces taste like ass, man. I hate that." So he assigned me the top secret mission of watching the cereal boxes to see who was cutting the tops open. So I did it real sneaky-like; I threw out the old boxes of Count Chocula and replaced them with brand new ones. Then I just hung around the kitchen for a day or so and watched everyone come and go. And, as it turned out, it was Red doing that crazy shit with the Count Chocula. Elvis never did forgive him for that.

So then, when Sonny and Red came out with their book of lies, Elvis just got really pissed. He kept talking about how much he wanted to kill them. Before the book had even come out, Frank Sinatra told us he could get some guys to "make sure the book never comes out," but Elvis said no. I think he thought the boys would remain loyal and pull out of the deal before the book hit stores.

He was wrong. *Elvis: What Happened?* sold over a million copies in two weeks.

Elvis said, "Bo, it's just you and me, man. We gotta go kill them sumbitches...kill 'em dead as hell, man." He was stoned when he said it, but he meant business. It was about ten o'clock at night and we were in his room at Graceland watching one of those old Francis the Talking Mule pictures on TV. It was *Francis Goes to West Point*, I think. Elvis always did like those movies. He'd just laugh and laugh, and sometimes he'd laugh so hard he'd piss his pants. It was really something. Anyway, Elvis went to the closet and pulled out two M-16 assault rifles. He handed one to me and said, "This is gonna be just like Vietnam, Bo. We're gonna go in there and kill them S.O.B.s tonight." I asked him what we should do about their kids, but Elvis said not to worry about them. "They deserve to be shot for being the kids of those no good bastards."

Elvis went and opened the door and started down the stairs. I was right behind him, trying to talk him out of this. I didn't want Sonny and Red to die, but mostly I just didn't want Elvis and me going to prison. I hear they do bad things to pretty guys like us in the pen, and I didn't want no part of it. I said, "Elvis, listen, man, you can't do this." He said, "I'm gonna be dead in three weeks. Who gives a damn if we get caught? The C.I.A. will come and get us out like they did last time." I told him, "What about your image, man? You don't want the kids to think Elvis Presley is a murderer." At that point, Elvis got real ticked and turned around and got up in my face. He shoved me into the wall and aimed his M-16 at my nose.

I said, "You can shoot me if you want, Elvis, but I ain't going with you to kill those cocksuckers." Elvis looked at me real funny. Again, he was not a guy who was used to being told no. "You're not going with me, man?" I said, "No, Elvis, I'm not." He thought about it for a moment and then he said, "Well, what are you gonna do then?" I said, "I'm going back into that room to watch Francis the goddamn Talking Mule and finish off that box of Ho-Hos." He tilted his head, put down the gun, and said, "I'll be damned if Ho-Hos don't sound pretty good right about now, man."

So we went back to the room and ate Ho-Hos and laughed at that talking mule. And that was the end of it. Elvis seemed to forget he wanted Sonny and Red dead, at least for that night.

SONNY WEST: We didn't write that book to hurt Elvis. We hoped it might show him how bad he was fucking things up. We wanted to hold a mirror up to his face, you know? We thought it might be the wakeup call he needed to turn things around and get his life back on track.

RED WEST: I know a lot of people think that book helped to kill Elvis. I'd like to think that's not true, but maybe it is. Who the hell knows?

BO WHITAKER: A few days passed. Elvis had been working with the C.I.A. to get everything ready for his fake death. We were only about a week away from the big event, and Elvis went bonkers about the whole damn thing again. He came to my room, made up like some kind of damn Rambo. He had guns and knives and throwing stars strapped all over his body. He had an AK-47 slung over his back and he was carrying a hunting rifle. I took one look at him and I knew what he was there for. He didn't even have to say a word.

So I said, what the hell, and I grabbed my pistols. We went out driving in Elvis' Lincoln. I don't know where Elvis was actually planning to go, because Red and Sonny were both out in California doing a publicity tour for their book. Elvis had on those great big sunglasses and a black cape. I was driving, and we just drove around for about a half an hour without saying anything. I'd say it was about four in the morning, and it was really grim. Then he looked at me and said, "Sonny and Red betrayed us, man. How can you go on living with the knowledge of what those rat fucks did to us?" I said, "What choice do I have, Elvis?" And he said, "We can kill 'em both. Right now. We'll go and murder them and then it'll all be over, man."

I had been with Elvis for a lot of years now, and I was about the best there was at redirecting him. I wanted to get his mind off Sonny and Red and on to something productive, so I said, "Maybe we should kill someone to be your body double in that casket." Elvis got real serious and said, "You know, I never thought about that. You're right." He thought for a moment and then he said, "Maybe Sonny or Red could be the ones made up to look like me in that casket." I talked him out of that. I convinced him that they didn't look similar enough to pass as him.

Now the big question was, where could we find someone who looked enough like Elvis that he could kill them in Memphis at four in the morning? So we just drove around looking for people who were out in the streets alone. Elvis had me pull the Lincoln up next to a homeless guy. "How about him?" Elvis says. The homeless guy says, "How about me, what?" But Elvis ignores him. "I dunno," I say. "He doesn't look much like you." Elvis turns back to look at the bum. "Could you turn around?" The bum says, "Why?" Elvis just says, "I wanna see something." So the bum is turning around and Elvis finally says, "No, his ass is too fat. Even with the fat suit on, he's not gonna look right." I didn't have the heart to tell Elvis that no one would be able to see his ass in the casket. The bum is really confused by all this. He says, "Well, can I have a dollar?" So Elvis gives him his gold rings and we drive off into the night, looking for someone to kill.

Finally we came up with the bright idea to go to the all-night supermarket and watch people there. Elvis is watching from the Lincoln in the front parking lot, and he sees a man going into the store. "That guy kind of looks like me," he says. It was at a long distance, and I couldn't really tell one way or the other, but I said, "Sure, he looks just like you." So we walked into the supermarket and followed the poor bastard around the store so Elvis could get a good look at him. It's about four-thirty now, and no one is in the store. It's just that guy and us. So me and Elvis bought some apples and a bag of Lemon Heads to make it look legit.

Elvis is whispering to me, "He looks just like me." That guy didn't look anything like Elvis. Hell, he was Mexican, and he had to be sixty-five if he was a day. But Elvis was sure this guy looked like him. So we paid for our stuff and walked back out to the Lincoln. We waited for the guy to get into his car and pull out before we started following him. Elvis has an eight-track of his last album playing, and I'm eating Lemon Heads, and we're following this poor S.O.B. around the city. Finally the guy parks his car outside a little apartment building. The place was a real shit hole, man. The guy took his groceries out and went inside.

We got out and followed him. There was no one inside the hallway but us and the Mexican. So Elvis takes out his .38 and he points it at the guy and makes him let us into his apartment. Elvis asks him if he's alone, and the guy says yeah, it's just him and his pet monkey. Elvis says, "You got a monkey, man?" The guy says yeah, and Elvis asks him what the monkey's name is. "Bonkers," the guy says. "His name is Bonkers." Elvis stands there staring at the guy with his pistol trained on him while I look around the dingy little apartment to make sure no one else was there. I look around, and sure enough, it was just the three of us and that monkey. The guy says, "Aren't you Elvis Presley?" Elvis says, "Not anymore, buddy. You are." The guy doesn't know what to make of this, but he doesn't have much time to think about it because Elvis shoots him in the chest. The guy falls down dead at once. The monkey is sitting on the couch, and he just watches us without making so much as a peep.

Elvis and me roll the dead Mexican up in a rug and carry his body back out to the Lincoln. No one is around, so there's no one else we have to shoot. We're getting back in the car and Elvis says, "What about the monkey?" I look at him and say, "What do you mean?" He says I should go back in there and take care of the monkey. So I go back in there and I take out my pistol, but man, that monkey was so damned cute. I just couldn't do it. I couldn't bring myself to kill that little fucker. So instead I took him home with us. Elvis was real irritated about it, but I brought him back to Graceland and renamed him "David Cassidy."

BOOTS PELTIER: Operative #67357 called me early in the morning one day and said, "I killed your man for you." I had no clue what he was talking about. I said, "You did *what?* Who did you kill?" He says, "I killed the man we can plant in Graceland for my death. We'll say he was me. We can make him up to look just like me, and no one will be the wiser." I asked him if the person looked like him, and he said yes, except for being a Mexican.

BO WHITAKER: Boots Peltier told Elvis there was no way he could use that body. Elvis asked why, and Boots said, "Well, for one, he's Mexican." Elvis said, "So what, man?" And Boots said, "You're not Mexican." Elvis said, "Charlton Heston played a Mexican in *Touch of Evil.* If he can do it, so can I."

BOOTS PELTIER: I finally convinced him there was no way we could use a Mexican with a hole blown in his chest that would be a week old by the time of operative #67357's impending death. He said, "Well, what do I do with this body now?" So I sent a "cleaner" over to dispose of the body discreetly.

BISHOP: The Central Intelligence Agency sent me in there to clean up the mess. I had heard all the tales about how brilliant operative

#67357 was, but he seemed kind of dumb to me. I went out there to the mansion and they had the dead Mexican propped up in the front seat of Bo's old Chrysler, and he was wearing a fake mustache. I asked them why they did that, and they said it was to fool people into believing he was still alive. I asked them what good that would do, and operative #67357 just said, "Then people don't know he's dead, dummy." I guess he had a point, but it seemed to me like it would have been easier to just hide the body until I could get there.

BO WHITAKER: Boots told us there was a cleaner coming out to the house, and that he was the best the C.I.A. had. He said the guy was known only as Bishop, and that he was a legend in the agency. But man, he seemed kind of stupid to me. I had this idea we could just drive him around town in my Chrysler and then crash him into a tree. That would make it look like he had an accident, but Bishop said we couldn't do that on account of how he had a bullet hole in his chest and was driving my car. But I don't know. It seemed like a solid plan to me.

BISHOP: I put the body in the trunk of the car and drove it to a safe location. Then I removed the body, chopped it into a hundred tiny little pieces, and shattered the skull into a lot of itty bitty pieces. Then I buried all of that in twenty or so different holes out in the middle of nowhere. Each of the holes were ten feet deep and covered with ten pounds of limestone. It was a thorough job.

BO WHITAKER: Bishop was just sloppy as hell, man. I'm surprised no one ever found that dead Mexican's body. Elvis was real irritated with the guy, too. He just kept going on and on about how we could have just hung him from a tree out in front of Graceland and then say we found him there.

BISHOP: Speaking candidly, those guys were stupid as fuck. I don't know how they got into the C.I.A. in the first place. They had to have been related to someone high up in the agency. They had to have been related to somebody. I wouldn't have given those two idiots a job cleaning up dog shit, let alone working as operatives for the C.I.A.

BO WHITAKER: I think Bishop was pretty impressed with us. He was real serious about everything, and he didn't use any of our ideas, but I could tell he was thrilled just to be working so close to two real smart operatives like us. We were pretty hot shit back in those days. You know, I'll bet Bishop used our ideas to get rid of bodies somewhere else. I think he was just too insecure to admit that we had come up with ideas that were better than his, on account of his bein' a cleaner and all.

BISHOP: Bo said *what?* Are you serious? [Laughs.] Like I told you, idiots. Both of them. Fuck those guys. That's the kind of shit that eventually made me leave the C.I.A. First they made George Bush director of the C.I.A., and then they had these numbskulls running around playing secret spy guy or whatever. It's just embarrassing.

BO WHITAKER: Once we had that mess behind us, we still had to make plans for Elvis' fake funeral. Elvis sat down and wrote out real detailed notes about what he wanted his funeral to be like. He said he wanted to be buried in a copper casket, just like the one they buried his mama in. Then he wanted seventeen white Cadillac limousines to carry the family and friends to and from the funeral. He was real specific about the whole thing. It had to be Cadillacs, and there had to be seventeen of them. Man, Vernon looked all over for those Caddies. There were only three of them in Memphis, so they had to track the other fourteen of them down. Then Elvis wanted to be buried in the white suit his daddy had given him.

There was one hitch, though. Elvis forgot to say who he wanted to officiate the funeral, so Vernon got his wife Dee's minister to do the honors. That really pissed Elvis off. He kept saying, "I don't even know that fuckin' guy. I only met him once, and that was at Vernon's wedding." So Elvis got real smart and came up with a plan. He wrote another letter saying that his friend Rex Humbard had to do the services. Then I took it to Vernon and said, "Look what I found!" Vernon was kind of irritated about that, but he wound up letting both Dee's minister and Rex Humbard speak at the funeral.

Then there was the music. Elvis said, "Man, there's got to be some good music at my funeral, man." So Elvis made a list of old-fashioned quartets that he liked. He had J.D. Sumner and the Stamps, the Statesmen, Jake Hess, and James Blackwood written down on his list, and all of them ended up performing there.

But the hard part of the whole death was having Elvis' girlfriend, Ginger Alden, find the body on the toilet. Somehow Elvis convinced the C.I.A. to let him tell Ginger what was happening. He still wanted to be with Ginger, and he thought she would be a good one to find him dead. So, somehow, he got the C.I.A. to agree to this, and he told Ginger the whole thing.

GINGER ALDEN: One night we were sitting around in Elvis' room at Graceland, playing Scrabble. Elvis was never very good at Scrabble, and I used to beat him handily. This would always piss him off and cause him to curse and break things. Well, that night he seemed particularly down—no, I guess you could say he seemed distracted— so I was trying to let him win. It was hard, though, because he kept playing three letter words for five or six points total. I was even letting him use brand names, which is against the rules. I let him use "G.E.," which he said was short for General Electric. But shit, I wound up beating him anyway. It was a fairly close game, but you know, there's only so much you can do to throw a game against someone who's as terrible as he was.

Well, I thought he was gonna get pissed off and go shoot a TV or something, but he just got real quiet. He said, "Ginger, I'm gonna tell you something that no one else knows... Well, Bo knows, but he's the only other one." And then he told me this crazy story about how he'd been working for the C.I.A. all these years and was going to fake his death. I thought he was kidding, but I eventually figured out he was dead serious.

"Ginger," he says, "I want you to be the one to find my body." Well, I thought that was the most romantic thing anyone had ever told me, so I said yes. He promised me that we would be together forever and it would only be us. Well, us and Bo. To me, that sounded like heaven. I had always known that Elvis hated being in the spotlight all the time, and I thought this might give us the opportunity to finally break free. Sure, he'd be gone killing dictators or whatever, but I figured it would just be like him being on the road, which I'd already become accustomed to.

Of course Elvis broke up with me about two months later. He said I was only twenty and he needed a more mature woman. "At least twenty-two," he said. And then he told me if I said anything about him being alive he'd kill me. I know that sounds harsh, but it wasn't like that at all. He said it in a real sweet way. So I waited all these years to tell anyone my secret.

BO WHITAKER: Ginger did her part and said she found Elvis dead there on the crapper. I don't know where the C.I.A. got the body that doubled as Elvis, but it looked pretty good. It wasn't an exact double like Cletus had been, but it was pretty close. And it had one characteristic we hadn't thought about when we'd shot that Mexican— it was fat like everyone thought Elvis was. It was perfect. Then they wouldn't have to put the fat suit on the dead guy. Why hadn't we thought of that?

So the C.I.A. sent their guys in to take care of everything. All the documents were forged, and as far as anyone knew, Elvis was really dead. We were supposed to be out of Memphis when all this happened, but Elvis wanted to be there to see the thing. He said, "Man, when am I gonna be able to see my own damn funeral again?" So we stayed in town.

People came from near and far to see Elvis' body and to mourn outside Graceland. So Elvis hired a taxi cab to drive him up and down the street all day long so he could watch the mourners.

Excerpt from Careless Love: The Unmaking of Elvis Presley *by Peter Guralnick:*

> For the viewing, scheduled to last from three to five o'clock, the body was moved to the foyer, underneath a crystal chandelier just inside the door. White linen was laid out on the floor underneath the casket, and outside, the lawn was a sea of flowers. Wire reports described the scene as verging on mass hysteria, as "four at a time fans filed by the stone lions guarding the door, past the casket and back out the door into the 90-degree heat. Several mourners fainted on the marble floor and had to be carried out. A quarter mile away, down a driveway with a sheriff's deputy every few yards, a throng, stretching a mile on either side, pushed and shoved

to be next through the gates.... Hundreds fainted in the heat. Many, revived with rubber gloves filled with ice, staggered back into the crowd and fainted again. Radios blared Presley's greatest hits as three police helicopters hovered over the mansion. Thirty National Guardsmen were called out to help the 80 policemen and 40 sheriff's deputies try to control the crowd.

BO WHITAKER: Of course Elvis being Elvis, he had to be a part of all that, man. So he went out there and stood in line for hours so he could get a glimpse of his own dead body right there surrounded by his fans. I couldn't go with him because I'd be spotted by Vernon and the other guys, so Elvis went out there alone. He hated being surrounded by people he didn't know, and he later told me being out there scared the hell out of him. So here was Elvis, dressed in one of his black sequined outfits with a cape and glasses, but with the blond hair and mustache. I guess those people just figured him for another crazed fan. No one seemed to give him a second look.

Elvis said he had a few conversations in the line about how great his music was. He said one of his songs would come on and everyone around him would be crying, and he'd just say, "Man, that Elvis sure was something, huh?" And then ten or twelve other fans would get into it and start telling him how damn great he was. Elvis lived for that kind of attention, but he hated being that close to the fans. Later on he said, "Man, some of my fans are crazy, man. They're just nutty." He said putting on a fake voice was easy; he said he just tried to talk like Burt Reynolds. He said the hard part was pretending to cry. "I'm a damn actor, man," he said, "but it was hard as hell making myself cry real tears for someone I knew wasn't dead. They all thought the guy they were mourning was dead, so they were sad, but I was happy because I knew they all loved me, and also I knew I was getting out of that life."

I asked him how he made himself cry. He said, "Well, I just thought of the saddest things I could imagine and used those things to make me cry." I asked him what kinds of things he meant, and he said, "Well, mostly I just imagined that Scooby Doo wasn't real. That choked me up a lot, man." He said he also made himself cry by imagining that there were no more TV dinners in the world. He said the thought of that made him about as sad as he had ever been. He liked those a lot—especially the ones with the little tacos. Elvis loved little tacos. He used to pretend like he was a giant eating normal-sized tacos. That always made him laugh. I asked him if he thought about his mama's death when he was trying to make himself cry, but he said no. He said, "Bo, Mama's death is a happy thing. She's up there in the sky with Mr. Jesus."

Since Elvis couldn't attend the actual funeral itself, I went and watched the damn thing. Elvis had me wear an earpiece so I could hear him talking to me from down the street. I was also wired with this little microphone on my sleeve. So during the funeral, Elvis would ask me every couple of seconds, "What's happening now?" So I'd whisper into my sleeve and update him. I got some weird looks from people, but no one had any idea what the hell was going on.

How could they have known who I was talking to? Elvis was dead.

And that ended the life of Elvis Presley and began his second life as Jon Burrows, C.I.A. assassin.

CHAPTER TWELVE
TRUTH OR CONSEQUENCES (1978)

BO WHITAKER: After we faked Elvis' death, Elvis got real depressed. I'd ask him what was wrong and he'd say, "I'm dead, man. Elvis Presley's gone." Then I'd remind him that now he was a C.I.A. assassin with a license to kill and that would cheer him up some. Elvis bought a new mansion down in New Mexico. It was in a little city called Truth or Consequences. Elvis said he wanted to move there for two reasons: 1) he said he'd kind of liked the climate when we were stationed out at Area 51, and 2) he liked the name of the town. He said it would be good karma to live somewhere named that.

The new mansion was pink stucco and it had 14 bedrooms. It wasn't as big as Graceland, but there were only the three of us living there—Elvis, me, and David Cassidy the monkey. We all had pretty good-sized rooms, and I found some real nice wallpaper with bananas on it for David Cassidy's room. Elvis really loved that mansion. He said it was the coziest house he'd ever lived in. He named it Little Graceland. On occasion he'd comment that he kind of missed some of the guys, or Priscilla, and he *really* missed little Lisa Marie, but this new life as a C.I.A. assassin seemed to agree with him. Elvis just liked killin' people, man.

There wasn't a lot of work coming in, but he was dispatched to kill someone about every six or seven weeks. So to keep ourselves busy, we entered a local bowling league down there at Carl's Bowl Mor. Our team was called the Quickie Mart Strikers on account of we was sponsored by Quickie Mart and we threw a lot of strikes. Elvis started relaxing a lot more, too. Where he would never take a drink of alcohol before, he started drinking the occasional beer and trying to fit in with the guys. There were four of us in all—Elvis, me, Carl, and Rudy. Carl was a used car salesman, and Rudy was a deejay at this little country radio station about thirty miles away. Obviously we couldn't tell them we were C.I.A. assassins, so we made up backgrounds for ourselves. We told them we'd owned a chain of fast food restaurants on the East coast, man. That seemed to satisfy them, and nothing more was ever said.

RUDY SHATZINGER: Jon Burrows and Bo Whitaker were really good guys. Me and Carl liked them a lot. They never told us so, but we were pretty sure they were gay lovers. My mama told me never to judge anyone, and I never thought twice about it. But they lived together in a pink mansion and they had a pet monkey they dressed up in human clothes. I always assumed they just pretended that monkey was their own child since gay people couldn't adopt kids back in the Seventies.

CARL BRADSHAW: Oh, yeah, they were totally gay. They were the first gay friends I ever had, but they were alright. They were on the level, you know? We were like a family. We were a team. We were the Quickie Mart Strikers. We didn't win that league or anything like that. Hell, we weren't really very good at all, but we drank a lot of beer and had a good time every Sunday night.

BO WHITAKER: Did I mention the thing about Elvis and the monkey? No, I guess I didn't... Elvis and David Cassidy hated each other with a passion. Truth be told, David Cassidy wasn't very nice to me either. He would get mad and erupt into a fuckin' rage, man, and he'd throw his shit at us. Sometimes I would try to hug him and he would scratch me all over my face. I always looked beat up.

CARL BRADSHAW: I hate to be the one to say it, but I'm pretty sure Jon abused Bo. The guy always had bruises and scratches all over his face. He'd blame it on the monkey, but I'm pretty sure it was Jon doing all that. I mean, who the hell would keep a monkey that acted like that? But hey, who am I to judge? I know lots of guys who fight with their wives. I personally don't believe in doing stuff like that, but you know, it was none of my business so I kept my mouth shut. Besides, Jon was the best bowler on our team, and I didn't want him defecting over to one of the other teams, like the Zip-In Car Wash Kings. They were the best team in the league, and I'll be damned if I wanted Jon throwing strikes over there with those evil sons of bitches. So if he wanted to beat up Bo, so be it. I wasn't gonna say anything.

BO WHITAKER: Life was pretty good there in Truth or Consequences. Elvis had the house all decked out the way he liked it. There was a music room with a nice big hi-fi eight-track player in it. We had a huge thirty-inch color TV set in the main room, where we could sit back and watch *Hee-Haw* and Elvis' movies. We used to watch *Roustabout* just about every damn week. Elvis really loved that one. He kept saying, "You know, I shoulda won a damn Academy Award for that one, man." The Academy had screwed Elvis over time and time again. Hell, everyone knows he should have gotten Academy Award nominations for *King Creole* and *Blue Hawaii*. *Everyone* knows that. Shit, if you asked those Siskel and Ebert guys who should have won the most Academy Awards and never even got nominated, I guarantee you they'd say Elvis. He was just an amazing actor. I mean, look, he pulled off this C.I.A. operative stuff for almost a decade and no one knew a thing. He even faked his death. He definitely would have won an Academy Award for that one, man. But hell, they just give awards like that to those artsy-fartsy fancy movies like *Lawrence of Arabia* and *Doctor Zhivago*. Elvis never had a chance out there in Hollywood.

And you know what? As big a pain in the ass as making those movies was, I think that was one of the things Elvis missed the most. He used to point at the screen and say stuff like, "You know, I should have been in this movie right here, man. Why didn't they offer me the role in *North by Northwest*? I'm better than Cary Grant." He really missed doing the movies, and I think it hurt him real bad that he never got the credit for being the great actor that he was.

So what were we talking about before I got off on that? The mansion? Oh, right. Little Graceland was just a real nice place to live, man. There was a video game room filled with pinball machines and a stand-up pong game. We had table tennis and a pool table and everything.

CARL BRADSHAW: Their house was ugly as hell. The walls were painted pink, and there was Elvis Presley memorabilia everywhere. They were real big Elvis fans from what I could gather. Jon even dressed like Elvis. And that was funny to me, because, you know, I really didn't like Elvis Presley at all. I preferred stuff like Elton John, Leon Russell, and Billy Joel—the stuff with the piano in it, you know? But I never told them that I didn't like Elvis because I didn't want Jon beating me up the way he beat up Bo.

RUDY SHATZINGER: It was the ugliest house I'd ever seen. It was like Liberace threw up and out came that house. It was definitely a house owned by a couple of gay guys. And again, I have nothing against that, but their sense of taste was unlike anything I had ever seen before. Everything was just gaudy as hell.

I always thought this was funny; Jon had a room he was really, really proud of that he called the Art Room. He would always tell us that he had a lot of really valuable pieces of art up there, but for the longest time he wouldn't let us see them. He said it was too big a secret for such a little city as Truth or Consequences. I wondered what he had in there. Maybe a few Kandinskys, a Goya, a Jackson Pollock or two... So finally I got tired of hearing about this room in such vague terms, so I convinced Jon to take us up there and show us his art. He was real hesitant about it. He made us swear on our mamas' souls that we wouldn't tell another living person about the art we saw in that room. Then he had this real elaborate security system that took about ten minutes to shut down so you could go in there.

CARL BRADSHAW: That art wasn't art at all. There was a huge—and I mean *huge*—painting of dogs playing cards. Jon kept saying, "This is my prize possession. I don't know what it's worth, but I paid a fortune for it." I always wondered how much he paid for that damned thing because it couldn't have been worth more than thirty or forty bucks. But Jon just kept saying, "It's funny, see? It's dogs playing cards. The reason it's funny is because dogs don't play cards! Get it?"

RUDY SHATZINGER: He had all these black velvet paintings of matadors and clowns like they used to sell in the parking lot at Wal-Mart. There was even a framed caricature of Bo. It was one of those charcoal drawings you get at the carnival. He just kept saying, "It's a one of a kind. It's the only piece of art like that in the world."

Those guys were really out there sometimes, but they entertained the hell out of me and Carl.

BO WHITAKER: Elvis was really afraid Carl and Rudy were gonna steal those paintings. He kept saying, "Carl was eyeballin' my damn dog painting. It was weird. He didn't even laugh." And I knew just what he meant. I mean, who wouldn't laugh at a damn painting of dogs playin' cards? That shit was hilarious, man. But I kept telling him, Carl and Rudy are good guys. They would never steal from us. Then he'd say, "Maybe they know art thieves like that guy in *The Thomas Crown Affair*. Maybe they'll just take a cut of the profits and let him do all the damn work." Elvis was real paranoid about that art, but you know, it was worth a fortune and he didn't wanna lose it.

CARL BRADSHAW: I don't know why they cared about that stuff. All those paintings combined were worth maybe seventy-five bucks. But, you know, they were really strange guys. That was what made them fun to be around. I think maybe they were on drugs. I saw Jon pop a few pills from time to time, but for all I know it was prescription stuff.

BO WHITAKER: Things went on like that for a while. Then, in late 1978, Elvis decided he wanted to have plastic surgery done. He said he wanted to look like someone else. I said, "Who?" And he said he didn't know; maybe Rod Taylor. So the C.I.A. sent a plastic surgeon from New York to Little Graceland to work on Elvis' face. Elvis looked at hundreds of books filled with pictures of different noses and lips. Finally he decided on some features, and the surgeries began. The whole thing was supposed to be a series of surgeries that took place over a six-month period.

DR. CHARLES FENDRICK: I performed all of the surgeries for Mr. Burrows. At first he said he wanted to look like Charles Bronson. Then he decided maybe he would like to look like Jesus. But finally he settled on individual features that would make him look like someone new altogether.

It was a series of five surgeries over a six-month period. I flew to New Mexico for each individual surgery, which we performed right there in Mr. Burrows' home. The whole series of procedures went without a hitch.

BO WHITAKER: Elvis had already had two of the surgeries when the break-in occurred. His face was still wrapped in gauze except for mouth and eye holes. He looked like Humphrey Bogart in that movie where he gets plastic surgery and wears a gauze mask through the whole damn movie. He kept goin' around doing Bogart impressions. But he couldn't remember any of the dialogue from that movie, so he would just make up shit like, "I ain't got no face. Look at me—I'm faceless!" You know, stuff like that.

So one night, real late, maybe three, four o'clock in the morning, the security alarm goes off. Someone's in the damn house! I was still awake. I was watching an old *Andy Griffith Show* episode. It was the one where Opie made a mistake and had to learn a lesson. It was a real good one. So anyway, I jumped up and ran out in the hall. Elvis was already out there. He said, "Someone's in the house, man. I'll bet they's here to steal the damn art!" By this time the alarm had shut off. The house was still pitch black. So Elvis and me make a run for the gun room, where we kept all our weapons. We ran in there and each of us grabbed a rifle, but it was too late.

We came out of that room and there were two guys standing there holding pistols to our faces. They startled the shit out of us. They said, "Put down your guns." I dropped mine, but I could tell Elvis didn't wanna do it. He wanted to have a damn Mexican standoff right there, but they had the drop on us, so he had no choice. He dropped his rifle. Then one of the guys says, "Thank you, Mr. Presley," which of course shocked both of us because as far as everybody knew, Elvis was dead. That's when we knew it had to be Russian spies sent to kidnap Elvis on account of his being one of the top C.I.A. assassins.

They made us turn around. We did, and then they struck us over the heads with their pistols. When we woke up, we were tied to chairs in the basement. Our heads hurt like hell, and we were tied really tight. Then we looked over and saw that David Cassidy was tied to a chair, too. And he looked real pissed about the whole thing. No one was in there with us, so we tried to scoot around and untie our hands, but neither of us had any luck. David Cassidy didn't even try to untie his hands. Stupid fucking monkey. We tried to get loose for maybe thirty minutes or so.

Then a group of people came into the basement and stood over us. All of them were packing guns. There were eight or nine of them, and two of them were women. One of the guys came forward and introduced himself as Del Newman. He said he was the leader of a group that called themselves C.R.E.E.P. Elvis says, "You're Russians, right? You're Russian spies sent here to kidnap me because I'm valuable to your country because of the things I know."

DEL NEWMAN: I explained to him that we were members of a group known as C.R.E.E.P., or The Coalition to Resurrect the Entertainer Elvis Presley. Elvis seemed really confused by that. He kept asking if we were Russians. I said, "No, we're from Tennessee."

BO WHITAKER: This guy Del Newman said that a woman in their group had recognized Elvis when they were in line at Graceland, waiting to see Elvis' body. I remember telling Elvis it was a bad idea to go out there, but did he listen to me? No. He never listened to anybody. He was stubborn as a damn mule.

LESLIE MARTIN: I had been standing in line, waiting to see Elvis' body, when I spotted this guy in line. He looked like Elvis but with blond hair and a mustache. He had a cape on, and wore those big sunglasses that Elvis always wore. So I followed him, and eventually concluded that he was really Elvis. I didn't know how or why they might have faked his death, and I wondered whose body was in that casket. But it certainly wasn't Elvis', because Elvis was right there walking amongst us.

DEL NEWMAN: There were nine members of C.R.E.E.P. in all. There was Max Morello, Glenn Toback, Ilsa Werner, Lefty McKenna, Jeff Wolcott, Leslie Martin, Miguel Mendez, Casey Cooper, and myself. We had originally been members of a local Elvis fan club. But after Leslie came and told us what she'd seen, we all devoted our lives to capturing Elvis Presley and showing the world that he was still alive.

BO WHITAKER: So after they explained who they were, Elvis asks what they want from him. "You want to kidnap me, is that it?" They said yes, they wanted to kidnap him and expose him to the world. This made Elvis real upset, man. He said, "I gave and I gave and I gave to my fans, and now all I want is to be left alone. Is that too much to ask?" But one of the women in the group said, "You mean too much to too many people to just disappear. What are we supposed to do without you? We don't know what to do." Elvis tried to convince them to go on with their own lives and forget about him, but they wouldn't budge. They were there to kidnap us, no matter what.

DEL NEWMAN: We were all real tired, so we went back upstairs to get some sleep before we would leave at sunrise.

BO WHITAKER: They left us downstairs without a guard. We tried like hell to get those ropes untied, but we just couldn't seem to get them. Then Elvis says, "Bo, look at your damn monkey." So I looked over and saw that David Cassidy had wiggled his way out of his ropes. He was just standing there on his chair looking at us. Elvis said, "Hey there, monkey, are you gonna come over here and help us get free?" David Cassidy scratched his head and, for a minute there, he kind of looked like he was taking this all in. Then, all of a sudden, he jumped down off his chair, reached back, and flung a huge handful of monkey shit all over us. He did this three or four times. Elvis looked over at me—he had a big glob of monkey shit on his cheek—and I could tell he wasn't too happy about what was going on. He said, "Goddamn, man, make that monkey stop throwing all that poo." I asked David Cassidy to stop, but he just kept hurling shit at us. Finally he stopped. I guess he must have run out of shit to throw.

Then, completely out of the blue, he jumped on top of me and started clawing my face, and his claws were just really grinding that monkey shit into my flesh. It was terrible. I screamed real loud, and the upstairs door opened. A man came running down with a knife out. He said he was gonna take care of David Cassidy. Meanwhile, David Cassidy was still clawing at my face, just ripping it to hell. I've still got a couple of scars from that night... So the man rushes toward the monkey with his knife, but the monkey goes crazy and bats it away. Then he swings up and kicks the man in the face. As he does that, his feet wrap around the guy's head, man, and that monkey is clinging to him and clawing at his face. Then the man fell back and hit his head on something and was knocked out cold.

Elvis says, "There isn't much time, monkey. I need you to pick up the knife and cut through these ropes." It takes a few minutes, but finally the monkey looks like he's got it figured out. So David Cassidy picks up that knife, man, and he's just staring at it intently. He kind of waddles over towards Elvis, and he's standing right behind him now, right where Elvis' hands are tied. "That's it, monkey," Elvis says. "Now cut through the rope." And right then, David Cassidy sliced a nice big cut into Elvis forearm. Elvis started to scream, but managed to stop himself so no one else would come downstairs. "That's it, monkey," Elvis says, and his voice is kind of wavering, man. He's in pain. And David Cassidy raises the knife up again and just slices into Elvis' forearm like he was slicing through hot butter. Elvis moans loudly, but not too loud.

So I say, "Why don't you try my ropes, David Cassidy?" So the monkey waddled over to me and sliced at my arm, but missed and cut the rope. He didn't cut all the way through it, but it was enough that I was able to wiggle my wrists until the rope finally snapped. Then, once I got loose, I helped Elvis get untied. I grabbed that knife from outta David Cassidy's little furry hand, and Elvis pulled a .38 from the unconscious man's waistband. "Let's go kill these cocksuckers, man," Elvis said.

So me, Elvis, and David Cassidy made our way up those stairs. Elvis had the gun up, and he pushed that door open real careful-like. We all stayed together, and Elvis stayed in the lead. He moved toward the right, and we followed. There was no one in the kitchen. Elvis then led us down the first floor hallway to the guest bedrooms. He opened one and saw a man sleeping there. "Wakey-wakey, man," Elvis said. The guy sat up and Elvis shot him in the head. He opened the next bedroom door and there was a woman in there. She was already standing and was fully dressed. She started to go for a gun, but David Cassidy ran in the room and jumped on her and started clawing at her face. She screamed loud as hell; between that and the gunshot, everyone was sure to be awake now.

We left David Cassidy there to fight with the woman, and Elvis and me made our way down the hallway. We kicked in a few doors, but we didn't see anyone. "I'll bet they's in the art room," Elvis said. "Let's go upstairs." So we made our way upstairs, and now David Cassidy was right there with us again, just like he was a part of the team. I remember he had that woman's blood all over his face... He looked real scary, like some kind of demented, crazy monkey, and he had that look in his eye—the same look that Elvis got sometimes—when he wanted to shed more blood. Maybe not, but that was my interpretation of his look. But then it's damn hard to read a monkey's facial expressions. Have you ever tried it? You just never know what them little sumbitches is thinkin'.

Harum Scarum was on in the front room, but there was no one there watching it. Elvis stopped and watched a few minutes of it before we went upstairs to kill everyone. "This is a damn good movie, man," he said. He just laughed and laughed like he'd never seen the damn thing before, let alone been in it. I remember him pointing that .38 at the TV and saying, "I should have won the damn Academy Award for that sucker right there, you know it? That was a complex role, man." I agreed with him, and then we continued up the stairs.

I pushed the door to the gun room open, and there was a man sitting in there smoking a joint. He looked startled at us. How in the hell he could have missed all the ruckus downstairs I'll never know. Maybe he just thought it was part of *Harum Scarum*. Or maybe he was just too high to know what the fuck was going on. Elvis said, "Didn't anyone ever tell you drugs are bad for you, son?" The man looked at him with his mouth hanging open, but didn't say shit. Elvis said "drugs kill," and then he said some silly tough-guy movie shit like, "And so do I." I dunno. It was something like that. Anyway, he shot that fucker clean in the throat. The guy was still alive, writhing around on the goddamn floor, and David Cassidy just went nuts. He jumped on the guy and started slamming his head into the floor as hard as he could. Elvis said, "I hate that monkey, man, but goddammit I respect him."

We went into my room, and there was a man lying in my bed jerking off! That really pissed me off. "Hell no!" I said. "I'm the only guy gets to jerk off in my damn bed!" I ran in and jumped on top of him, and just started punching him in the face. I wanted to use my Samurai training, you know? At first he didn't know what was going on; he was flailing around, and his cock was all hard and shaking around all over the place. I punched him in the throat, but then he pushed me back off the bed onto the floor. Before I could get to my feet, he jumped up and karate kicked me in my face. If you've never been Karate kicked by a sucker with bare feet and long-ass toenails, let me tell you, it fuckin' hurts like hell, man. So he's all jumping around and twirling and kicking like a little blond, naked Bruce Lee. He stands over me with his arms up like a crane and one leg raised like he's about to deliver some deadly kick. Finally, just before he could kick, Elvis interrupted. He said, "Fuck this," and he shot the guy in the chest.

I said, "What did you go and do that for?" And Elvis says, "I saved your ass, son." But truthfully, I was just about to whip that guy's ass. I know Elvis thought he was saving me, but I would have won that fight fair and square. But fuck it, that's how Elvis and me were back in those days; we were always there for one another.

So we step back out into the hallway, and there's a guy running down the stairs. I took that knife I lifted off the guy in the basement and threw it at him, and I'll be damned, it stuck right in the guy's back. Elvis smiled and said, "We're some damn tough Samurais, man." We kind of high-fived each another and went on down the hallway to look for more S.O.B.s to kill.

The door to the art room was open. Elvis grumbled that he never did trust security systems. We went in there, and there was a guy with a .45 in there. He started to talk some shit, but Elvis shot him in the face. The guy fell back, and his brains shot all over the wall behind him. "Look at that," Elvis said. "It looks like a painting by one of them abstract expressionists." I didn't know what that meant, but I kind of laughed so Elvis wouldn't think I was dumb or something.

We stepped back out into the hallway, and the group's leader, Del Newman, was there. He was just standing there. He said, "I'm a huge fan of yours, Mr. Presley. That's why we did all this. Because we love you." Elvis said, "You got a funny way of showin' it, man." And he raised the .38, lowering it towards the man's head. Del Newman got down on his knees and begged. "I'm so sorry, Mr. Presley. Surely we can work something out. Surely we can pretend that none of this ever happened?" Elvis touched the man's forehead with the pistol and squeezed the trigger. *Click!* He was out of bullets! Well, Elvis decided that was a sign from Mr. Jesus, so he rounded up Del Newman, the woman who'd spotted Elvis at the wake, and the guy from the basement. He made them all get down on their knees downstairs in the living room.

DEL NEWMAN: I thought I was dead. Just as sure as shit, I thought I was a goner.

LESLIE MARTIN: At that moment, I couldn't even imagine a scenario in which we got out of that room alive.

BO WHITAKER: Elvis says, "I'm gonna let you cocksuckers live. Not because I want to, but because Mr. Jesus wants it that way."

DEL NEWMAN: At first I thought Mr. Jesus was the name of the fat guy with Elvis. It took me a moment to realize that he was talking about the *real* Jesus. I'd never heard anyone refer to him as Mr. Jesus before.

BO WHITAKER: So Elvis tells them they're gonna be allowed to live. "But if I find out you told just one other person about me, I'll track you down and murder your entire family. I'm serious as hell, man. Don't test me." And the guy from the basement can't believe it. He's just happy as hell. "You're not gonna kill us?" And Elvis said no. The man started to thank Elvis and me for letting him live, and then, out of nowhere, David Cassidy leapt all the way from upstairs down onto the man and started chewing into his face! I was gonna run over and pull David Cassidy off him, but Elvis told me not to. "Mr. Jesus works in mysterious ways, son." So David Cassidy killed that man by eating off his face and tearing into his throat. It was really gross.

So Elvis let the two remaining people go, and you know, we never heard from them again. That was the end of C.R.E.E.P.

CHAPTER THIRTEEN
OPERATION VIPER'S NEST (1980)

BO WHITAKER: In November 1979, Iran took about fifty Americans hostage from the American Embassy there in Tehran. President Carter wasn't about to stand for that that shit. Several efforts to rescue the hostages had been made, and they had all failed. The most public attempt was known as Operation Eagle Claw. That resulted in the deaths of several American servicemen and the destruction of a couple U.S. aircraft. It also cost Carter reelection, man. Operation Eagle Claw took place in the spring of 1980. Elvis and me got the call to take part in Operation Viper's Nest in late November. By that time, the hostages had already been over there for a full year.

BOOTS PELTIER: The mission was simple: a team of C.I.A. assassins were to be sent in to kill the Ayatollah Ruhollah Khomeini, who was the leader of the Iranian revolution that had overthrown Mohammad Reza Pahlavi, the Shah of Iran.

Personally, I kind of questioned the logic behind this mission. I believed that the killing of the Ayatollah would have pushed the Iranians to murder those hostages. But what the hell did I know? Perhaps there were other forces at work that I didn't know about. But none of that was my concern. My concern was putting together a team of elite killers to take out the Ayatollah.

The C.I.A.'s top assassin was a man named Chalky Wilson. He was tied up on some other mission. Rather than waiting for the completion of that mission, the agency thought it best to send in their number two and three assassins. The second best assassin on the C.I.A.'s payroll was Jon Burrows. The third best was a woman named Erika Lindskey.

ERIKA LINDSKEY: I was thrilled to get the call. I'm one of those people who really love their job. When I was a C.I.A. assassin, I ate, slept, and drank assassinations. I truly lived for that. So when I was offered the chance to take out a piece of shit like the Ayatollah, I was all for it.

BO WHITAKER: Elvis and me were real excited about the thought of killing the Ayatollah. Besides, we figured what we always figured— it was an all-expenses paid vacation to a different country. Sure, Tehran was a dirty war zone, but how many Americans ever get to say they went to Iran? The only part of the job we weren't excited about was having to work with another assassin. Normally we worked alone. "What the hell do we need another gun for?" Elvis asked. "This is bullshit, man. This is pure bullshit." Then, when he found out the other assassin was gonna be a woman, he went through the roof. I remember him really screaming and ranting about it. He said, "Why would they even train a woman to be a damn assassin? Killing's a job for men. Women should just stay in the kitchen and make pastries. I figure a woman could do just about anything she wanted except for being an assassin. And the President. That's no good either." Then he thought about it for a moment and added, "And professional baseball player. No women need to play professional baseball. The only balls they need to handle are mine." We both kind of laughed about that. Elvis was a real funny guy when he wanted to be.

He was also really, really sexist. I tried to point it out to him a few times, but he never could believe he was capable of bein' a sexist. He just saw himself as being a "good old-fashioned Southern boy." The thing was, he kinda objectified women. He was only capable of seeing them as one thing—sexual objects. Now I like having sex with women as much as the next guy, but I also know that they're just about equal to men when it comes to most things. But not Elvis, man. He just couldn't see things that way.

You want an example? Okay, here's one, off the top of my head: one night there was a story about a woman astronaut on TV. They was makin' a real big deal about her being the first female astronaut in the history of NASA. It was, you know, a big thing. It was a breakthrough. I was kind of excited about it. But do you know what Elvis said when he saw that woman in her NASA suit? He said, "She's kind of cute. I wonder what her asshole tastes like." I laughed, but I thought it was pretty damned sexist.

But man, Elvis saw *every* woman as a possible sexual conquest. Nobody knew that better than Col. Tom Parker. No matter how fat or ugly a gal the Colonel hired to be his secretary, Elvis would make it his personal mission in life to have sex with her. He just couldn't help himself. He had to have them. He just *had* to. Then, after Elvis had sex with 'em, things would become real messy and the Colonel would have to fire them. I think he really hated to do that. So to put a stop to that shit, the Colonel hired a transsexual to be his secretary. You know, it was a guy with a schlong who looked like a woman. She had tits and everything, and to tell the truth, she...he...I'm not sure what to call her...was pretty attractive. But I had no interest. I mean, you know, she had a cock and balls. She might have looked like a woman, but she was packing down there, if you know what I mean. But do you know what? Elvis couldn't help himself. He had sex with her anyway. Of course he never would admit to it, but it was pretty obvious when the Colonel fired her and hired an old man to be his personal secretary. And that put an end to it.

But if you asked Elvis if he was sexist, he'd say, "Hell no, man. I ain't no damn sexist." His argument was that he treated women even better than he treated men. He'd say, "You know why I know I ain't no damned sexist, man? Because I always tip a female waitress. And if she's cute, I tip her a little extra. But I never tip a male waiter. Never." So that was Elvis' reasoning, and I didn't argue it any further. I mean, it wasn't gonna get me anywhere, and hell, Elvis wanted me to say yes and agree with him. Again, I wasn't a "yes man." I didn't say yes all the time—I just never said no.

BOOTS PELTIER: Operative #67357 Jon Burrows threw a fit when he found out he was going to be working with a female operative. I assured him that she was one of the very best—almost as good as he was—and that he had nothing to worry about, but he just kept ranting about how women should be barefoot and pregnant, and not carrying weapons. That was his exact quote, that they should be barefoot and pregnant and not carrying guns. I thought that was a real chauvinistic thing to say for 1980, but that's just the kind of guy Burrows was. He didn't care for much of anything or anyone. He just enjoyed killing people.

ERIKA LINDSKEY: When they told me I would be working with Jon Burrows, I was really excited. I mean, he was a legend in the agency. Everyone loved to share tales about what he and operative Bo had accomplished in their short time in the Central Intelligence Agency. Their work inspired us all. They gave us something to aspire to. They were our heroes.

BO WHITAKER: Elvis didn't like it one bit. He kept saying, "Maybe we shouldn't even go on this mission, man. Maybe we should just let 'em send someone else to take out the fuckin' Ayatollah." I told him it would be a waste of a really great opportunity to kill someone terrible if we didn't do it. I said, "If we stay home, what the hell are we gonna do?" And Elvis said, "Well, maybe we could get some bowling in with the guys." But I just kept telling him it was a bad idea. I mean, I wanted to go to Iran and I really wanted to take out that cocksucker Ayatollah. Then Elvis came up with a new idea. "Maybe we could save those hostages ourselves. Maybe we could take out the Ayatollah, and then go in there and free those hostages. We'd be goddamn heroes, man." I knew the C.I.A. didn't like rogue work, but it sounded pretty good to me. I mean, those hostages had been there for a full year and they deserved to come home. I asked him how we might pull off such a thing, and he just said, "I dunno, man. We'll just have to wait for the opportunity to present itself." When Elvis had a great idea, he really had a great idea. He was a fucking visionary, man. I knew the moment I heard his idea that this was something really great that we could accomplish by ourselves.

So finally Elvis gave in and decided he would go to Iran even if we had to work with a woman assassin. "Maybe she'll have nice tits," he said. I agreed. That was one way to look at the bright side of things. Tits is always a good thing. But don't get me wrong, I ain't no sexist, man; I just like tits.

BOOTS PELTIER: It was a really unheard of thing for operatives to turn down missions, but there for a minute it looked like Burrows and Bo were going to do just that. Then, at the very last second, Burrows called me and said, "Count us in, son. We're gonna go in there and take out that cocksucker Ayatollah." Then he went on this long rant about how patriotic it would be for he and operative Bo to take out the Ayatollah. "We don't do this work for credit, son, but we would be goddamn heroes if we were to pull this off." I reminded him that the agency wouldn't allow them to receive any public credit, but he just kept saying they would be heroes. Frankly, I just wanted to get him off the telephone, so I kind of agreed with him. I shouldn't have, but talking to Jon Burrows was as difficult as anything I had ever done. I was trained to endure the most brutal tortures the enemy could dish out—and I could easily have done it—but I couldn't stand talking to that goddamn Burrows. I just hated it.

BO WHITAKER: We flew on a passenger plane to Iran. We were dressed like Iranians, and we had Iranian credentials. Neither one of us could pronounce our fake names, so we had to hope no one asked us what they were. We just figured we'd mumble something if we were asked. We had brown makeup on our faces, hands, and arms. We were both a little skeptical of wearing brown makeup after the whole Black Panthers fiasco, but I'll be damned if it didn't work. Neither of us could speak a lick of Arabic, so we just nodded and played mute. But no one tested us. No one said so much as a word to us.

I was mostly afraid of how David Cassidy would be seen. We put a little turban on him and made him some fake credentials. We also stuck a fake beard on him. I remember that it didn't match his fur; the beard was black and his fur was brown. But you know, we figured no one would notice. We put David Cassidy in a little robe and he looked just like a little furry Iranian—no offense intended to either Iranians or monkeys. I kind of worried when David Cassidy took a shit in his seat, tossed it on top of some of the other passengers, and knocked a tray from a stewardess' hands and threw it, but no one said anything about any of it. I guess maybe that's how they behaved over there in Iran. I dunno. I didn't see anyone else throwing their shit around the plane, man, but who knows? Maybe I missed it.

It took something like twenty hours to get there. It was a real long flight, and there was no movie on it. It was just boring as piss, man. It was also a long time to not speak. Even David Cassidy kept his mouth mostly shut, so no one figured out he was a damn monkey and not an Iranian. Finally the plane landed and we were met at the airport by an operative named Reza. At first we couldn't identify him because there were several people holding up placards with Arabic written on them, and we didn't read Arabic. You know, it just looked like chicken scratches to us. So we just stood there looking around like a couple of morons. But then, finally, he came over to us and whispered in English, "Hey, guys, it's me, Reza." I'm not sure how he identified us. He must have had photographs of us so he could see what we looked like. I asked him later how he knew it was us. He just looked us over and started laughing. I don't know what that was all about, man. Those Iranians are some strange sumbitches, so who the hell knows?

Reza drove us to a hotel. During the drive, David Cassidy went crazy and scratched my ear so hard I thought it was gonna tear off. Reza said, "Real nice monkey you got there." That was when I knew he had to have been briefed about us. I mean, how else could he have seen through David Cassidy's clever disguise and known that he was not an Iranian, but a damn monkey? Elvis asked to hear some Iranian radio in the car. "I wanna see what Iranian rock and roll sounds like, man," Elvis said. Then he turned to me and said, "Maybe we'll hear me on the radio." Elvis always got a real kick out of hearing himself on the radio, especially in other countries. Reza turned the radio on, but it didn't sound like rock and roll and it sure didn't sound like Elvis. It was just some guy wailing and making weird sounds. It sounded like something between a wailing banshee and a cat who's just had his nuts run over by a damn lawnmower. Elvis was a little bit disappointed that he wasn't on the radio. Later I made him feel better by reminding him that he had been dead for three years now. I said, "They probably played you on the radio here all the time back when you was still alive, man." He started to perk up and then got sad again. I asked him why he was sad and he said, "You think people don't listen to me anymore now that I'm dead?" It was real hard to keep Elvis happy sometimes.

REZA RAHIMI: Being Iranian myself, the Central Intelligence Agency had stationed me in Iran for the past seven years. Even in Iran, we had heard tales of the great operative Jon Burrows. He was said to be one of the greatest assassins who ever lived—maybe even better than Chalky Wilson himself. But then when I saw them at the airport, I thought they were the two biggest dumbasses I had ever laid eyes on. They were just stupid beyond belief. And there was that stupid-ass monkey dressed like an Iranian man. What were those guys thinking? But then, what can I say? They pulled it off. Maybe they really were the geniuses everyone had said they were, but they certainly didn't seem like it.

BO WHITAKER: When we got to the hotel, Reza checked us in and took us up to our room on the second floor. He pointed out this real big building down the street and told us that we would be watching that place from the window of our hotel. "That's one of the Shah's old palaces," Reza said. "The Ayatollah lives in all of them now." So the job was that we would just watch and wait until the Ayatollah showed up at this particular palace, and then we would punch his ticket. Elvis asked Reza where our rifles were. "Under the bed," Reza said. "I trust that you can assemble them yourselves?" That kind of pissed Elvis off. He didn't like no Commie foreigners suggesting that a damn killer like himself couldn't assemble a rifle. Reza told us he would be back the following day with Erika Lindskey, the other assassin. "The woman," Elvis said with contempt in his voice. Reza just looked at him and said nothing. Even a damn Commie Iranian like Reza thought Elvis was a sexist. Reza left us with radio equipment to call in, and some codes to use when we did. We never could figure out the damn codes so we didn't use the radio at all.

We set up our eagle's nest in the window and started watching that damn palace through our rifle scopes. About two minutes after we set up, Elvis said, "I see him! I see the Ayatollah!" So Elvis fired down there and shot the man right through his temple. Then, as a crowd of people started to gather down there, Elvis said, "What the hell?" I said, "What?" And he said, *"I see him again!"* So Elvis shot another man. We were real excited about having already finished the mission, but it later turned out that neither of those guys was the Ayatollah. They were just random Iranian guys, but to us they all looked the same.

ERIKA LINDSKEY: I had to dress like a man to fly on the plane and go unnoticed. That part was difficult. They put brown makeup on my face, my arms, and my hands. They also put a fake beard on me and gave me some credentials. I could pronounce my name perfectly, but if they checked to see if I had a penis I'd be found out. The plane trip was long and boring. There was no movie on the plane, and I had decided not to bring a book so as not to tip anyone off that I was a female American. I read through a couple of the onboard flight magazines the airline provided, but they were mostly just filled with articles on how best to keep a woman submissive and how best to please Allah. Being a bit of a women's rights kind of gal, that rubbed me the wrong way. To tell the truth, it just made me even more anxious to put a bullet in the Ayatollah.

Finally the plane landed, and I was met at the airport by an operative named Reza. He whisked me out of the airport before anyone could have a chance to find out my true identity, and he took me to the hotel where I would be staying with operatives Jon Burrows, Bo, and David Cassidy. On the way to the hotel, Reza asked me, "Have you met Jon Burrows yet?" "No," I said. "What's he like?" Reza just chuckled. "What?" I asked. And he said, "Jon Burrows is probably the second stupidest man I have ever met in my entire life." This kind of surprised me. After all, Jon Burrows was a personal hero of mine. I thought about it for a moment and then I asked, "Who's the first stupidest man you've ever met?" Reza chuckled again and said, "Operative Bo." Again I was really surprised by this. There was no way those guys could have been that stupid and have accomplished all they'd accomplished at the Central Intelligence Agency. I just chalked it up to Reza having differences with them.

Reza and I talked about the United States for a few minutes. Reza said he had gone to college at Berkeley and had majored in literature. I found that fascinating. I asked him what his favorite part about the United States was. He turned to me and looked me straight in my eyes. "American pussy," he said, and then he winked. Goddamn men, I thought. They were all the same.

Hopefully operatives Jon Burrows and Bo would be different.

REZA RAHIMI: Operative Erika Lindskey was quite an intelligent woman, and I had heard that she was one of the greatest assassins the agency had ever trained. And on top of that, she had great tits.

BO WHITAKER: Elvis and me had been playing hangman for a while. It was a real slow day. I really hated playing hangman with Elvis because he cheated. Hell, he cheated at every game he'd ever played, from hangman to high-stakes Chutes and Ladders. Elvis was a natural born cheater. I knew he was cheating—hell, it was obvious—but I let him get away with it. After all, he was Elvis.

We were debating whether or not we should have a contest to see who could piss the furthest out of the window when Reza knocked on the door. I looked out through the peephole and reported to Elvis that it was Reza and Erika Lindskey. "Great," Elvis said. "Just great." I hoped that Elvis would be on his best behavior, but that was probably too much to hope for. Besides, his best behavior wasn't much better than his worst.

ERIKA LINDSKEY: My first impression of operatives Jon Burrows and Bo? They looked like real dullards. I looked at Reza, and we exchanged a look. I could tell that he was thinking, I told you so. They looked like Southern shit kickers. I'd heard a million or so stories about Burrows—probably mostly made up—but the one thing that struck me then that I had never heard before was how much he talked like Elvis Presley. I hated Elvis Presley. I just thought his music was the most atrocious shit ever. I preferred the Beach Boys, John Lennon, and Elton John, but what did it matter? Burrows was still an attractive man, even if he did talk like Elvis.

BO WHITAKER: Elvis was muttering under his breath about not wanting to work with a woman. He wasn't trying to hide it. In fact, I think he wanted to be heard. It was really embarrassing.

REZA RAHIMI: What a dumb shit Burrows was. I disliked him from the git-go. He was just a huge pile of steaming shit, as far as I was concerned. My second impression of him was even worse than the first had been, and I would not have believed that possible. But here he was blatantly disrespecting operative Erika Lindskey right in front of her face. I just thought he was a terrible, terrible person, and I thought he looked goofy as hell with that fake blond hair.

BO WHITAKER: Reza introduced us all. At first Elvis refused to acknowledge Erika's presence. But then, slowly but surely, he started to come around after Reza left. It was probably her tits, I think, that did it.

ERIKA LINDSKEY: While we were watching out the window and eating pork and beans straight from the can, we all started to get to know one another. Burrows asked me what kind of music I liked. I told him that I really liked the Beatles, and was a huge fan of John Lennon's solo stuff. And then he just went ape shit. He stood up, started yelling about John Lennon being a cocksucker, and he broke the recliner all to hell. Then he picked up the television and threw it on the ground. It just broke all over the floor. Then Burrows said something about the TV being a cocksucker. It was just ridiculous. I asked operative Bo what all that was about and he just shook his head. "He's not really much of a Beatles fan," he said. I could understand not liking someone's music, but this was really silly. It just made no sense whatsoever. When Burrows was in the bathroom trying to pull the toilet out of the floor in his anger, Bo leaned over to me and said, "If he asks you about Elvis Presley, you be sure to say you like his music. Don't say anything bad about him. Not one word, man." I grinned. "Or what?" I asked. "Or it'll be ten times worse than this," Bo said.

I hate to admit it, but Burrows' breaking the room all to hell kind of turned me on. Maybe it was because I had already had my head filled with so many tales of Jon Burrows and his amazing exploits, but it really made me horny. Again, I'm embarrassed to say that, but it was true.

BO WHITAKER: Erika acted really nice to me and at times I thought she was flirting with me. I really believed there for a minute I had a chance with her. But, you know, it happened the same way it always did... Eventually she fell for Elvis. I mean, who could blame her? He was Elvis fucking Presley. In the end, every woman wound up falling for him. Sometimes it depressed me that Elvis could act so crappy towards a woman and still wind up taking her to bed—trust me, it was not that way for me at all—but in the end I realized that I had David Cassidy to keep me company. Sure, he scratched and bit me all the time, but I think he just did that because he loved me.

ERIKA LINDSKEY: Bo had some sort of unnatural gay love thing for that monkey. I can't really explain it, but I'm certain he had done some sort of sexual acts with that monkey. I think that's why the monkey was so mean to him all the time; I think he resented being raped by Bo. And maybe I'm just imagining things. Maybe that never happened, but you know, I'd bet money that it did.

BO WHITAKER: Over the next few days, Erika and Elvis got closer and closer. Pretty soon they would just leave me out of the conversation altogether. So I'd look to David Cassidy to entertain me, but then he'd just do something like scratch me across my eye or bite a hunk out of my thigh. He was always doin' shit like that.

ERIKA LINDSKEY: There was something about Jon Burrows that really grew on me. I can't say exactly what it was, but there was a sort of animal magnetism between us. He wasn't really a charming man, and he wasn't very intelligent, either. But he just had this sexiness to him that was unlike anything I had ever encountered before.

We had been there for maybe three days when Burrows and I kissed for the first time, and it was magical. Just magical.

BO WHITAKER: I was really sad the first time they kissed. Then it got to the point where they would make me go sit in the bathroom by myself while they had sex. I would try to get David Cassidy to come into the bathroom with me to keep me company, but he wouldn't go. I guess he just wanted to watch them have sex. I don't know, man. It was really, really horrible. I mean, here was this beautiful woman that I had a crush on, and Elvis was right outside the bathroom pounding away at her in my bed. I thought that was really rude of him, so I asked him not to have sex in my bed anymore. You know what he said? "What? Do you expect *me* to sleep in the wet spot?" So he just kept having sex with Erika in my bed. I could hear her moaning in pleasure and he was saying these really nasty things to her. He would call her names like "sexy fuck monster" and she would yell things like "give me that cock." One time they played this role playing game where Elvis pretended he was the Ayatollah and Erika would scream, "Fuck me, Ayatollah! Fuck me!" It was really hard to take.

The bathroom was really goddamn boring. I mean, sometimes I had to take a shit, so then it wasn't so bad. I would actually have something to do in there. But then, when that was over, it was horrible being in there with that smell. Especially since all we had to eat was pork and beans every day. It was just awful, man.

Finally I said, "What happens if the Ayatollah shows up at the palace and you two are going at it and I'm locked away in the bathroom?" Elvis said that was a good point. So from then on, I would be sitting at the window, watching for the Ayatollah, while Elvis railed Erika on my bed.

ERIKA LINDSKEY: It was really gross having sex with Bo in the room. I didn't really mind the monkey being in there, with the exception of the one time he masturbated in the corner while we were doing it. But I didn't care for Bo being there. I was fairly certain he was watching us make love. It was just...gross.

BO WHITAKER: We had been in Iran for about a week when Elvis snapped. He woke me up in the middle of the night. "I can't take it no more, man," he said. "We gotta leave Iran and go on our own mission." I was confused. "Our own mission?" "Yeah," he said. "An ultra-top-secret mission." I looked at him, still not understanding what the hell he was talking about. "An *ultra*-top-secret mission?" Elvis nodded. "Even more secret than what we do for the damn Central Intelligence Agency, man. This is gonna be our own thing."

I told him I didn't think we should leave Iran without informing Boots Peltier first, but Elvis said to hell with that. He said we had to go immediately. So I said, "Okay, fine." After all, he was Elvis and I was Bo. I was the second banana and I did whatever Elvis said we were gonna do. Besides, the truth is that I was happy to have Elvis back to myself. I'd be happy to live in a world where I didn't have to sit there and watch for the Ayatollah while Elvis and Erika shot their love juices all over my bed.

Elvis held up a big syringe filled with a clear fluid. "What the hell is that?" I asked. At first I thought it was some drug he was gonna inject himself with. But it wasn't. Elvis smiled. "Why, son, this is X9." So I asked him what the hell X9 was. He explained to me that it was a top secret drug he had gotten from one of his contacts. His plan had originally been to sneak up on the Ayatollah and use it on him so we could capture him. "So what are we gonna do with it now?" I asked. He said, "We're gonna inject it into Erika's neck so we can get the hell out of here without her stopping us." I wasn't sure about that plan. "It won't kill her?" I asked. "Nah, man," Elvis told me. "My guy says this'll just knock her out for eight or nine hours. That should be plenty of time for us to get away. I asked him where we were going, and he told me I'd have to wait and see. Again, Elvis could be real sneaky when he wanted to be.

Erika was still asleep. Elvis leaned over her and injected that X9 right into the side of her neck. Her eyes opened for a moment and she started to wake up, but then she fell right back to sleep. I guess that X9 was some real potent shit, man.

ERIKA LINDSKEY: When I woke up, I had a vague memory of Jon Burrows injecting that drug into my neck. My neck hurt like hell. I got up and looked around and found that operatives Jon Burrows, Bo, and David Cassidy were all gone. That was the last time I ever saw any of them. Jon and I had had great sex that night and had gone to sleep in each other's arms. I thought everything was fine. I have no idea what made him decide to get up in the middle of the night and inject that shit into my neck and then leave. But he did.

Sometimes I still think about Jon Burrows and wonder what ever happened to him. I never heard another agency rumor about him ever again. He just disappeared right off the radar.

BOOTS PELTIER: Erika Lindskey called me in the evening and she was frantic. She said Operative #67357 Jon Burrows, operative Bo, and that goddamn monkey had taken off. Once again Jon Burrows had gone off the reservation. I knew the agency wouldn't take kindly to that. In fact, I figured they'd probably have him killed. But who knew? He was one of their elite assassins, their fair-haired golden boy, so maybe they'd give him a break. I just hoped he didn't do anything stupid while he was running around out there.

ERIKA LINDSKEY: We never did manage to assassinate the Ayatollah. He never came back to the palace, and after operatives Jon Burrows and Bo left, the agency decided to pull the plug on the whole thing. I really would have liked to have killed the Ayatollah—that would have been one hell of a feather in my cap—but Burrows fucked that up for me and I never got the chance to do anything that big again. So even though I loved Jon Burrows like I've never loved another man before or since, I kind of hated him for having ruined my one opportunity to be an agency legend like he was.

CHAPTER FOURTEEN
THE ULTRA-TOP-SECRET MISSION (1980)

BO WHITAKER: We arrived in New York City on December 6, 1980. It was a Saturday. At that time I had absolutely no idea what Elvis had planned for us. All I knew was that it was some sort of "ultra-top-secret" mission, and that we were going rogue again. I kept asking Elvis what the hell this was all about, but he just kept telling me to wait and see. We got a room at the Ritz-Carlton, and Elvis said we wouldn't be there much.

That afternoon Elvis made a few secretive telephone calls. Again, I had no idea who he was talking to or what he was talking about. He was back in super-secret spy mode, and it was as annoying as it had ever been. Realizing I wasn't going to get anything out of him about this mission, I finally decided to just sit back and enjoy the ride, man. I knew that when Elvis was good and ready to tell me what the hell this was all about, he'd do so.   That day Elvis bought a car—a 1976 Caddy—from a used car dealership. Elvis kept bitching about the color. The car was maroon. "I really hate driving a Cadillac that isn't pink," he told me. "It almost defeats the whole purpose of driving a damned Caddy." I suggested that maybe he could have it painted, but Elvis said no, he didn't wanna do that. "We're gonna ditch this car after the mission is over," he said. "This is a mission-only automobile, man."

Later that night we sat at the curb and staked out a recording studio called the Record Plant. "Who's in there?" I asked, but it was no use. Elvis just told me to keep quiet and watch the damn building. We sat there and watched that building until late that night. Sitting in the car that long was driving David Cassidy nuts. He kept tearing the stuffing out of the seat and throwing it on our heads. And the car smelled pretty bad because he'd pissed and taken a shit or two in that backseat. It was a less-than-ideal setup for a stakeout.

I think it was about eleven or so when Elvis finally saw a couple leaving the studio in a black limo. "That's them," he said. Elvis had been watching them from down the street through a pair of binoculars. Since I didn't have binoculars, and basically have pretty crappy eyesight to start with, I had no idea who the couple was. "Who is it?" I asked. And again Elvis said nothing. We followed the limo to West Seventy-Second street, which was dark as hell. The limo stopped outside an apartment building, which was surrounded by a smattering of people milling about. I had no idea why there would be people just standing around at such a late hour.

"Maybe I ought to just go inside there and do what has to be done," Elvis said. Again I pushed. "What has to be done, man?" Elvis just grinned and said nothing. We then went and got some hamburgers (and a banana milkshake for David Cassidy) and headed back to our hotel room. Elvis made a few more hushed phone calls, which I couldn't make out.

The next morning we were up bright and early. I think it was about seven o'clock. I really wanted to sleep longer, but Elvis insisted that we return to our ultra-top-secret mission. We went for breakfast first. We both had blueberry pancakes with syrup. I still remember that breakfast, man—it was good as hell. Then we drove back to the apartment building on West Seventy-Second street. Elvis parked a ways down the street and watched the building through his binoculars. There were still people standing around outside the building, as if they were waiting for someone. We sat there for several hours and Elvis kept talking about how we were on a stakeout just like in the cop movies. "I could have been a damn cop, you know," Elvis said several times. We listened to the radio while we waited and one of Elvis' songs came on. I think it was "(Marie's the Name) His Latest Flame," but I can't say for certain. Anyway, that seemed to cheer Elvis up quite a bit. I remember him singing along with himself on the radio and commenting about how "goddamn good" he sounded.

Around three p.m., the limosine returned to the front door and the couple we had seen the previous day reemerged from the building. At first the crowd of people gathered around them, so I couldn't see who it was. Elvis sat down the binoculars and started the Cadillac's engine. I picked up the binoculars and looked at the couple through them. At first I still couldn't see who they were. The man was writing on album covers and magazines being handed to him. I figured he must be someone famous, which would have explained why Elvis was being so secretive. Then crowd parted a bit and the man looked up. That was when I saw who it was we was tailin'—it was John Lennon, and his wife, Yoko Ono. My mind was going crazy with thoughts. What could this be about?

I put down the binoculars and looked at Elvis, who was grinning like a damned fool. I said, "Are you gonna team up with John Lennon and make a new song?" Elvis just said, "Nah, man." So I asked him what the hell this was all about. And Elvis said, just as calm and cool as could be, "We're gonna kill John Lennon." That surprised the hell out of me. Elvis and I had killed a lot of people by that time, but they were mostly bad people who had it coming. As far as I knew, John Lennon hadn't done anything to anybody. So I asked Elvis why he wanted to kill John Lennon. When I asked this, John Lennon and Yoko Ono climbed into the limo and it pulled away from the curb. Elvis started following them again. "Why are we doing this, Elvis?" I asked.

Elvis had never liked the Beatles. That was no secret. I guess he saw them as his only competition, and Erika Lindskey's mentioning how much she liked Lennon's music had only made things worse. Elvis didn't mind being "dead," because there was no one who could take his place. But Lennon had just made a comeback and released a new album, *Double Fantasy*, and I guess Elvis thought he might somehow take his place in the public's mind. Again, I don't know all of this for sure, man; it's just a guess. Then Elvis said, "The guy's a damn menace. On top of that, he's one of *them*." "*Them*?" I asked. Did he mean the Beatles? And then Elvis said, "He's a fucking Commie heathen, man."

We followed the limo back to the recording studio where we had first found John and Yoko the day before. We sat in silence and watched the building all day, occasionally listening to the radio and eating cheeseburgers. Late that night, around ten or so, the limo returned and John and Yoko walked out of the building. We followed them back to their apartment building.

"When you plannin' to do this?" I asked. Elvis said he wasn't sure. "I'll know when the moment is right," he said. I asked him how he planned to kill John Lennon. Elvis said he'd been thinking about that for a while now. "I thought about stabbing him," Elvis said. "But that's too damn messy. I hate stabbin' people. It's just a major pain in the ass and it makes a big old mess, man. It's not really my thing." Then Elvis said, "I thought about taking a piss in the toilet and drowning him in my piss, but I changed my mind." Before Elvis could go on, I said, "You really hate him, don't you?" Elvis said, "Yeah, man, I hate that cocksucker." I asked him why, but Elvis just sat there. A few minutes later he said, "What if I killed him the way they killed me... What if I made it look like he had a heart-attack taking a dump?" He thought about this for a moment and then said, "I think I'll probably just shoot him with my .38. That oughta do the trick." John and Yoko went back into their apartment, and Elvis and I returned to our hotel for the night.

Elvis was real moody. I knew something was up when he didn't break our TV set. I mean, he never stayed in a hotel room and didn't break a damn TV, you know? He just kept to himself and read the Gideon Bible that was on the nightstand. Occasionally he would read a passage out loud or say something about having Mr. Jesus on his side, and then he would go back to reading. I remembered John Lennon saying that the Beatles were bigger than Jesus, and how that had pissed Elvis off. Then I remembered that line about there being no heaven in the song "Imagine." Elvis didn't particularly like that, either. That's when I kind of figured it out; Elvis was justifying this mission of his by telling himself that he was doing Mr. Jesus's work. I stayed up late into the night and watched some old movie. I can't remember what it was...something with Charlton Heston in it, I believe. Elvis was still awake, reading that Bible, when I fell asleep around four or so.

We got up at seven again. Elvis stood in front of the mirror in his underwear and muttered to himself. "Today's the day, cocksucker." I think he was talking to an imaginary John Lennon. I didn't say anything. I just tried to ignore him. Elvis was kinda creepin' me out, man. I was just hoping that I didn't have to help him murder John Lennon. I was never a fan of John Lennon or the Beatles—I mean, they had a couple of songs that I had kind of liked, and I liked Wings— but I felt real bad about Elvis wanting to murder the man. Hell, he never did nothing to nobody as far as I could tell.

We went and ate breakfast. I had the blueberry pancakes again, but they didn't taste so good that day. Elvis didn't eat. He seemed nervous, fidgety, and I wondered if maybe, deep down inside, he knew what he was doing was wrong. But if he did, he never said so. After I finished my pancakes, we got back in the Caddy and drove over to John and Yoko's apartment building. We sat there and watched as nothing happened for hours and hours. Finally, around four, John and Yoko came out and walked toward a car—it wasn't their normal limo; it was a Buick, I think. They signed a few autographs and then got into the car. Elvis and me followed them back to the Record Plant again, and then there was more sitting around and waiting. Finally Elvis said, "Fuck this," started the engine, and drove away. At first I thought maybe he had come to his senses and decided not to shoot John Lennon, but then I saw that we were going back to the Dakota apartment building where John and Yoko lived.

"I'll just sit and wait for them," Elvis said. "Then, when they get here, I'll just get out and walk over to them. Then, *blam!*, I'll shoot him dead." I thought about this for a minute and then asked Elvis what he would do if John Lennon recognized him. Elvis looked at me as if I was from another planet. "How would he recognize me?" Elvis said. "I got blond hair and a new face, so nobody can recognize me." I figured he was probably right, so I said nothing. "Besides," Elvis said, "even if he does recognize me, it won't matter. After all, he'll be dead. Who's he gonna tell?" I sat there for a moment, sad about being involved with this whole thing. "You know, John Lennon's got kids," I reminded him. But Elvis just laughed and said, "Everyone we kill has children, son. The world will be a better person with a Commie cocksucker like him gone." And that was it. We didn't talk anymore. In fact, I think Elvis turned up the radio to let me know we were done talking.

About a half an hour before John Lennon and Yoko Ono arrived at the apartment building, a Beatles song came on the radio. David Cassidy got real excited. I don't think I mentioned this before, but that monkey was a huge Beatles fan. So David Cassidy started jumping around and snapping his fingers. Elvis looked real irritated. That's when I knew for sure that he was gonna go through with this. Hearing that song—"Nowhere Man," I think it was—seemed to remind him how much he hated John Lennon and the Beatles. Then another thought occurred to me: after killing John Lennon, would Elvis then track down each of the other three Beatles and kill them, as well? I hoped not. I didn't want to be a part of that nonsense. I mean, Elvis was my friend and my boss and I would have followed him to the ends of the earth, but I wouldn't have liked doin' that particular bit of nastiness. Thankfully none of that ever happened.

John and Yoko returned to the apartment building around ten-thirty. "I'll be right back, man," Elvis said, climbing out of the Caddy. "This'll only take a minute." As he approached John and Yoko, I found myself praying to Elvis's Mr. Jesus that he would somehow stop Elvis from committing this murder. But it didn't work. Elvis walked up behind them just as they reached the door to the apartment building. I heard him say, "John Lennon." John turned around and Elvis shot him five times. I heard Yoko scream, and soon Elvis was back inside the car with me and we were pulling away.

"I'm surprised you didn't shoot Yoko, too," I said. Elvis laughed. "No, I actually like her." "Why?" I asked. He turned and looked at me and said, "Because she broke up the damn Beatles." Then I thought about the whole thing and asked Elvis if we needed to get rid of the gun. Elvis laughed again. "No," he said. "Get this: there was some dumb kid sitting there against the wall, trying to read a book in the dark." "So?" I asked, not understanding what he was saying. "So," Elvis said, "I handed him the gun before I came back to the car."

YOKO ONO: I didn't get a good look at the man who shot John. Everything just happened so quickly, it was all a blur. But as time has passed, I have had dreams about the shooting. In the dreams, everything slows down and I can see the man. He was blond. He wasn't Mark David Chapman at all. This is gonna sound crazy, but his voice sounded like...Elvis Presley.

BO WHITAKER: Mark David Chapman, the guy Elvis had given the gun to, was apparently this crazed Beatles fan from Texas who had come to New York to stalk John Lennon. After Elvis gave Chapman the gun, Chapman took credit for the shooting. Yoko said she didn't get a good look at the shooter, so Chapman took the fall. I guess it's what he wanted, man. I guess he wanted to become famous or something—to be forever linked John Lennon. I don't know, but Elvis was in the clear. Elvis was kind of irritated though. Even though he wanted the kid to take the fall for him, he hated doing things and not getting the credit for them. He especially hated seeing other people getting credit for something he'd done.

BOOTS PELTIER: The agency knew at once that Jon Burrows was responsible for the murder of John Lennon. Of course they didn't say anything publicly. After all, Elvis Presley was supposed to be dead and the C.I.A. didn't want to be connected to John Lennon's murder. That was when serious discussions began about the future of operative #67357 Jon Burrows. He had apparently gone crazy and was using his talent at killing to murder innocent people. The agency couldn't stand back and allow that to continue—even if this was Jon Burrows.

BO WHITAKER: The shooting was all over the news, man. Even though John Lennon hadn't been as big a star as he once had, his murder became as big as the assassination of John F. Kennedy. All of a sudden it seemed that by murdering John Lennon, Elvis had made him even more famous than he had been before. That really infuriated Elvis, but there was nothing he could do about any of it now.

We returned to Truth or Consequences to wait for the backlash.

CHAPTER FIFTEEN
ASSASSIN VS. ASSASSIN (1980)

BO WHITAKER: Elvis knew what was coming. He said it almost immediately after getting off the telephone. "They're gonna eliminate me," he said. "Those goddamn cocksucking sons of motherfuckers are gonna have me killed, man." I wasn't prepared for news like that. I asked him, "Do you think they'll have us *both* killed?" Elvis said, "Probably. But it don't matter none—you gotta stay and help me fight because I'd do it for you. You and me, we're a team. If someone comes after one of us, they gotta contend with the both of us, man." I thought about it for a minute and then asked, "And David Cassidy, too?" Elvis looked at David Cassidy, muttered something about "stupid fucking monkey" under his breath, and then said, "Yeah, I guess David Cassidy, too."

I'll tell you the truth, if Elvis had said David Cassidy couldn't come along with us, I would probably have just walked out right then and there. I mean, we were a team—not just Elvis and me, but all of us, including David Cassidy. And you don't just break up a good team, man. I mean, look at the Eagles... They all had solo careers, but most of their songs kind of suck without each other. When you break up a good team, you end up with something a whole lot less than you began with, man. That's how I saw it. Sure, David Cassidy was a fucking asshole to me a lot of the time, but he was my friend and I wasn't about to just leave his little furry ass there.

Then Elvis said, "That's not even the worst part of it, Bo." And I thought, hell, what could be worse news than finding out the Central Intelligence Agency wants you dead? And then he said, "They'll be sending Chalky Wilson to eliminate us." When I heard those words, I thought I was gonna be sick.

Chalky Wilson. Ask any C.I.A. operative and they'll rattle off a hundred or so tales about the fuckin' guy. He's a legend. He was more than a legend—he was *real*. He was like the boogeyman times ten. He was like Johnny fuckin' Rambo times twelve. He was a really bad dude, and if you found yourself in that guy's crosshairs, you were royally fucked. Chalky Wilson didn't miss, and Chalky Wilson didn't allow his targets to walk away alive. No, the guy was pure perfection—the single greatest assassin the C.I.A. had ever trained.

Where did he come from? No one knew. He was a black guy, but stories about his background depended on who was telling the damn story. Some people said the guy was from New York City, others said London, and still others said Africa. The truth is that no one knew shit about Chalky Wilson except that they didn't want to wind up as one of his targets. Sure, Elvis was the second best assassin the C.I.A. had, but it was a distant second. It was like saying Scottie Pippen was the second best player on the Chicago Bulls roster. Sure, Pippen was good—maybe even great—but Michael Jordan was the best *ever*. And that was Chalky Wilson.

Some operatives said he was the greatest assassin in the entire world, man. Who knew if that was true, but he was definitely a guy you didn't wanna fuck around with. And now here Elvis was telling me that this guy was gonna be coming to kill us? This wasn't the best news I'd ever gotten. And here it was still eight or nine in the morning. When you start out your morning with shit news like that, the rest of the day doesn't stand a goddamn chance.

To tell you the truth, I was scared as hell, man. I don't think I'd ever been that scared before; not even when Elvis put a sheet over David Cassidy's head and tried to tell me he was a little stinky ghost. That was scary, but it was nothing compared to this.

Elvis said, "Well, the first thing we need to do is to have some kind of plan so we don't get caught with our pants down. We gotta be ready for that cocksucker, man. We're gonna have to kill him." I heard those words and I thought about what they meant. Before I could say it, Elvis beat me to the punch. "We kill Chalky, we'll never be able to rest again for the rest of our lives, man. The C.I.A. will just keep sending killer after killer to terminate us. They won't be as good as Chalky, but eventually someone'll get lucky." Elvis paused and then added, "And that's just if we're lucky enough to beat Chalky, which is a big fucking 'if', man."

Elvis and me decided it was best to go to the city and set up a base of operations. So we went back to New York City to set up camp at the Ritz-Carlton. The thought was that we'd just sit in there in our room and wait for Chalky to show up. We hoped maybe we'd get lucky and he wouldn't come, but we both knew the truth—Chalky was gonna come knockin'. It was only a matter of when.

We went to the airport, bought tickets, and boarded our plane. It was a Delta flight, I think. David Cassidy had to ride in cargo inside a cage on account of how he was a monkey and all. The plane was filled to capacity, and there was about seven, maybe eight black guys onboard. Since neither of us knew what Chalky looked like, we had to be extra careful not to get killed right there on the damn plane, man. So we were sitting there, Elvis reading the *New York Times* funny papers, and me coloring a page from a *Dukes of Hazzard* coloring book. But we were both kind of looking around, too, watching those black guys. There was one black guy who looked especially suspicious. He was sitting about three rows up from us, on the other side of the plane. He kept looking back. What the fuck did he have to look at us for? So we came to the conclusion pretty quickly that he was Chalky Wilson.

So Elvis comes up with a plan. He says, "You go to the bathroom at the back of the plane, act like you gotta take a shit or something. Then I'll watch and see if he tries to follow you back there. If he does, I'll come up behind him and hit him over the head with my giant belt buckle. Then we'll kill him in the bathroom and toss him out of the plane." The plan sounded solid, so I went along with it. I mean, we were on a friggin' airplane. How the hell else was it gonna go down?

I got up and made my way to the bathroom. When I was getting up, I saw the black guy looking over his shoulder at me again. So I go to the bathroom and shut the door for a minute. I'm looking in the mirror there and noticing that I'm starting to grow a little bit of a unibrow, which kind of bummed me out. I was thinking about plucking those hairs, but then there was a knock on the door. Was this Chalky, sent to murder me? I stood there for a moment, not moving. Then there was a second knock. I started to open the door just a crack, and I could see the black guy standing there looking at me. Just as I caught a glimpse of him, Elvis smashed his belt buckle over the man's head. But the man didn't fall. He just yelled out in pain.

"What the fuck are you doing?" he yelled. Then his flailing arm came in through the crack in the door, and I slammed that goddamn door on his arm as hard as I could. The man made another loud noise. I opened the door and Elvis was standing over the guy, about to smash him over the head with his gold belt buckle again. "Who are you, goddammit?" Elvis asked him. "I'll kill you, you stupid sumbitch. Now you tell me who the fuck you are."

ROBERT OWENS: I had no idea why these white guys were beating the shit out of me. I kept trying to stop them, but they just kept hitting and kicking me. It was real fucked up.

BO WHITAKER: Elvis said it again. "Who the fuck are you, man?" The guy kind of shook his head like he was trying to clear his vision and said his name. I can't remember it now—

ROBERT OWENS: I said, "My name is Robert Owens. Why the fuck are you doing this to me?"

BO WHITAKER: Elvis says, "You're Chalky, goddammit!" And the guy just keeps saying, "Who the fuck is Chalky? I don't know no Chalky." So Elvis says, "Well, then why did you come back here?" The guy grinned kind of sheepishly and says, "Well, I thought you guys were gay. You kept staring at me, you're both dressed kind of flamboyantly, and you're obviously lovers. So I thought—" Elvis interrupts him and says, "You thought *what*?"

ROBERT OWENS: I told him I had made eye contact with the fat guy and I thought we had made a kind of a connection. I thought maybe we could join the Mile High Club there in that bathroom. I'd done it a couple of times before, but it didn't work out this time. They insisted they weren't gay, which was fine. I never would have approached them if I had known they were straight. It was really dangerous being gay back in those days. You never knew who might just try to attack you or something just because you were gay or you insinuated that they were gay. It could be really scary.

BO WHITAKER: I thought it was weird the guy thought we were gay. At first I thought maybe he was Chalky, and was just trying to convince us to let him go. Then I noticed that he didn't have a gun or a knife. So finally we let him go.

ROBERT OWENS: The big guy let me go so long as I promised not to tell anyone what had happened. Shit, I had no problem with that whatsoever. I didn't want any trouble. So I kept my mouth shut and went back to my seat.

BO WHITAKER: That whole thing was kind of strange, but you could never be too careful. Since no one knew what Chalky Wilson looked like, he could have been any black guy. You just didn't know, man. So we finished that plane trip, and the black guy never even so much as looked back at us after that. I felt kind of bad we had roughed him up, but again, we couldn't take no chances.

We found our luggage at the airport and hailed a cab. The cabbie was from somewhere in the Middle East, and Elvis was just sure he was a Communist. He kept asking the guy, "Are you a damn Commie, man?" And the guy kept looking at us real weird and saying, "Commie? No, no Commie." But Elvis was convinced. Normally he wouldn't have taken a cab that might have belonged to a Commie, but this was a special circumstance. It was more important that we get to the hotel and get out of sight than it was to ride Commie-free. So finally we got to the Ritz-Carlton and Elvis tipped the cabbie a quarter. "Gee, thanks," the cabbie said. Elvis told him he was lucky he was getting anything seeing as how he was probably a damn Commie. Then the guy said, "I should have charged you more since you have a monkey." But Elvis said, "He's got a little suit on. Can't you see he's a little furry guy? That ain't no monkey. Hell, that's my brother-in-law, Earl."

So we check into the hotel, and we're both looking around nervously. They gave us a couple of keys to a room on the third floor and we went on up. It was a nice room, but you know, we weren't there for a vacation. We were there to protect ourselves from Chalky Wilson. First thing Elvis did was shut the curtains. He says, "I got a plan." So I said, "Okay, man, I'm listening." Elvis says, "We need a mannequin to prop up in the window dressed like me." So I suggested we call down to room service and see if we could get a mannequin. Hell, we'd asked for stranger things at hotels when we were on tour. But Elvis said, "Nah, man, you gotta go get the damned mannequin." I said, "Chalky Wilson's out there. I'm not going to get the damn mannequin. You want the mannequin, you go get the sumbitch yourself." So Elvis says, "Okay, then let's flip a damn coin, man." So I agree to that and Elvis flips it. "Tails," he says. "You gotta go get the damn mannequin." And you know, I think he might have been bullshitting me because I never even got to see the coin for myself.

"Well," I asked. "Where the hell am I gonna get a goddamn mannequin?" And he says, "You just go to one of the department stores and you offer 'em a hundred bucks for a mannequin. They'll give you one. They got 'em to spare." So I did. I didn't wanna leave that hotel room, but I did. I was gonna take David Cassidy with me, but Elvis said I would probably stand out more with a monkey—even if he was dressed in human clothes. I guess he was right. Anyway, I took a cab to a nearby department store and bought a mannequin. When I was coming back to the hotel, I ended up with the same Middle Eastern cabbie that Elvis thought was a Commie. When I put the mannequin in the seat, the guy says, "First you bring a monkey into my cab, and now you bring this big mannequin?" I said, "Hell, no, man. That's my brother-in-law, Earl." I thought it was kind of a funny joke, but the man didn't laugh. He just muttered, "Goddamn fucking Americans." It was a good thing Elvis wasn't there to hear that. If he'd have heard a damn foreigner disrespecting America, he'd have Karate chopped him right in the back of the head, man."

So I got back to the hotel, and Elvis was taking a bubble bath and David Cassidy was just sitting on the bed watching *Magnum P.I.* That was David Cassidy's favorite show. He really liked that one. So anyway, we sat up that mannequin in a chair by the window. We put Elvis' big oversized sunglasses on that sucker, and put a cape and a great big belt buckle on him. I'll be damned if that mannequin didn't look just like Elvis. Then we pulled back the curtains and ducked out of sight. Elvis hid beneath the window, and I hid in the bathroom next to the hotel door. David Cassidy just sat in the bathtub. I hooked the TV up in the bathroom so he could watch his soap operas. He especially liked *The Young and the Restless*.

We had been camped out in that room like that for two days before the bullet finally came zipping in through the window. It struck the mannequin right in the side of the head, breaking the sunglasses. Elvis moved real quick, pulling down the mannequin out of sight so it looked like he'd really been shot. Then we sat and waited for Chalky Wilson to come in and verify that Elvis was dead. We all moved into the bathroom entrance. I had to turn off *The Young and the Restless*, which really got David Cassidy steamed. He attacked me, which wasn't really very quiet. He scratched me across my face, but luckily I was able to shut him up pretty quick. We all sat there in that little bathroom entrance, waiting for Chalky.

A few minutes later, we heard a knock on the door. Man, that was some scary shit. It was like sitting there and waiting for the boogeyman to come in and get your ass. This was maybe even worse—*this was Chalky fucking Wilson!* Well, when nobody answered the door, we could hear him going to work on that lock. Elvis and me and David Cassidy all looked back and forth at each other, but no one said a word. Hell, I don't even think we so much as breathed during those few minutes. Finally, after about three or four minutes, we heard the door unlock. Chalky opened the door a crack until the chain lock was taut, then burst in through the door. We were going to jump him when he walked in, but he walked right past us without even looking at the bathroom. Can you believe that? Greatest C.I.A. assassin ever, my ass! Me and Elvis would definitely have checked the bathroom first.

So Chalky walks past us and goes over to the window and leans down over the mannequin, lying on the goddamn floor. Elvis and me come out of there with our pistols drawn. "Drop your gun, Chalky," Elvis says. Chalky nods, turns around, and drops his gun.

Approximated conversation between Elvis Presley and Chalky Wilson, recreated from the memories of Bo Whitaker:

WILSON: How'd you know it was me?

PRESLEY: I'd have been offended if they'd sent anyone else, Chalky.

WILSON: Man, this should have been an easy job.

PRESLEY: What do you mean?

WILSON: You're already dead, Mr. Presley. You died two years ago, remember?

PRESLEY: How do you know who I am?

WILSON: Don't you recognize my face?

PRESLEY: You do look familiar to me, but then a lot of black guys look alike to me.

WILSON: I'm gonna forget you just said that.

PRESLEY: We know each other?

WILSON: We've met before.

PRESLEY: I don't recall... Oh, shit, I see it now...

WILSON: You see who I am.

PRESLEY: If you had longer hair...and facial hair... You look like...

WILSON: Right.

PRESLEY: *Jimi Hendrix?!*

WILSON: Now you got it.

PRESLEY: But I thought you were dead. Hell, you died ten years ago!

WILSON: Just like you did, right?

PRESLEY: Are there others like us?

WILSON: Just Jim Morrison. He works for the F.B.I.

PRESLEY: Really?

WILSON: Yeah. But I was the first.

PRESLEY: How'd you get in?

WILSON: The C.I.A. recruited me. How'd you get in?

PRESLEY: I had to go and apply. Those cocksuckers never recruited *me*.

WILSON: I wouldn't take it too hard now. I mean, you're a legend in the agency. You're one of the best ever.

PRESLEY: And soon, after you're dead, I'll be *the* best ever.

BO WHITAKER: Elvis aimed his sequin-handled .45 at Chalky's face. I saw the muscles in his hand tense up, and he squeezed the trigger. *Click!* It was a goddamn misfire! Before I even realized what had happened, Chalky leaped through the glass window and disappeared from sight. "Get him!" Elvis yelled. I said, "Don't you think he's dead?" Elvis said, "No, he's Chalky Wilson. He's not dead." So we ran to the window and looked down, and sure enough, there was Chalky hanging from the window a floor down. So I climbed out the window and started climbing down towards him. Elvis fired down at Chalky, but missed. "You climb down, and I'll run down the stairs and meet you there," Elvis said. I thought that was kind of a dick move, but shit, I was already out on that ledge. What the hell else was I gonna do?

I let go of the ledge and fell, hoping to catch the ledge where Chalky was hanging. I missed, and the ledge slipped through my fingers. I kept falling, and I grabbed Chalky's legs and hung there in the air from his feet. "Dammit, man," he said. "I wasn't even after you. I was just after Elvis." I said, "Really?" And he said, "Yeah, but I'm gonna have to kill you now." He kicked me in the face and I lost my grip. I was scared as hell, man! I tried to catch the ledge on the next floor, but missed. I wound up falling into some brush. I was scratched up, but it was nothing new to me—it was just like another day hanging out with David Cassidy.

I looked up and Chalky was gone. In the time it had taken me to fall, he'd climbed in through the goddamn window. I got to my feet and started to run, but realized I'd lost my gun somewhere in the bushes. So there I was hunting for my gun, and about a minute later I see Chalky high-tailing it past me. I still don't have a gun, but I broke into a sprint and started chasing him down the street. He turned and shot at me a couple of times, but his shots were wide; none of them hit me. I was running down the street after him, man, lookin' around for a rock or something to attack him with. I was empty-handed. If he had known that, I'd be dead today.

I chased Chalky into Central Park. There were people all around, and yet no one paid us any mind. At least not at first. I guess shit like that happens all the time in New York City. Well, I was running, and I tripped and fell. I looked up, and Chalky was coming back for me. I turned myself around and sat up, still sitting there on the sidewalk. Chalky walked until he was standing over me. "It was nice knowing you, operative Bo," he said. He raised the gun to my head. Just as he was about to pull the trigger, a gunshot rang out and Chalky was struck in the side. We both looked back and there was Elvis with David Cassidy. Man, was I ever happy to see those no-good S.O.B.s.

Chalky raised his weapon, but Elvis shot him in the leg, and Chalky fell down hard. Chalky raised his pistol and shot me in the chest, just to the right of my heart. It hurt like hell. Boy, did it burn... Elvis shot Chalky in the arm this time, and Chalky returned fire at Elvis. Elvis shot Chalky in the other arm, and Chalky kind of slumped back on the pavement, his legs under his body like a little kid in kindergarten class. Elvis stepped towards him. Chalky said, "If I had to die, I'm glad it was you, Elvis." Elvis nodded respectfully, raised his pistol, and *click!* It misfired again! "Goddamn pistol," Elvis said. Chalky started to stir, but David Cassidy leaped on top of him and started slamming his head into the pavement in this real brutal way.

I asked Elvis if we should stop him, but Elvis said, "It's Mr. Jesus' will, Bo. Mr. Jesus wants David Cassidy to kill Chalky. It's out of our hands." So we just stood there and watched David Cassidy bash Chalky's brains out all over the pavement. Then David Cassidy started chewing on his face.

Elvis knelt down over me. I told him I thought I was gonna die, man. "Bullshit," Elvis said. "You still got business to take care of. You and me, we can't die, man. We're gonna live forever." Then Elvis said, "I gotta go now." I said, "You're leaving me?" And he said, "I gotta go. It'll be better for everyone. The C.I.A. ain't never gonna let me go, Bo. I don't want you to die on account of me." I said, "Will I ever see you again?" Elvis kind of grinned and said, "Maybe one of these days, son." I had tears in my eyes and wondered what the hell I was gonna do without my best friend. Then Elvis said something I'll never forget; he said, "Bo, I'm taking your monkey with me."

And he left. That was the last time I ever saw either one of them. I think about them all the time, but you know, life has gone on. The C.I.A. offered me a job working as an operative by myself, but I gave all that up. Mostly I was just doing that to make Elvis happy. So I took some time and healed up real nice, and then I got a gig working as a roadie for Tom Petty. I worked for him for almost ten years, man. Since then I've worked for a lot of rock stars, from Motley Crue to Jackson Browne. Things have never been as good as they were with Elvis, but you know, life is good.

EPILOGUE

Elvis Presley a.k.a. Jon Burrows never resurfaced after 1980. However, there have been countless sightings in which people claimed to have seen the dead rock star/C.I.A. operative at locales ranging from bowling alleys to 7-11 convenience stores. None of these sightings have been confirmed. It is unknown whether Presley is still alive at this time, but the mysterious deaths of many interview subjects within this book (as well as author Jonathan Woodson and Hill House Publishing chief Tony Piccolo) provide reason enough to suspect he is still at large.

According to sources which asked to remain unnamed, the spacecraft known as X9736, or "Big Blue," was stolen from Area 51 in 1982. Since that time, literally hundreds of people around the world have claimed to have seen an unidentified spacecraft shaped like a sideways taco. In each of these reported sightings, the unidentified spacecraft was pink.

ACKNOWLEDGMENTS

The author would like to thank Kerri Rausch, Ron Riley, Gary Lee Vincent, Marilyn Allen, and the late Jonathan Woodson.

ABOUT THE AUTHOR

Andy Rausch is a freelance journalist, celebrity interviewer, and film critic. He is the author or co-author of nearly twenty books on the subject of popular culture. These include *Making Movies with Orson Welles*, *The Films of Martin Scorsese and Robert De Niro*, and *The Wit and Wisdom of Stephen King*. He is also the author of the novels *The Suicide Game* and *Riding Shotgun*. He has also worked as an actor, film producer, composer, casting director, and as the screenwriter of the cult film *Dahmer vs. Gacy*. He is a regular contributor to *Screem* magazine, and his work has appeared in such publications and online journals as *Film Threat*, *Shock Cinema*, and *Bright Lights Film Journal*. He resides in Parsons, Kansas.

OTHER GREAT TITLES FROM

Burning Bulb

PUBLISHING

WWW.BURNINGBULBPUBLISHING.COM

ANTHOLOGIES
BIZARRO AND TRANSGRESSIVE FICTION

THE BIG BOOK OF BIZARRO

The Big Book of Bizarro brings together the peculiar prose of an international cast of the most grotesquely-gonzo, genre-grinding modern writers who ever put pen to paper (or mouse to pad), including:

NIGHT OF THE LIVING DEAD horror writers John Russo & George Kosana; HUSTLER MAGAZINE erotica contributors Eva Hore, Andrée Lachapelle, & J. Troy Seate and established Bizarro genre authors D. Harlan Wilson, William Pauley III, Wol-vriey, Laird Long, Richard Godwin and so many more!

From Alien abductions to Zombie sex, The Big Book of Bizarro contains OVER FIFTY STORIES of the most outrélandish transgressive fiction that you'll ever lay your capricious and curious hands upon!

WARNING: This book may be one of the most controversial and dangerous books you'll ever read.

WESTWARD HOES

Nine outlaw writers rode into town from obscurity to pen nine tantalizing tales of horror and fantasy, and leaving once they branded their own personal marks on the weird western genre and became living legends of the American Frontier experience.

Like drunken Indian scouts, the writers fervidly tracked down and captured the Western genre, tore off its fashionable veneer and ravished its exposed essence.

So belly up to the bar with your favorite soiled dove and enjoy perusing these thrilling tales of Old West debauchery, danger and desire; compiled by the publisher of The Big Book of Bizarro and featuring the bizarro novella *Big Trouble in Little Ass* by Wol-vriey.

ANTHOLOGIES
BIZARRO AND TRANSGRESSIVE FICTION

THE BIG BOOK OF BIZARRO SPECIAL KINDLE EDITIONS

VULGARITY FOR THE MASSES

A whole history of madness and struggle lie ahead for the disfigured children of Adam in this collection of nine tales from J.S. Lawhead.

Available at

GARY LEE VINCENT'S
DARKENED
THE WEST VIRGINIA VAMPIRE SERIES

DARKENED HILLS

When evil descends on a small West Virginia town, who will survive?

Jonathan did not start out his life to become a rambler, it just worked out that way. William was a troubled youth with something to hide. Both were from Melas, a small town tucked away in the West Virginia hills... a town where disappearances are happening more and more frequently.

After the suicide of a wanted serial killer, the townsfolk thought the nightmare was over. But when a centuries-old vampire is discovered they find out the hard way it's just getting started. Dark secrets can only stay hidden for so long and when the devil comes to collect, there will be hell to pay. Can Jonathan and William find a way to stop the vampire before it's too late? Find out in *Darkened Hills!*

DARKENED HOLLOWS

In the heart-stopping sequel to the award-winning *Darkened Hills*, Jonathan and William must return to West Virginia to face possible criminal charges stemming from their last visit to the damned town of Melas, where both had narrowly escaped the clutches of a vampire seethe.

And as livestock start mysteriously getting murdered with all of their blood drained, worried farmers are searching for answers - leaving the local Sheriff and his deputy racing against time to learn the cause before a more violent crime is committed.

www.DARKENEDHILLS.COM

GARY LEE VINCENT'S
DARKENED
THE WEST VIRGINIA VAMPIRE SERIES

DARKENED WATERS

When the world goes to hell, the chosen must arise!

As Talman Cane orchestrates a flood of epic proportions in this third installment of the *Darkened* series the towns of Melas and Tarklin are caught completely off guard by the deluge. Hell-bent on finishing what they started, the evil brothers return to the lunatic asylum to take care of the witnesses and add to the ever-growing army of the undead.

Aided by Lucifer himself and the insane vampire demon Legion, the stage is set to channel all of the forces of hell to come forth. In an all-out race to survive, Jonathan, William, and Amanda soon discover they are up against impossible odds as Lucifer opens the Gateway to Hell, ushering in the zombie apocalypse and the End Times.

DARKENED SOULS

Melas and the Madison House are about to be rebuilt.
True evil is about to be reborne!

Young ex-priest and vampire-killer William is drawn back to the West Virginian town that almost killed him, where his vampire arch-enemy Victor Rothenstein still stalks the earth.

The town of Melas lies destroyed after the battle of the End of Days. But why is wealthy Jackie Nixon so eager to rebuild it using the bone dust of murdered souls?

Terrible evil has visited before, but the Gateway to Hell is about to be reopened in a horrific climax. And this time – it's personal.

WEST VIRGINIA-THEMED
HUMORROROTICA
BY RICH BOTTLES JR.

HELLHOLE WEST VIRGINIA

From the heights of Mothman's perch high atop the Silver Bridge in Point Pleasant to the depths of Hellhole Cavern in Pendleton County, evil lurks within the shadows as the sun sets upon the haunted hills and hollows of West Virginia.

Bizarro author Rich Bottles Jr. blows the coffin lid off horror genre clichés with this tour de force cast of Eco-friendly vampires, beach-yearning zombies and sex-starved she-devils.

LUMBERJACKED

If you are easily offended or do not possess a truly depraved sense of humor, this story may not be the light summer reading fare you desire. As for the four feisty female freshmen stranded on top of West Virginia's third highest mountain, they have no choice but to experience the sick, twisted debauchery and perverted mayhem described deep inside the tight unbroken bindings of this horrific missive.

Lumberjacked takes the reader to a nightmarish world where character development and aesthetic integrity are prematurely cut short by the swinging axes of maniacal lumberjacks, who are hell bent on death and destruction in the remote forests of Appalachia. And at the climax, when paranoia crosses over to the paranormal, Lumberjacked makes Deliverance look like a family raft trip down the Lower Gauley.

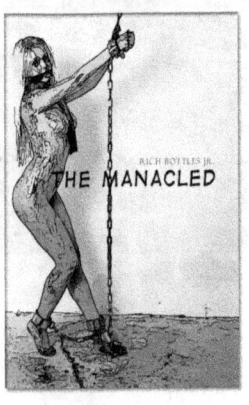

THE MANACLED

What happens when twin brothers lease out the former West Virginia State Penitentiary with the false purpose of filming a documentary on supernatural phenomena, but their true intention is to make a pornographic movie?

Chaos ensues as the disturbed spirits of murdered convicts, along with the reanimated dead from the neighboring Indian Burial Mound, take their vengeance on the unwary and undressed trespassers.

Zombies, ghosts, mobsters and porn collide in this bizarro tale from horror author Rich Bottles Jr.

WOL-VRIEY
BIZARRO AND TRANSGRESSIVE FICTION

BOSTON POSH

Boston Posh: A Bud Malone Thriller! Why are the white robots trying to kill Malone?
In 2028 AD, the USA is a nation ravaged by hungry dragons and dinosaurs. In Boston, Massachusetts, private eye Bud Malone is hired to rescue a kidnapped heiress. But nothing is as it seems. Malone works to unravel a tangled web involving Boston Chinatown, a 200-year-old woman with a 9-year-old body, white humanoid robots, a human-liver-eating psychopath, a golem, a porcelain dragon, and a snake goddess with a crush on him. There's also a woman obsessed with chicken sex.

Then Malone meets Posh Lane, a gorgeous call girl who's desperate to quit her pimp. Romantic sparks ignite between Posh and Malone, but Posh's past suddenly catches up with her in a BIG way. To save Posh, Malone agrees to run a quest for Earth's new rulers, the Forks. The quest: recover ex US president Jefferson Lincoln's liver for them. Malone has no idea that agreeing to the Fork's odd request will send him on the weirdest trip he's ever been on in his life. *Boston Posh* - A total mind fuck! Reality like you've never dared imagine it!

VEGAN ZOMBIE APOCALYPSE

In the post-apocalypse worlderness, zombies rule the earth. They're allergic to meat, and brains literally make them explode. Zombies now eat blood potatoes, parasitic tubers grown in the flesh of humancows corralled in maximum security farms. The necros, barbaric human nomads travelling the worlderness in floating villages, worship the zombies. The necros both eat the zombies, and wear clothes made from them; they live in houses built of bricks of undead flesh. They also keep zombies as sex slaves. Two fugitives meet in the ancient ruins of Texas. The first is Soil 15-f, a womancow who's escaped her farm a week before she's due to be killed and her blood potato crop harvested. The second fugitive is Able Kane, former head necros food technician, now sentenced to death for heresy. But Soil is no ordinary humancow. Unknown to herself, she's the vegan zombie agricultural revolution, and the zombies desperately want her back. And the necros equally desperately want Able Kane dead. He's fled with a forbidden discovery which will reshape the world for the worse if used. And Able is just hardheaded/misguided enough to use it.

With android zombinators and the head necros assassin (Able's ex-girlfriend Morphia) after them, Soil and Able Kane have no choice but to climb the lemon tree to Haeven, residence of the zombie god Necro. And by anyone's reckoning, Soil and Able Kane are the two people in the worlderness who should never have been let into Heaven.

MINOR CONFESSIONS OF AN ANGEL FALLING UPWARD

by Planner Forthright, as edited by Joey Madia

Confession. Revelation. Rant. *Minor Confessions of an Angel Falling Upward* is all of these... and more. Set in modern times and spiraling back to the swirl of Pre-Creation, this postmodern blend of genre-bending pop-prose and socio-political commentary is a classic tale of the (anti-)hero's quest for Reason and Redemption in a Universe gone mad.

Who is Planner Forthright? A fallen angel made Man. A once-winged evil with un-Divine purpose on this Plane. A cannibal prince chosen to inherit a castled landscape of destruction and despair. An Alchemist of sorts—a mental magician; a mortar-and-pestle wizard converting carbon lies to golden Truth, whose language is his own. A Vampire by nature and condition whose been walking the waters and thorny highways of our planet for over 40 years. And he's seeking a way out...

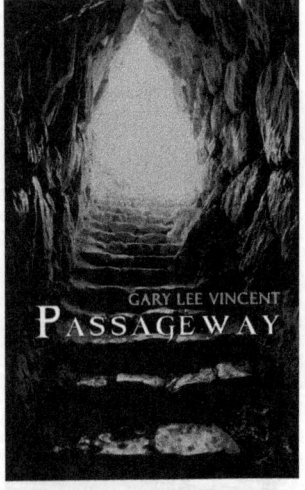

PASSAGEWAY

by Gary Lee Vincent with illustrations by Andy Hopp

When an archeological dig goes horribly wrong, the team is trapped in an alternate world where evil awaits them at every turn. Find out who will survive the *Passageway!*

From Gary Lee Vincent, the author of supernatural vampire thriller *Darkened Hills*, comes an unforgettable tale that spans four continents and takes the reader to the very realm of Hell itself.

Skeleton warriors, zombies, other undead beings and werewolves are allvery real inside the *Passageway!* In this Bizarro-genre tribute to H.P. Lovecraft and Indiana Jones, this deadly tale will keep you guessing and leave you breathless to the end!

THE TWELVE STEPS

by Zachary Crabtree

"A Man who Cannot Keep Awake Cannot Keep it Together." There is always something that pulls an alcoholic deeper into his unquenchable thirst - something degenerative to the human spirit. Indeed, there have been incidents in my life that carry tragic significance to me, yet I know they pale in comparison to the tragedies experienced by others.

When the jagged pieces of a disfigured past become a troubled, broken-up, glass-bottled mosaic in one's present life, all the innocent souls affected along the way become entangled in one's conscience; while the depression, pills, manic behavior and soul-searching coalesce in a series of twelve steps.

Alcohol affects the lives of hooligans, stubborn old fools, lovers, and families torn apart by drunk drivers - drunk drivers like me.

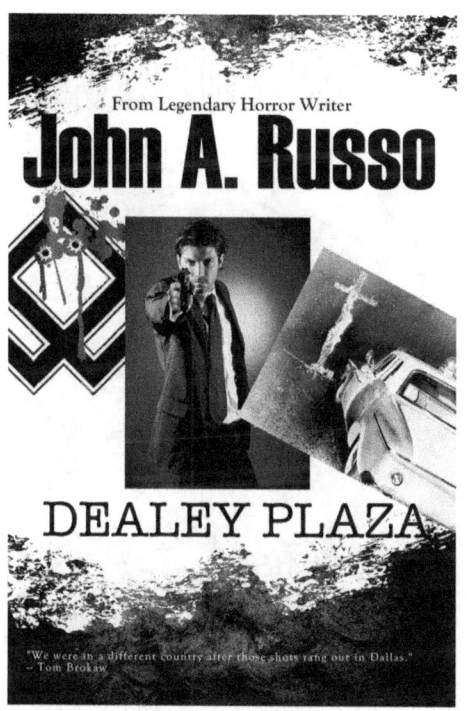

THE TAILSMAN

BURNING BULB

COMICS

From the creators of *The Big Book of Bizarro* and *Westward Hoes* comes a new comic unlike anything you have ever seen!

He's hot on the trail, looking for some *tail...*

Sly Franko was a man of the West, a forger of the wild frontier. Like the Country Western song that would be written years after he died, the words, "Faster horses, younger women, and more money," seemed to be the anthem of this horn dog cowboy.

Franko would ride into town on a blazing saddle, find the closest saloon to wet the whistle, belly up to a good card game, and find him a hot-loving hussy to get his cowpoke on with.

However, Sly might have met his match when a visit to bathroom leads to terror and death. Can Sly and his poker buddies solve the mystery before more of the townsfolk are murdered? Find out in this exciting premier issue of *The Tailsman!*

WWW.BURNINGBULBCOMICS.COM

www.ingramcontent.com/pod-product-compliance
Lightning Source LLC
Chambersburg PA
CBHW070920180626
46817CB00003B/1149